Praise for the Cutthroat Business series

"Move over Stephanie Plum, there is a sassy, sexy sleuth in town! If you enjoy your cozy mysteries with a good shot of romance, and a love triangle with a sexy bad boy and a Southern gentleman in the mix, then you will love this. Very reminiscent of the Stephanie Plum books, but the laughs are louder, the romance is sexier and there is a great murder mystery to top it off."

—*Bella McGuire,* **Cozy Mystery Book Reviews**

"...a frothy girl drink of houses, hunks and whodunit narrated in a breezy first person."

—*Lyda Phillips,* **The Nashville Scene**

"VERDICT: The hilarious dialog and the tension between Savannah and Rafe will delight fans of chick-lit mysteries and romantic suspense."

—*Jo Ann Vicarel,* **Library Journal**

"... equal parts charming and sexy, with a side of suspense. Hero and heroine, Savannah Martin and Rafe Collier, are a pairing of perfection."

—*Paige Crutcher,* **examiner.com**

"...hooks you in the first page and doesn't let go until the last!"

—*Lynda Coker,* **Between the Pages**

"With a dose of southern charm and a bad boy you won't want to forget, *A Cutthroat Business* has enough wit and sexual chemistry to rival Janet Evanovich."

—*Tasha Alexander, New York Times bestselling author of* **Murder in the Floating City**

"A delicious and dazzling romantic thriller... equal parts wit and suspense, distilled with a Southern flavor as authentic as a mint julep."

—*Kelli Stanley, bests*   *ward winner,* **c Dormienda**

Also in this series:

Savannah Martin has always been a good girl, doing what was expected and fully expecting life to fall into place in its turn. But when her perfect husband turns out to be a lying, cheating slimeball—and bad in bed to boot—Savannah kicks the jerk to the curb and embarks on life on her own terms. With a new apartment, a new career, and a brand new outlook on life, she's all set to take the world by storm. If only the world would stop throwing her curveballs...

It's late February, just two months after Savannah Martin and Rafael Collier finally worked things out between them, and Rafe is already sneaking out of bed in the wee hours.

Catching fellow realtor Tim Briggs rinsing blood from his hands in the office sink makes for a welcome distraction, and when Tim disappears just as one of his clients is found dead in a nearby park, Savannah throws herself into the investigation with abandon.

But even the murder mystery taking place right under her nose can't completely distract her from worrying about personal problems. Has Rafe changed his mind about their relationship, or is something else going on? And what are the chances of Savannah coming out of this latest debacle with her life—and her heart—intact?

CHANGE OF HEART

Jenna Bennett

CHANGE OF HEART
SAVANNAH MARTIN MYSTERY #6

Copyright © 2013 Bente Gallagher

Interior design: April Martinez, GraphicFantastic.com

ISBN: 978-0-9899434-3-7

MAGPIE INK

One

I t was Rafe's fault. If he hadn't snuck out of bed before six, going God knows where, I wouldn't have been in the office at the ungodly early hour of seven, and I wouldn't have seen Tim washing blood from his hands in the bathroom sink.

It was a Saturday morning in late February, just about two months after Rafe had crashed my mother's Christmas Eve shindig at the Martin Mansion in Sweetwater to tell me that it was Christmas, when all good girls got what they wanted, and that if I wanted him, I could have him.

He didn't have to tell me twice.

We'd only rarely been out of bed since, let alone out of each other's sight, or at least it felt that way. Rafe was out of work, basically, so he could spend every waking moment with me. The undercover job he'd worked for the past ten years—the one the Tennessee Bureau of Investigations had sprung him from prison to do at twenty—had finally come to a close. He had, almost singlehandedly, brought the biggest SATG—South American Theft Gang—in the Southeast to a screeching halt, and had blown his cover sky high in the process. Once the holidays were over and I'd gone back to work, he'd helped me with my real estate business when I needed him, and the rest of the time he'd spent working on his grandmother's house on Potsdam Street in East Nashville, painting and scrubbing, getting it ready to list and sell.

I wished I could believe that's where he was, getting an early start on the weekend's labor, but it wasn't. I'd driven past, taking a big, long detour through the Potsdam area, and there'd been no sign of the Harley outside the big brick Victorian, and no sign of life inside.

I pulled into the circular driveway anyway, and crunched my way up to the front steps. I even parked the Volvo and got out, traipsing across the gravel to climb the stairs to the porch to press my nose against the wavy glass in the heavy carved front door. There was nothing to see, and the door didn't yield to my touch. I got back in the car again, and sat for a minute, torn between anger and concern.

If he wasn't here, where was he? Where had he gone so early, and without telling me?

Maybe I should have followed him as soon as I opened my eyes and saw him sneak out. However, he's much better at sneaking around than I am, a result of those ten years spent undercover. He's caught me before, and the result was unpretty and embarrassing. And I still had a few shreds of self-preservation and dignity left. If he didn't want me to know where he was, I wasn't about to run after him. There are limits to how desperate I wanted to seem. And besides, I wanted him to think I trusted him, even if I, in my heart of hearts, worried what he might be doing that he didn't want me to know about.

I thought about going back to the apartment to wait, about just staying there until he came home, whenever that was, to see what he had to say for himself. But if he took a long time, I'd be climbing the walls by the time he got there, and anyway, I didn't want to make him think I didn't have anything better to do. After two months of togetherness, I still wasn't so sure of him that I wanted to take any chances.

So I drove to the office instead. I often do floor duty on Saturday mornings anyway. It was how I hooked up with Rafe in the first place. He'd called the office one Saturday morning in August, to tell me that our queen bee, real estate maven Brenda Puckett, had stood him up for an appointment—at the house on Potsdam Street, as it happened—and when I went out to meet him, we'd found Brenda dead in the library, with her throat cut from ear to ear.

It's a long story. I'd been a bit leery after that of doing Saturday morning floor duty, but I didn't have so many clients yet that I could afford to give up any opportunities, so I toughed it out most weekends. It's usually a bit later than 6:55 that I pull into the parking lot, but I could just as well sit in the office as I could at home, I figured, and with luck, there might be something there that would distract me. Like work. Or a phone call.

Or Tim, bent over the sink in the bathroom, his face as pale as death while bright red-tinted water swirled down the drain and away.

I saw him as soon as I came through the back door. The bathroom is back there, off the hallway, and he hadn't bothered to close the door. I guess he didn't expect anyone to show up so early. And the sound of the back door opening must have been lost in the gurgling of the water going down the drain, because when I appeared in the doorway behind him, and he realized I was there, his whole body stiffened in surprise. The eyes that met mine in the mirror were wide: bloodshot and terrified.

"I'm sorry," I said automatically, "I didn't mean to startle you."

And that's when I noticed the red water sluicing down the drain.

I noticed a few other things too. He looked a bit less than his best, dressed in a faded long-sleeved T-shirt with the sleeves pushed halfway up his forearms, and a pair of seen-better-days jeans, with his hair in disarray and the aforementioned bloodshot, dark-rimmed eyes.

On someone else, it might not have been a big deal. But Tim is very particular about his looks. He's gay, he'd gorgeous, and he has an image to uphold. I've never seen him look anything less than perfect: absolutely polished and put together. My mother would adore Tim; apart from the gay thing, that is.

But this morning he looked like he'd lived through the night from hell, and had woken up with a hangover.

"Is that blood?" I asked.

"No," Tim said, in the mirror.

"It looks like blood."

The water was running clear now, and Tim turned it off. "I had a nosebleed."

So it *was* blood.

Not that I'd been in much doubt, really. I've seen a lot more of it than someone like me—a gently bred Southern Belle—should have to.

Although as far as the nosebleed went, what I could see of his face showed no sign of trauma, and also no sign of having been washed. His hands and forearms were wet, but not his face or neck. And when he reached for the hand towel hanging from the hook beside the sink, he dried his hands and arms, but not his face.

It was fairly obvious he wasn't thinking straight, to use a nicer expression than flat out lying. Another clue that something was wrong. Tim is usually pretty cunning, and doesn't miss much.

"Something going on?" I asked.

He busied himself hanging the towel back on the hook, without looking at me. "What would be going on?"

"That's what I'd like to know."

He turned and faced me, finally. "What are you doing here?"

"It's Saturday morning," I said. "I do floor duty on Saturdays."

He glanced at the Rolex wrapped around his wrist. Waterproof, I guess. "At seven o'clock?"

"Rafe went somewhere early."

When Tim didn't immediately smack his lips and make some X-rated remark about my boyfriend, that only reinforced my impression that something was seriously wrong. Tim's had a crush on Rafe since the first time they met, back in August, and when word got out that Rafe was dead, Tim was pretty upset about it.

Not as upset as I was, of course, for the eight hours or so I believed it to be true, but Tim was kept in the dark for months, and he was pretty miffed when he found out the truth. He does miffed quite well, too. But he had truly been upset when he thought Rafe had died, and for that I could forgive him a bit of petulance. There were few enough people in the world who had grieved over Rafe's supposed demise. My own mother, for instance, had been more upset to discover that he was still alive than she was when she thought he was dead.

Anyway, the fact that Tim didn't take the opportunity to salivate all over the mention of Rafe, only made me more certain that something was wrong.

"It's not like you have any room to talk," I pointed out. "You were here before me."

"Early appointment," Tim said, after a second.

Looking like that?

I didn't say it, but he flushed. "New construction."

New constructions, houses in the process of being built, are often danger-zones, full of sawdust and plywood and dirt and nails, so it makes sense to dress down when you're escorting someone around. Even so, I would have thought Tim could do better than ripped jeans and a faded T-shirt.

"By the way," he said, "now that I have you here..."

"Yes?"

"Can you sit an open house for me tomorrow?"

I blinked. Talk about a quick change of subject.

There was nothing unusual about the question, though. I often sit open houses for Tim on Sunday afternoons. Usually he doesn't wait until the day before to ask, but it's happened before, when he's had something come up suddenly. I'm happy to sit open houses for anyone who asks me. So far, in the just over six months I've had my real estate license, I've managed to nail down a few buyer clients and actually bringing them to closing, but I haven't had a listing of my own yet. Mrs. Jenkins's house, the one Rafe was working on—or rather, not working on this morning—was supposed to be my first. I host other people's open houses in the hope of snagging a new client, and because a lot of realtors find open houses to be at best boring and at worst a waste of their time. They're usually happy to pass them off to newer agents, like me.

"Which house is it?"

Sometimes he lets me have my pick of a few, and I choose the one that sounds most promising, but in this case he rattled off an address. It was in the same neighborhood as the office—Historic East Nashville—and not too far from my rented apartment on the corner of 5ᵗʰ and East Main.

"Sure," I said. "I'm happy to."

"Thank you." Tim's baby-blues flickered, as if he were looking for a way out. I guess I had sort of captured him there in the bathroom, and he had nowhere to go except past me. I took a step out of the doorway. "I should head up front." To the reception area and the front desk.

Tim nodded.

"Are you sure nothing's wrong?"

"Positive," Tim said, with a look on his face that said the opposite. But if he didn't want to tell me, it wasn't like I could knock him down and sit on him until he did. It would be unladylike. And although I've gotten better in that regard—I'd totally knock Rafe down and sit on him until he told me where he'd gone this morning—Tim was different. So I let him walk out of the bathroom and down the hallway to the back door. "Thanks, Savannah," he told me over his shoulder.

"You're welcome," I said. "Tim?"

He turned around in the doorway, with the door already open and the colder air from outside flowing into the hallway. "Aren't you going to freeze without a coat?"

It was February, after all. I was wearing a wool overcoat myself.

"It's in the car," Tim said, but not in a way that made me believe it; more in a way that made me think he'd forgotten to put one on—had forgotten all about it until I asked—and now he was making an excuse.

There was nothing I could do about it, though, so I just nodded. "Have a good day."

Tim's lips twisted, but not in a smile. "Oh, sure." He stepped out and let the door close and lock behind him. I turned off the light in the bathroom and hallway, but instead of heading for the other side of the building and the reception area, I stepped into the office to the right of the hallway for a moment, and walked over to the window. Tim's baby-blue Jaguar was parked nose-forward in the lot, with its rear against the brick wall. Now I watched as the lights came on and cut through the dusk outside before the car rolled out of the parking space and toward the exit to the street. It wasn't until it was moving away from me that I could see the rear clearly, and the smear decorating the trunk. Red, like blood. Palm and five fingers, as if someone had put his hand there and slammed the lid closed.

There was a logical explanation, I told myself. Maybe Tim hadn't been lying. Maybe he'd really had a nosebleed. Maybe he'd walked into a door. Maybe he'd gotten into a fight with someone, and they had popped him in the nose. Just because his nose wasn't swollen, and just because I hadn't noticed any blood on his face, didn't mean he was lying. He could be telling the truth. Someone could have hit him, or he could have accidentally hit himself. With his nose throbbing and blood streaming, he could have parked the car—carefully backed it into a parking space, a tiny voice in the back of my head pointed out—before getting out and staggering toward the door to the office. Catching himself on the trunk of the car on his way past for balance while somehow managing not to get a single drop of blood on his sweatshirt.

No, that didn't make a lot of sense. The car had been parked nose out, with the trunk up against the brick wall. There'd be no way to get behind it, and no reason why Tim would try. It was just a couple of yards from the driver's side door to the back door to the office, with no obstacles in between. Tim would have had no reason to go to the rear of his car. Unless there'd been something in the trunk he'd wanted to get out, but then he probably wouldn't have parked so close to the wall in the first place.

But it was none of my business. If he'd wanted to tell me what was going on, he would have. My curiosity has gotten me in trouble plenty over the past six months. I decided I'd just leave this one alone.

It wasn't like I didn't have enough other things to worry about, after all.

IT WAS AFTER SEVEN O'CLOCK. RAFE had to realize I'd be awake by now, and worried about where he was. Why wasn't he calling?

Was he doing something he didn't want me to know about?

Was he seeing someone else?

He hadn't exactly lived a celibate life. I didn't know much about his past, but I did know that. Women find him attractive, and they tend to be fairly obvious about it, so he can pretty much have his pick. He'd even slept with a woman named Carmen just a few months ago, after he and I had been together. After I'd gotten pregnant and had lost his baby.

I'd dealt with it—pretty much—since I hadn't had a choice. It was either accepting it or losing him, and that wasn't an option at all. And besides, sleeping with Carmen had been part of the undercover operation he was involved in, nothing personal. Not something he'd wanted to do; something he'd had to do to preserve his cover. She'd have thought it strange if he didn't, since the man he was pretending to be—a hired gun by the name of Jorge Pena—would certainly have taken her up on the offer. I hadn't been concerned about it, honestly. Carmen ended up in prison along with all the other criminals, and Rafe hadn't said a word about her, other than the very first time I'd asked, point blank, whether he had slept with her. He'd told me not to worry about it, that it was all part of the job. So I hadn't.

Until now.

I didn't really think he'd gone to visit Carmen Arroyo in Southern Belle Hell—the Tennessee Prison for Women—but was it possible there'd been another woman I didn't know about?

Over ten years of undercover work, it was pretty impossible that there hadn't been someone. We hadn't really talked about it, though. He knew all about my sex life—married at twenty three, divorced at twenty five, after my husband cheated on me with his paralegal because he claimed I was frigid. Single for two years until I met Rafe. The sum total of my sexual experience at this point consisted of those two relationships, and Rafe knew it. His was rather more extensive, I suspected, but I didn't want to think about it, so I'd never asked him just how many women he'd bedded in the twelve years since he'd left Sweetwater.

As far as I was concerned, our sex life was good. Enthusiastic. Satisfying. And lest you think I'm too much of an idiot to know a good sex life when I see one, I did actually realize that my marriage to Bradley was lacking in that respect. Bradley wasn't the only one dissatisfied; he was just the only one who saw cheating as a solution.

I had no such problems with Rafe. I wasn't frigid at all, and he didn't seem dissatisfied with me. If he was seeing someone else, it certainly hadn't manifested in any way in our sex life.

I had reached the lobby and had dumped my bag on Brittany's chair—she's the receptionist, but not on Saturdays—and was in the process of hanging my coat on the coat tree beside the door when my bag chirped.

It wasn't a call, just the phone signaling a text message, but I dove for it anyway, and pushed buttons with hands that shook.

It was from Rafe's number, of course. I had assumed it would be. It wasn't very informative, however.

Rise and shine, Goldilocks.

Rise and shine? Did he imagine I was still in bed?

Where are you? I texted back. No sense in wasting time with preliminaries, after all.

After another minute, the phone signaled another message. *Had to go somewhere.*

No kidding. I already knew that. The question was— *Where?*

I hit send, and waited.

And waited some more.

Gotta go, came back. *Love U.*

Sure.

I didn't bother to respond, just tucked the phone away in the bag, while I muttered under my breath about the fact that he wouldn't tell me where he was or what he was doing.

After a moment, however, I changed my mind and pulled the phone out again. I'd spent too much time worried about Rafe's safety, and that was before we got to the point in our relationship where we were now. I didn't want to go backwards. And besides, he'd told me he loved me. So chances were he wasn't in bed with someone else.

Love U 2, I told him. *Stay safe.*

This way, at least he knew. If something bad was going on, I wanted the last thing I said to him, the last thing he heard—or read—from me to be that I loved him.

Two

didn't hear anything more after that, and I didn't expect to. He was doing something, something he didn't want to talk about, and he'd avoid me for however long it took.

Needless to say, I was worried.

Worried enough that, about nine thirty, I lowered Brittany's copy of Cosmopolitan to the desktop and pulled the phone back out again.

What you need to understand is that Rafe spent ten years deep undercover, surrounded by the dregs of humanity; dregs who might, at any moment, figure out that he wasn't one of them and act accordingly. I have it on good authority—his own words—that he used to wake up in the morning never sure whether he'd survive the day. He didn't plan any kind of future because he never knew when someone might pull out a gun and shoot him.

Since August, I've spent considerable time worrying about that, and about him. At first, I didn't even know what he was doing; I just knew that he was dealing with unsavory people, people who might hurt him. I thought he was a criminal, and that he was in imminent danger of arrest by the police. Then I realized he was one of the good guys, and that made things even worse, because the bad guys have no qualms about killing good guys who try to catch them. I'd spent many a sleepless night wondering if I'd ever see him again. Once I thought he'd died, and the eight hours until I realized he was still alive, rank as some of the worst of my life. The fact that something might be going on now—that somehow, he might have gotten sucked back into the world of crime and undercover work—was enough to make me break out in a cold sweat.

So I called someone else, someone who might know if something like that was going on.

The phone rang a couple of times and then was answered. "Metropolitan Nashville Police Department, Homicide. Tamara Grimaldi speaking."

"Detective," I said, while my mind registered the fact that she sounded both harried and preoccupied.

"Ms. Martin."

"Don't you think you should start calling me Savannah? You don't call my brother Mr. Martin, do you?"

She didn't answer.

The detective and my brother Dix have developed some form of relationship over the past few months, since my sister-in-law was murdered back in November. Sheila and Dix lived in Sweetwater— Dix still does—but it happened in Nashville, so Tamara Grimaldi was assigned the case. Or claimed the case, I think, when she realized the victim was a Martin from Sweetwater. She told me she assumed it was a distant cousin of mine, certainly not my brother's wife, but she ended up working the case and solving the murder, with a little help from yours truly. And during the process, she and Dix bonded, in part over my relationship with Rafe, I think. This was around the same time Rafe's son David went missing, and I had my miscarriage and lost his baby. Rafe's, not David's.

I don't really know what sort of relationship they have now—Dix and Tamara, not Rafe and David—but I do know she gave his daughters Police Barbies for Christmas. My mother was horrified, of course, but Abigail and Hannah were thrilled. And I do believe they talk regularly, but of course it's too soon for Dix to get involved with anyone again. He's only been a widower for a few months.

At any rate, they talk. And I'm pretty sure she calls him Dix, not Mr. Martin. And the detective and I have known each other a lot longer than she and Dix have, so I did think it was about time she started calling me Savannah.

She didn't. She also didn't say anything about Dix. Instead, she said, "What can I do for you?"

There was no sense in beating around the bush, so I just blurted it out. "I wondered if you might know where Rafe is."

There was a beat, then— "No?"

"There's nothing going on that you know about?"

The detective hesitated. "Not on our end. As far as the Metropolitan Nashville Police Department is concerned, he's a civilian. And as far as I know, he hasn't broken any laws lately."

As far as I knew he hadn't, either.

"He left before six this morning. Didn't kiss me goodbye. Did his best to sneak out quietly."

"I imagine his best is pretty good?" the detective said dryly.

"I only woke up because one of the neighbors was in the hallway outside when he opened the door, and Mr. Sorenson said good morning. If it hadn't been for that, I don't think I would have realized he was leaving."

Grimaldi didn't answer, and I added, "The phone didn't ring, so no one called him this morning. Or texted. He must have known yesterday that he was going out. But he didn't tell me about it. I'm worried."

The detective was quiet. I could hear sounds in the background: faint voices talking, a buzz that might be cars going by in the distance.

"I'm sorry," I said belatedly, "is this a bad time?"

"Not at all," the detective shot back. "The corpse isn't going anywhere. Not until I'm done with it."

Gah. "I'm sorry."

"Don't be," Grimaldi said. "Talking to you gives me something more pleasant to think about for a few minutes."

Sure.

"It's no one I know this time, I hope?" Entirely too many people I knew had died recently. My colleague Brenda Puckett, her assistant Clarice, my friend Lila Vaughn, Mrs. Jenkins's nurse Marquita, my sister-in-law...

"I don't think so," Grimaldi said. "Does the name Brian Armstrong ring any bells?"

It didn't, I was happy to realize. It was quite a relief to be able to say so, too. "What happened to him?"

"He was stabbed," Grimaldi said. "Last night sometime. And dumped in Shelby Park."

Shelby Park? "That's just up the street from here. He wasn't gay, was he?"

Grimaldi was silent for a second. "Why?" she asked eventually, her voice politely curious.

"No reason." My mind had just made a quick and dirty connection between a stabbed body in Shelby Park, a quarter mile away from the office, and the blood on Tim's hands.

"Sure," the detective said. "Spill, Ms.... Savannah."

Damn. I mean, darn. I back-pedaled as quickly as I could. "East Nashville is just a very diverse neighborhood, is all. Lots of people with alternative lifestyles live here. I wondered if he was one of them. That's all."

"Uh-huh." It didn't sound like she believed me, but she let it go. "To answer your question, he doesn't seem to have been. Not according to the pictures in his wallet, anyway."

"Family pictures?"

"Wife," Grimaldi said. "Twenty years younger and bottle blonde. The photograph is inscribed *Until death do us part*."

Ouch. "Have you spoken to her?"

"Not yet. We got the call less than an hour ago. A jogger running around the lake found the body. Wrapped in a sheet and lying on the side of the road."

"Maybe he was on his way home from a toga party last night, and someone tried to take his wallet."

"I should have been more specific," the detective told me. "I didn't mean that he was wearing the sheet. I meant that he was rolled in it. Probably for transportation."

In the trunk of a car?

I bit my tongue before I could blurt out the thought. "You mean, someone stabbed him somewhere else," I asked instead, "and then rolled him in the sheet and dumped him in the park?"

"That's about the strength of it."

"I guess you'll be looking at the wife, won't you?"

"Always," Grimaldi confirmed. "The significant other always tops the list."

"So if something were to happen to Rafe, I'd be your number one suspect?"

"In Mr. Collier's case," Grimaldi said, "I think I'd make an exception. You'd never hurt him, and there are so many others who'd be delighted to try that I think we'd have more suspects than we'd know what to do with."

She paused for a second before she added, "Are you worried?"

So much so that my voice cracked on the response. "Yes."

The detective pretended she hadn't noticed, bless her. "What are you worried about?"

"That he's with someone else. Or that something's going on and he's putting himself in danger again. That something might happen to him."

"He isn't with anyone else," Grimaldi said.

She sounded very sure. "How do you know?"

"Not because I know what he's doing. Because I know he cares about you. You didn't see him back in December, when Hector Gonzales had you on the phone, talking to us from that warehouse."

I hadn't. But I'd seen him come through the door to that same warehouse five minutes later, without a weapon, without a coat, and with a look on his face that said that if Hector had hurt me, Rafe would tear him limb from limb, or die trying.

It had almost come to that before it was over, too.

"Thank you."

"Don't thank me," Grimaldi said. "I'm just telling you the truth. He isn't with anyone else. Not for that reason, anyway."

Right. However, that made it even more likely that he was doing something dangerous. If it wasn't another woman, then he was probably involved in something he knew I'd worry about.

"Will you let me know if you hear anything?"

"Sure," Grimaldi said. "The MNPD has nothing better to do than keep tabs on Mr. Collier so his girlfriend won't worry."

"I'll tell Dix you're being mean to me," I said, and Grimaldi snorted.

"I'll let you know if any information comes my way. But I don't have the time to track him down right now. I have a dead man in front of me and his wife to notify of his death. I'm afraid your concern over Mr. Collier will just have to take a back seat."

Of course. "Please. Take care of your dead man and his wife. I'll just sit here and be glad I don't have your job."

And grateful that I wasn't on the receiving end of such news. The same news I had spent months dreading. The news I was just getting past worrying about, now that Rafe wasn't involved in anything dangerous anymore.

Tamara Grimaldi's voice gentled, so although I hadn't said anything, she must have heard those thoughts in my head. "I'll let you know if I hear anything."

"I appreciate it," I said, and let her go back to her unpleasant task.

AT NOON, I LEFT THE OFFICE and went home. I had fielded a half dozen phone calls by then, none of them from anyone I wanted to talk to, and for all intents and purposes the morning had been a colossal waste of time. The only good thing about it was that I hadn't been sitting at home with nothing better to do than stare at the walls.

I had given up reading tawdry romance novels a few months ago. Partly because I had Rafe in my life—and my bed—and I had no reason to live vicariously through anyone else. He was more than tall, dark and handsome enough for me, and far superior to any two dimensional book hero. But more than that, I stopped reading when my favorite tawdry romance author, Barbara Botticelli, was killed, and I realized that not only did I know her, but I wasn't the only one who had pictured Rafael Collier when one of her tall, dark and handsome bad boy heroes walked onto the page. She had, too.

She was David's mother, pregnant at sixteen after a one night stand in high school. Rafe had had no idea he'd knocked her up, and hadn't known that David existed until recently. Elspeth—Barbara's real name—hadn't either, at least according to what information I'd been able to dig up. Rafe went to prison right after high school, and Elspeth hadn't seen him again until this past September. By then, she'd become a romance novelist. A very successful romance novelist. She wrote historical romances about sweet, sheltered, well-bred blondes swept off their feet by tall, dark, exotic rogues. Pirates, highway men, sheiks, and Native American warriors. The books had titles like "Stand and Deliver," "Pirate's Booty," and "Apache Amour." Deliciously over the top titles, swashbuckling stories, and larger-than-life heroes. I loved them—until I realized that Elspeth was still hung up on Rafe, and every one of the heroes in her books was modeled after him, or after what she imagined he might have grown into.

So that ruined it for me. I couldn't read a Barbara Botticelli book anymore without imagining Elspeth in the role of the heroine. Before, I'd always imagined myself, and if the hero bore a striking resemblance to Rafe—long before I was willing to admit to anyone, including myself, that I was attracted to him—that was between me and my conscience. They were just romance novels, after all. Vicarious pleasure. I wouldn't ever get involved with him for real.

But I digress. It was months since I'd picked up a romance novel. That afternoon I was so desperate for comfort and for a distraction from the worry that I actually stopped at the grocery store on my way home and bought a gallon of ice cream and a book. It wasn't a Barbara Botticelli, it wasn't a historical, and I made sure the hero was a well-dressed blond gazillionaire, not your classic tall-dark-and-dangerous bad-boy alpha hero, and when I got home I sank onto the couch with the ice cream bucket and the book on my lap.

I got a stomach ache from the ice cream after a while, so I put it away, but I kept reading. It was a long book, and pretty engaging, so I didn't realize how late it had gotten until I looked up and realized it was dark outside. A quick glance at the clock told me it was time for dinner. Since the stomach had settled some from my ice cream lunch, I went ahead and nibbled on some crackers and brie. There was no sense in making anything more elaborate when I was cooking for one.

I hadn't heard from Rafe again, although I had jumped at every sound from beyond the apartment door. Steps in the hallway had my heart speeding up. Once, when a car backfired on the street outside, I dropped the book and ran to the balcony doors, terrified I'd see my boyfriend, the man I loved, gunned down in the street below.

I didn't. It was just a car. So I went back to my book and back to waiting.

Eventually the book ran out of pages and I went to bed, and by then the worry was at peak, not to mention that I was starting to get angry again, on top of it. How dare he just walk out in the morning and stay gone all day with no word on what he was doing or where he was? We were committed to one another, weren't we? We had a relationship. Didn't he realize he owed it to me to let me know what was going on? If it had been me, wouldn't he have wanted to know what I was doing and that I was safe?

But maybe he wouldn't. Maybe he didn't care. Or maybe he trusted that I'd be careful and that I wouldn't take stupid chances.

The trouble with that comparison was that Rafe always took stupid chances.

Of course he didn't consider them to be stupid, just necessary, and maybe he was right. But they seemed stupid to me, since my only concern was his survival.

I found myself more than halfway wishing he was in bed with another woman, because at least he'd be safe that way.

And then I pushed it all aside and just prayed that he'd come home in one piece.

I WOKE UP IN THE DARK after midnight, when the weight of another body hit the bed behind me. For a second, it was startling and jerked me out of sound sleep. I'd slept alone for more than two years before Rafe, and part of me still wasn't used to sharing my bed with anyone. Especially someone who entered the bed after me. Rafe and I usually hit the sheets together, one on top of the other.

It took me less than a second to recognize him. My body knew the feel of his behind me, even when we weren't touching. I recognized the sound of his breathing and his smell: spicy and citrusy, all male. All Rafe.

Part of me wanted to turn to him, to make sure he was all right. To run my hands over his body and assure myself that he wasn't hurt. To yell at him for making me worry and for not telling me what was going on. But I didn't. Instead I lay quietly, waiting to see if he'd reach out instead.

A minute passed, the silence only broken by rustling as he moved around, trying to get comfortable. The cotton sheets slipped across his body with a whispering sound. He sighed softly as he settled into the mattress, as if maybe his body hurt. His breathing slowed into a steady cadence. I waited.

He moved again. The mattress dipped a little. He settled back, with another soft sound.

I lay, wide-eyed, staring into the darkness. I could see the red numbers on the digital alarm clock on the bureau tick over, from 12:47 to 12:48.

I was just about to give up when a hand found my shoulder, warm and hard. It skimmed over my skin, down to the elbow and back up, leaving goose bumps in its wake. "You asleep, darlin'?"

His voice was low, a bit rough, with an edge of fatigue. When the hand moved down a second time, he leaned in and his lips found my shoulder instead, his breath warm against my skin.

I let go of the anger and the righteous indignation. He was here. He was safe. He was mine. It didn't matter that he hadn't told me where he was going or what he'd been doing there. The only thing that mattered was that he'd come back, and safely.

I turned into his arms and lifted my face to his. He kissed me, and that was it for the next little while. I lost myself in the heat and the building excitement, the feel of his hands on my skin and his body moving against mine.

"I love you," I murmured against his cheek a bit later, when he had collapsed on top of me, his skin slick and his breathing ragged.

"Love you too." The words were half-lost in my hair, hoarse and breathless and edged with exhaustion.

I smoothed a hand down his back, over hot, slick skin and hard muscles. "Everything OK?"

He murmured something. It could have been anything, really. Yes or no or maybe. I waited for him to elaborate, but he didn't. His breathing slowed, and became deep and rhythmic.

"Rafe?"

There was no answer, just the sound of his steady breaths in my ear. He was dead asleep.

I thought about trying to wake him—trying being the operative word, since I wasn't sure I'd be able to; he seemed to hover just a scant inch from the edge of unconsciousness—but in the end I decided against it. Partly because I wasn't sure I could, yes, but also because I wanted him to rest. We'd have time to talk tomorrow.

I squirmed out from under him—he's heavy, and his weight made breathing hard—and curled up next to him instead. He didn't stir. I closed my eyes and settled in to sleep, with his steady breaths ruffling the hair at my cheek and the warmth of his body at my back.

Three

He was gone when I woke up. I don't know why that surprised me. And this time I hadn't even stirred when he left. The only evidence that he'd been there at all, was the scent in the air and the loose feeling in my body as I turned over in bed and stretched.

There was no "good morning" message today. I guess he felt he'd done his duty last night, in allaying my fears and convincing me not to worry. And he had, to a degree. If nothing else, I felt pretty certain I could trust that he wasn't with another woman, rolling around in bed with her. Not after the way he'd made love to me last night.

And in case you wondered: yes, it had been about making love. It wasn't just sex, or about getting release after what I had to assume had been a rough day.

When the phone rang just after ten, I thought it might be him. It wasn't. Instead it was Tamara Grimaldi.

As usual when the detective called, my first instinct was to fear for Rafe's safety. It was habit, hard to change at this point.

There may have been a tremor in my hand when I pushed the button to answer the call. "Detective?"

"Ms. Martin."

"Something wrong?"

"No," Grimaldi said. "I'm just checking in."

"He came home last night. Eventually."

"And did he tell you where he'd been?"

I blushed. "No. We... um... didn't get around to talking about it."

"I see." Her voice was bland to the point of being neutral. I blushed more furiously. There was nothing I could say, though, because the reason we hadn't talked about it was exactly the reason she thought we hadn't talked about it.

"I was happy to see him," I said in my defense.

"Of course you were. What about this morning? Did you talk then?"

"He's gone again."

There was a beat. "Snuck out again, did he?"

"And this time I didn't even hear him."

"You must have been tired from last night," Grimaldi said, and although I'm sure she wasn't smirking—because she rarely smirks—I felt pretty certain I could hear the smirk in her voice even so. Especially when she continued. "Have you thought about chaining him to the bed?"

Yes. Frequently. However— "It wouldn't work. He's too good at picking locks."

"I don't want to know that," Grimaldi said.

"Sorry. I don't suppose you were able to find out anything? About anything?"

"I'm afraid not. I spent yesterday working a case."

"The dead guy in the park? How's that going? Have you arrested anyone yet?"

"This isn't television," Grimaldi said. "In real life, it usually takes a bit longer."

"Does the wife have an alibi?"

There was a pause. "You do realize you're not supposed to ask me these things, don't you?"

"Sorry."

"I can't talk to you about what I'm doing. Bad enough when it's a case you're peripherally involved in, but when you're not, definitely not. I told you more than I should have yesterday."

"I'm sorry," I said. "I guess I just got used to asking. Since so many people I know have died lately, and you've dealt with all of them."

"You didn't know this one," Grimaldi reminded me. "Unless you've changed your mind about that?"

I contemplated telling her that I had, just because I wanted to know what was going on. I'd found myself involved—sometimes more than peripherally—in a few of Tamara Grimaldi's cases last fall, and I'd actually sort of enjoyed hearing her explain what was going on with them. I'd enjoyed tracking down a few killers myself, too. But it was probably better if I didn't lie. "I don't think so. The name didn't ring a bell. Was he local?"

"Not originally," Grimaldi said. "A Californian."

We'd seen a lot of those lately. Nashville had weathered the recent economic downturn fairly well, and quite a few people from the places that were harder hit by the bad economy had arrived in town over the past year or two. Many from California, but we'd also gotten our fair share of Floridians and people from Michigan. Of course, they came from other places too, and not only because of the economy. Nashville is a magnet for all the musicians and music industry people, and there are a lot of wannabes who hope to strike it rich in Music City.

"A musician?" I ventured.

"An orthodontist," Grimaldi said.

Interesting. Or at least it struck me as such. What could an orthodontist have done to make someone want to kill him?

"Wealthy?"

Grimaldi didn't answer—I must have come too close to classified information with that question—but it wasn't like I couldn't guess. "He probably was. Most doctors are well off. Do rich people get murdered more than poor people?"

"No," Grimaldi said. "Crime rates are usually higher in low income areas. Poverty breeds crime. But the crimes that affect rich people are different from the ones that affect poor people."

"How so?"

"If you're a welfare mom living in the projects," Grimaldi said, "your chances of being killed by a stray bullet from a gang-related drive-by shooting is much higher than if you're a doctor or a lawyer living in Belle Meade or Green Hills."

Naturally.

"When a doctor or a lawyer is killed, it's more often personal, and the stakes are usually higher. Your average crime-for-profit criminal will steal a car, or rob a bank, or break into a house, or take someone's wallet, with no real concern for who the victim is. It's more or less random. Your average citizen who gets tempted into committing murder may still kill for money, but not for a couple hundred dollars for a fix. It'll be bumping off Aunt Edna for the inheritance or doing away with a coworker for the promotion to the corner office."

"Is that what happened to Brian Armstrong?"

She immediately clammed up again. "We don't know what happened to Brian Armstrong. And I couldn't tell you if I did."

"But you don't think it was random violence."

"He wasn't walking through the park when someone came upon him and stole his wallet and his clothes and stabbed him a few times for good measure. He was killed somewhere else and brought there. Wrapped in a sheet."

"His own sheet?"

The detective was silent. I took that to mean no. So the man hadn't been in his own bed when he died. He'd been naked in someone else's.

The obvious suspects, then, were the wife and the other woman. If Grimaldi could find her.

"Seems like a pretty open and shut case," I offered.

"Seems that way," Grimaldi agreed pleasantly.

"Probably won't take you too much longer to arrest someone."

"Maybe not."

There was a pause. "I'll let you get on with it," I said.

"Most kind," Grimaldi answered, although it was she who had called me in the first place, not vice versa. I was just about to remind of her of that fact when she added, "Call me if you need anything."

The words got stuck in my throat. "Thank you," I said instead.

"And when you figure out what your boyfriend's been up to, let me know. I'm curious."

She hung up before I had the chance to tell her I would.

I SPENT THE REST OF THE morning hanging around the apartment, doing a couple of loads of laundry, and giving myself a shower and a pedicure.

Washing and folding Rafe's T-shirts—his other clothes too, but especially the T-shirts—was very calming. I love his T-shirts. I love it more when he's not wearing them, but there's just something about the way those T-shirts fit, and how soft they are, that gets my heart rate up.

It seemed he'd worn a black one yesterday. Plain black, short sleeved—he's not much bothered by the cold—and smelling faintly of spice and citrus and—I inhaled deeply—smoke?

Once it came out of the dryer, the smoke smell was gone, of course, and so were the other smells, but as I folded the shirt and put it on top of the others, I wondered where he'd been and what he'd been doing for long enough that the smell of smoke had permeated his clothing.

Around one, I headed out. First to the grocery store, for a tray of cookies and a big box of hot chocolate mix. I'd already tucked my fancy samovar into the trunk of the Volvo, and I was planning to serve hot cocoa and cookies at the open house. The weather was chilly and a bit nasty: not quite snowy, but with a sort of cold mist in the air. It was more like autumn weather, really, than something you associate with February, but the climate in Nashville is strange at the best of times. Summers are hot and muggy, we don't always have spring or fall, and it can be seventy five degrees in January. Or January can bring a few days of snow and a week or more after that of no school for the kids, since the school buses can't drive if the roads aren't perfectly clear.

All in all, what we had now wasn't too bad. It probably didn't bode too well for my open house, though. Open houses do well when the weather is overcast, the temperature neither too high nor too low. If the weather is too nice, people find other things to do. If it's too nasty, they stay indoors. We were borderline too nasty today, but maybe I'd be pleasantly surprised. And as locations went, it was certainly a very nice, desirable one.

The house Tim had assigned to me was squarely in the middle of East Nashville's historic district, on a street full of old turn-of-the-century Victorians and 1920s Craftsman cottages. It was a street you would expect to be treelined, with big, old, majestic oaks, but the 1998 tornado hit East Nashville hard, and took out a lot of trees. Some of the streets were down to brand new growth, only what had managed to grow in the last fifteen years.

My assigned house was neither a Victorian nor a Craftsman cottage. Instead, it was what's known as a historic infill: a brand new house, made to look somewhat old to fit with the guidelines in the historic overlay district.

It was two stories tall, with a stacked stone foundation and porch supports topped by square pillars. Very Arts and Crafts. It also had a steep, Victorian-looking gable with half-timbering, but there were no other Tudor accents. Instead of brick on the lower half, the whole house was covered with Hardiboard siding. So basically, it was a hodgepodge of different styles and elements, all of which—separately—had their counterpart somewhere in the neighborhood.

The house was big, though—almost 3,000 square feet—and the pictures of the interior had been beautiful. Real hardwood floors—they don't always put those in new construction; this had been an upscale one—granite and stainless steel kitchen with oversized, commercial refrigerator and gas stove, stacked stone fireplace in the family room... It was nicely furnished, too, at least according to the pictures. The family still lived there, or so I had to assume from what I'd seen of furniture and knick-knacks. It looked personal, not staged.

That can be a bit uncomfortable, to be honest, because sometimes the owners insist on sticking around for the open house, sort of incognito, to hear what people might say about their home. Or worse, *not* incognito, but because they want to be on hand to answer any questions anyone might have. It's always difficult to try to convince them that it isn't a good idea for them to be there. Not only because their feelings get hurt when people say bad things about the house, but because buyers want to be able to imagine *themselves* in the house, and if the current homeowner is standing right there expansively chattering about how the ceiling in little Tommy's room had a leak before the roof was replaced two years ago and how much they enjoy using the covered deck and permanent gas grill on cool nights... well, it does tend to destroy the illusion.

When I pulled up across the street and saw no less than three cars parked at the curb, my heart sank. Surely Tim had explained to them the importance of spending two hours elsewhere?

And not only that, but there were cars parked at the curb on the other side of the street, too, and for a half block in both directions. And when I took a closer look, I saw that the front door was open—only the glass storm door was closed—and people were standing around inside.

I checked the clock. 1:43. Surely they hadn't started the open house without me? It wasn't supposed to begin until two o'clock, but there was already a crowd here.

Had Tim changed his mind and decided to host the open house himself?

I looked around. The baby-blue Jaguar of his is pretty easy to spot, and I couldn't see it anywhere.

Had Tim called off the open house for some reason, and forgotten to tell me? Had the owners called it off and Tim didn't know?

Was he playing a joke on me? He does have his moments of maliciousness, although it was difficult to fathom how this could be aimed at me in any way. I might look a bit stupid if I came to set up for an open house that had been cancelled, but let's face it, it could have happened to anyone.

Sitting in the car peering across the street at the house and the open door, I dialed Tim's number and waited. It rang a few times on the other end, and then his voice mail kicked in. "You've reached Timothy Briggs with LB&A Realty. I can't come to the phone right now. Please leave a message..."

I waited for the beep and introduced myself. "I'm sitting outside the house on Forrest that you told me would be open today. And it's open, all right. Lots of people inside. But it's only a quarter to two, and there's no Open House sign in the yard. Did you cancel and forget to let me know? Did something happen? Call me, please."

I sat back and waited. He didn't call.

By five to two I was sick of waiting. I thought again about just turning the car around and going home. But I'd gotten dressed up, and anyway, I was curious. I'd double checked the address—twice— and this was definitely the place I was supposed to be. Tim's For Sale sign was in the yard. As I'd told him, the Open House sign wasn't. But something was clearly going on. People came and went, arriving and departing in glossy BMWs, Mercedes and Lexus, and it did look a bit like an open house of some sort. And I *was* supposed to be here. It would be OK for me to go up to the door and see if I could figure out what was going on.

I swung my legs out of the car and trotted across the wet street on high heels.

So far, everyone I'd seen coming and going had been dressed in their conservative Sunday best: heels and hose, suits and ties. Subdued colors. That should probably have clued me in. It didn't. But I did fit right in, in my black skirt and pumps and my businesslike striped blouse. When I stopped outside the storm door, hesitating, a lady inside turned and saw me, and beckoned.

I pulled the door open and walked in, smiling apologetically. She smiled back, her mouth full of something.

I looked around. I was in a foyer that opened into a formal parlor on one side and a formal dining room on the other. Straight ahead was a kitchen and, I assumed, a family room. The parlor had a grand piano in the middle of the floor, while the dining room table was set with food; a much bigger spread than the one I had tucked away in the trunk of the Volvo. There were finger sandwiches and stuffed mushroom caps, bacon wrapped dates and all sorts of vegetables and cheeses.

My stomach registered approval. I'd had a late breakfast but no lunch, and I was starting to feel empty.

It wouldn't be polite to attack the buffet before I knew what was going on, though. It looked a bit like a party, with lots of people standing around eating and talking—maybe twenty, maybe more; certainly more people than I'd expected to have at my open house on a gray and gloomy day like this one—but the atmosphere seemed very subdued, not at all celebratory. There was no music and everyone spoke in somber, low voices.

I turned to the lady who'd waved me in. "Hi. I'm Savannah."

She swallowed. "Lydia Hollingsworth. Are you a friend of Erin's?"

I hesitated. I didn't even know who Erin was—or Aaron, in case Lydia pronounced the name strangely. It was tempting to say yes, but safer to say no. "I'm afraid not."

"Oh, dear." Her eyes filled with tears, and her voice dropped to what was almost a whisper. "You knew her husband. I'm so sorry for your loss."

"Thank you," I said automatically. My mother trained me well. "I mean... no, I didn't. Our company is listing the house for sale. I'm the realtor."

"Oh." The tears evaporated. "You should have said so, dear."

And here I was under the impression that I just had. I looked around. "What's going on?"

"I guess no one told you," Lydia said, leaning closer. "He died."

Dear Lord, had I inadvertently walked into a funeral? And of someone I didn't even know?

Good thing my mother wasn't here; it was the kind of faux pas I'd never live down.

Lydia nodded. "A few days ago, from what I understand." She shook her head and clicked her tongue. "Poor Erin."

No doubt. I'd only had one husband, and for only two years. I hadn't liked him much towards the end, but I would have been upset to learn he had died, at least while we were married. And Rafe... we weren't married, but for those few hours back in September, when I'd though I'd lost him, let's just say I'd been a wreck.

The last thing a grieving widow would think to worry about, was getting in touch with a realtor to call off an open house. This wasn't Tim's fault. It must have slipped the unknown Erin's mind, and who could blame her?

Was there a proper etiquette for accidentally crashing a funeral of someone you didn't know? Sneak out before the family noticed, or pay your respects to the widow?

If Tim wasn't here, maybe someone should represent the company?

I squared my shoulders. We Southern Belles may look soft, yielding and docile, but there's steel underneath. "Where is she?"

Lydia was busy chomping on a chicken leg, so she merely gestured to a woman on the other side of the grand piano. I turned in that direction and examined the lady of the house.

She was about my age, and she looked great. Slender figure, tanned, set off to perfection in a black dress that just missed being too sexy by a hair. It was probably a cocktail dress that she'd pulled out of the closet on short notice, since she didn't look like the kind of woman who'd keep mourning attire tucked away, just in case she needed it.

She looked like she played tennis. In one of those very short skirts and with a diamond tennis bracelet twinkling around one wrist. A perfect combination of athletic and mercenary, with a little California golden girl thrown in for good measure. Heather Locklear in black crepe.

When I stopped in front of her, she looked me up and down. "Do I know you?"

It could have been my imagination, but I thought her voice had an edge of something more than hostility. It sounded like liquor. Maybe she had fortified herself for the occasion.

"I don't believe we've met," I answered politely, since a Southern Belle never descends to their level, wherever that may be. "My name is Savannah Martin. I work at LB&A. With Tim Briggs."

Something moved in her eyes for a second. Then the light must have come on, because her tone changed. "Oh, no. The open house."

"I'm sorry. I didn't know about..." I gestured around to the crowd.

"Didn't Tim tell you...?" She trailed off, since obviously he hadn't. If he had, I wouldn't be here. "I'm sorry, Ms.... Martin, was it? My husband passed away unexpectedly. The police called me yesterday morning. I called Tim... eventually. Maybe around four yesterday afternoon? It slipped my mind until then. Until I came back home and saw the sign in the yard."

Naturally. Cancelling an open house wouldn't have been the first thing on my mind, either.

"I'm sorry," I said. "He didn't call me. Maybe he didn't get your message." Admittedly, that wasn't like him. Tim is usually pretty good about answering his phone. My own experience of a few minutes ago notwithstanding. "Did he call you back?"

She shook her head. "I haven't heard from him."

That was strange, too, but I'd worry about it later. "I'm sorry for your loss," I said formally. "And I'm sorry for having intruded. I'll go now."

She didn't try to stop me. Instead, she walked me out the door and onto the steps, the skin on her arms pebbling in the cold air. She lowered her voice. "When you talk to Tim, tell him I have to see him next week. About the house. Now that Brian's gone... I mean, I'm sure there are issues to deal with when someone dies."

"Of course." I did my best to sound like I was paying attention, but it wasn't easy. "I'm sorry, but... did you say your husband's name was Brian?"

She nodded. "And I'm Erin. Erin Armstrong." She offered her hand, and I took it numbly while I ran the names over and over in my head.

Armstrong. Erin Armstrong. Brian and Erin Armstrong.

"Something wrong?" Erin said, from far away.

I pulled myself together and forced a smile. "Not at all. I'm sorry for your loss. I'd better go try to track down Tim."

She nodded, although I do think she may have looked at me a bit a strangely. "It was nice to meet you, Savannah. Do tell Tim I need to talk to him when he has a moment."

I promised I would and headed for the front door, my mind churning.

Four

The first thing I did when I got into the car was dial Tim's number again. There was no answer, again. Or rather, the voicemail kicked in and told me Tim's mailbox was full, so I couldn't even leave another message.

I sat behind the wheel for a few minutes after that, thinking.

Yesterday morning, I had found Tim rinsing blood off his hands in the office bathroom, a half dozen miles away from where he lived on the south side of town.

Sometime just before that, someone had stabbed Brian Armstrong to death, rolled him in a sheet, and dumped him in Shelby Park.

Now I had just learned that the Armstrongs were Tim's clients.

Add the fact that Tim wasn't answering his phone and hadn't called to tell me the open house was cancelled, and it all added up to a pretty damning picture.

Maybe I ought to call Detective Grimaldi.

I had the phone in my hand, but part of me rebelled against the thought of using it. I like Tamara Grimaldi—I like her better than I like Tim, if it comes to that—but he was, for all intents and purposes, my boss, and besides, I could be wrong. All the things I thought I knew hung together quite well, but what if Tim had really just had a nosebleed? If I sicced the police on him, he wouldn't be happy with me. And when Tim was unhappy, he could make everyone else very unhappy indeed.

Maybe what I should do was pay him a visit instead. Maybe something was wrong. Perhaps that nosebleed I had dismissed betokened a brain hemorrhage or some such, and he was at home, unconscious, unable to answer the phone. If I went there, I might save his life.

Or at least be able to give him a piece of my mind about not calling me to cancel the open house.

In pondering it, I realized I didn't know where he lived. I knew it was somewhere in the 12 South area—around 12th Avenue on the south side of town, in another historic district much like this one—but more precisely than that I wasn't sure. I'd offered to drop off some paperwork to him once, but he had declined, and so I'd never pinpointed it more specifically than just the neighborhood.

I could stop by the office to check the employee roster, but that would be going out of my way. First, I decided to try accessing the information from where I was sitting. Property assessments are a matter of public record, at least in Nashville, and our powers that be, in their infinite wisdom, have laid them out on the internet. And with all the iIntelligence these days, all I had to do was cue up the internet on my phone, go to the courthouse records system, and search Tim's name. The phone obliged me with an address.

It took me under twenty minutes to get there, on a lazy Sunday afternoon. Football season was over for the year, so there were no road closures due to Stadium traffic. I was able to slide right onto the interstate at Shelby Avenue, and it didn't take me long at all to exit again at Wedgewood. Pretty soon I was wending my way down 12th Avenue looking for Tim's street.

Like the Five Points area in East Nashville, 12th Avenue is all up and down little funky clothing stores and bars and coffee shops. On a sunny day in the spring, the sidewalks are full of hip young things with piercings and tattoos. Today, with the sky overcast and gray mist in the air, the area was pretty deserted.

There was no sign of life on Tim's street, either. Nobody working in their yards on such an unpleasant afternoon. No children playing outside, nobody jogging. People stayed inside.

Tim's house turned out to be one of the old Victorian cottages: extremely prissy, practically dripping with gingerbread trim, and painted—of course—his favorite baby blue. Like his eyes, or so he'd probably tell me if I asked. The landscaping was immaculate, green even in the middle of winter, and manicured to within an inch of its life.

I pulled the Volvo into the driveway and cut the engine. Everything was quiet. There was a porch light on, glowing yellow through the mist, but maybe that wasn't so surprising, given the general grayness of the day. Someone could be forgiven for keeping a light on on an afternoon like this.

I made my way out of the car and up the flagstone walkway to the porch. The skinny plank flooring was slippery with water, and my hand got wet from dragging through the rain on the banister. I shook off as much of the water as I could, but was forced to wipe the rest off on my skirt, which I did with a grimace.

There was no newfangled doorbell beside Tim's door; instead, he still had the original handle mounted in the middle of the heavy, carved wood door. When I twisted it, a chime rang through the house, pure and clear.

I took a step back, off the welcome mat, and waited.

Nothing happened.

After a minute I rang again. Then I tried the door. It was locked, of course. I did check under the mat—after surveying the neighborhood to make sure no one was watching me—but there was no key underneath. Ditto for the big flower pot in the corner. The porch swing was stripped of its pillows for the winter, so there was nowhere there to hide anything, and running my fingers across the top of the lintel likewise produced no results. Obviously, Tim hadn't seen the need to leave a hide-a-key on his porch, or if he had, he'd found a hiding place that was more inventive than I'd guessed.

That left the back door.

I made my way around the house to the rear, where, indeed, there was a kitchen door. Knocking on it produced no results either, and like the front door, it was locked. All I could see through the window was the laundry room. A washer, a dryer, a table for folding, and a sliver of the kitchen through the open door. Tim had dark espresso cabinets, stainless steel appliances, and a granite countertop. And no key hidden anywhere, that I could find.

If I'd truly been afraid for Tim's health and wellbeing, I would have broken the window and stuck my arm through to unlatch the door from inside. But I wasn't quite at that point yet. I was worried, certainly, but I wasn't yet at the point of wanting to commit B&E.

So instead I wandered through the misting rain to the garage. There was a window at the top of the roll-back door, but it was too high for me to reach. And this door, likewise, was locked. At least I got no movement when I slipped my fingers under the edge of it and heaved. And because it was an electronic door—or so I assumed—there was no handle I could tug.

As a last resort, I headed around the garage to the rear, the heels of my shoes sinking into the soggy ground, and finally came across a small door set into the side wall. It was locked too, but it had a window, through which I was able to ascertain that the garage was empty. Or not empty, exactly—there were gardening supplies and a bicycle and a variety of boxes and plastic crates stacked along one wall—but there was no sign of the Jaguar, nor of Tim.

He definitely wasn't here.

On the one hand, that was good news. At least I could stop worrying about him bleeding to death inside the house.

On the other hand, it was worrisome, taken in combination with Saturday's blood and dead body, the overflowing voicemail box, and the fact that he hadn't contacted me about the open house.

If I'd been able to get into his place more easily, I would have gone in. But since I couldn't, not without actually breaking in, I had a choice to make. Would I be better off calling Tamara Grimaldi right now and telling her what I knew—what I suspected—and let her make the decision as to whether Tim's house warranted further investigation? Or would it be better to wait a bit longer and see if Tim turned up at the weekly sales meeting at the office tomorrow morning? He was the broker-in-residence, so under normal circumstances he should be there. And it wasn't like I knew that something had happened to him. It was the middle of the afternoon, and there was nothing here that suggested foul play. Maybe he'd found a new friend and things had gotten a little rough, and that's where the blood had come from. Or maybe he really had killed Brian Armstrong, and now he was on the run.

But either way, Tim didn't seem to be in any immediate danger. And since I couldn't use that as an excuse to break into his house to make sure everything was all right, it was probably better just to wait until the morning to call Grimaldi. If he didn't show up at the weekly sales meeting, and he hadn't told Brittany that he'd be gone, then we'd have something to worry about. But until then, I could just be making things up.

I scribbled a note for Tim to call me on the back of a business card and tucked it between the door and the jamb on the back door. If he parked in the garage—and with the nasty weather, he probably would—he was more likely to enter the house through the back than the front. After a moment's hesitation, I added one to the front door, as well. Better safe than sorry.

I FULLY EXPECTED RAFE TO SLINK in after I'd turned out the lights and attempted to go to sleep for a second night in a row. Imagine my surprise when he showed up around dinner time, as I was curled in a chair in the living room, deeply invested in another romance novel I had picked up at the grocery story this afternoon along with the hot chocolate and the cookies. I was enjoying a cup of cocoa and a few of the cookies too, since they'd only go to waste if I didn't eat them.

The book was your classic tale of contemporary love, between the cold-hearted, money-grubbing billionaire and the sweet woman who turned him human. The tall, blond, gray-eyed hero had quite a lot in common with my ex-husband Bradley, not to mention Todd Satterfield, my brother's best friend and the man my mother had designated as my second husband.

My mother isn't terribly fond of Rafe. Not to put too fine a point on it, but if there existed a list of all the men in the world my mother could imagine me getting involved with, Rafe would not be on it.

There are lots of reasons for this, beginning with his mother, his father, his grandmother, the rest of his family, his illegitimate child, his skin color, his past, his present, the fact that he seduced me, the fact that he knocked me up, the fact that he left me, the fact that he came back, the fact that he's risked my life more times than mother is comfortable with—never mind the fact that he's saved it a few times too. Most of all, it's simply because he isn't Todd. Mother wanted me to marry Todd. She's dating Todd's daddy, Sweetwater sheriff Bob Satterfield, while my brother Dix remains Todd's best friend. If I were to marry Todd, it would set mother's world to rights. And when I chose Rafe instead, let's just say she wasn't best pleased. Our relationship became official on Christmas Eve, and she hasn't quite gotten over it yet. I've done my best to keep the two of them apart since then, since my life is a lot easier that way.

Anyway, I was sitting there reading when Rafe walked in. First I heard the key in the door, and then steps in the hallway. A couple of thuds were the sounds of his boots hitting the floor. A rustle was his leather jacket being hung on one of the hooks. And then I heard his footsteps padding down the hallway toward me, past the kitchen and the half bath, into the living room/dining room combination.

I looked up from the book, but I didn't say anything. He didn't either, for the first few seconds. We just looked at one another. And as usual, even in the midst of my worry and anger, the sight of him took my breath away.

It's not just because he's beautiful, although he is. LaDonna Collier was a blue-eyed blonde like me, while Tyrell Jenkins was black, and the combination is gorgeous. Rafe has golden skin, melting dark eyes, and hair the color of espresso. It's a coloring that has served him quite well in his ten years of undercover work. He can look African-American, he can look Hispanic, he can look Middle Eastern or Greek, and dressed up in a suit and tie, he fits in quite well with the upper crust, too, as long as he tones down that far-from-upper-class Southern drawl.

At the moment he was dressed in another black T-shirt that pulled tight across his arms and shoulders, and a matching pair of cargo pants. With his hair in its usual barely-there crop, and with the viper tattoo on his arm peeking out from under the sleeve of the shirt, there was nothing refined or civilized about him at all. He looked hot as hell, and he also looked dangerous. I recognized the getup from early December, when he'd used it to play bouncer at *La Havana* nightclub.

As if to complete the picture, he reached behind him to pull out a gun and lay it on the dining room table, as easily and without fanfare as if it were an everyday occurrence. For him it was. I wasn't quite there yet myself, especially since I hadn't seen that gun much lately.

I was still staring at it, trying to guess what its presence might mean, when he sauntered toward me, to brace his hands on the arms of the chair I was sitting in, one on each side of me. "Evening, darlin'."

When he leaned in to kiss me, I turned my face aside. "You smell like smoke."

There was a beat while nothing happened, and I could feel his breath against my cheek. Then he straightened. "Yeah?"

I already wished I could take it back, but it was too late. He didn't wait for me to answer, just turned on his heel. "Guess I'd better take care of that." He peeled the T-shirt up over his head as he sauntered toward the door to the bedroom and the shower beyond. Muscles moved smoothly under golden skin, and my tongue got stuck to the roof of my mouth. So much for pretending I was unaffected.

I thought he might disappear into the bedroom without looking back, but I guess he knows me too well. When he glanced over his shoulder as he passed through the doorway, the look on my face must have told him everything he needed to know, because he winked. "Hold that thought, darlin'."

No problem. I closed the romance novel and used it to fan myself.

When he came back into the living room a few minutes later, he was mostly dry and wholly naked except for a towel wrapped negligently around his waist. With each step he took, it dipped a little lower.

"That's not fair," I protested weakly.

He grinned. "Sure it is. A man's gotta do what a man's gotta do, darlin'. Can't have you holding out on me."

"I'm not holding out," I managed. Barely.

Truth was, I'd forgotten all about why I'd been upset in the first place. It's pathetic, and totally unbecoming a properly brought-up Southern Belle—mother would be aghast—but all he has to do is move close to me, and I go weak in the knees and lose my breath as every coherent thought blows out of my head.

The first thing he did was take the romance novel out of my limp hand and look at the cover. One eyebrow arched. The fact that he can do that, and I can't, is a source of constant annoyance to me, although between you and me, I love the look on his face when he does.

Because he knows me well, he knew exactly what had been in my mind when I bought the book. "Wish you'd married Satterfield after all?"

I shook my head.

"Then you don't need this." He tossed it onto the sofa and turned back to me. "Let's try this again."

I stopped breathing as hot dark eyes and sleek muscles crowded my vision. I could feel the heat of his skin through my blouse.

He didn't smell like smoke anymore. He smelled like soap, and mint toothpaste, and something else—spicy and citrusy—that's just him.

When he leaned in, I swear my eyes rolled back in my head. I could hear him chuckle, and then he kissed me.

"So what have you been up to this weekend, darlin'?"

It was an hour or so later, and we were still in bed. He had carried me there at some point—I'd been vaguely aware of floating—but nearer than that I couldn't say. Now we had caught our breaths again, and Rafe wanted to know what had been going on in my life during the hours he'd been MIA.

Some of my earlier pique returned. "Shouldn't that be my question?"

He grimaced and flopped over on his back, throwing an arm up to cover his face. Muscles bunched and the viper tattoo flicked its little forked tongue at me. "I should have told you."

"Yes," I said, "you should have."

He glanced at me, slantways, from under the arm. "I didn't want you to worry."

"How could you imagine I wouldn't? We've been together practically 24/7 for the past two months. Suddenly you're up and out at the crack of dawn? You don't call, and when you come back, you make sure I don't have the opportunity to ask you where you've been? And then you do it again the next morning!"

He made another face. "That's why."

"What's why?"

"We've been together almost 24/7 since Christmas. I'm going crazy."

It was as if the bottom fell out and my heart dropped down to my stomach. Not an easy thing to do when you're lying down.

"Oh," I managed, my lips stiff.

He shot me a look. "It isn't you, Savannah."

"Of course not." He was just used to more excitement than I could provide, was all. More women. More exciting women.

I'd always known it would happen, to be honest. I can't say I'd thought it would happen quite so quickly, but I had been waiting for it almost from the start. Part of me knew I wouldn't be able to hold his interest for long. He had assured me that the paltry sex life that Bradley and I had had, had been Bradley's fault and not mine, but I guess when it came right down to it, I wasn't woman enough to keep Rafe satisfied, either.

"I'm sorry, darlin'."

"Me too," I said, blinking away a couple of tears. Crying and clinging would surely be the worst thing I could do right now. Much better to let go gracefully, and have a meltdown later, after he was gone. I wouldn't be able to pull off feigned indifference—he knew me too well for that—but I could be nice about giving him his freedom.

"I just needed to do something to feel alive again."

"Right." I nodded, understanding incarnate even as my heart broke in two. I'd felt more alive in the past few months with him than in all my almost twenty eight years so far.

"I love you. And I like being around you. But it's just been too much, you know?"

"Sure."

"I need to get away once in a while. Do something different. I'm not used to this."

"Of course."

He turned over and leaned on an elbow to look at me. "You're saying all the right things. Why do I get the feeling you're not OK?"

"I don't know," I said.

His eyes searched my face. "Nothing happened. I was careful."

Sure.

"I didn't get hurt. No new scars. Feel free to check."

The smile that curved his lips lacked a little of its usual brilliance. It looked almost... tentative.

"Hurt?" I said. "Why would—?"

And then the brick dropped. I sat up, my eyes wide, clutching the sheets to my bosom. "What did you do?"

"I worked," Rafe said, looking up at me. "What did you think I did?"

I opened my mouth, but I couldn't get the words out. My cheeks colored, though, and his face changed. "Oh."

"I'm sorry," I said—muttered, really. "It isn't you. I love you. I trust you. I just... I know I'm not as exciting as some of the other women you've been with..."

"I wouldn't say that," Rafe said, with a curve to his lips that told me he was thinking about some of the things we'd just done.

"It's not like you've been complaining or anything. I mean, you've seemed pretty happy, actually. With me, anyway. I knew you were getting a little bored with the renovations. But when you left like that, all I could think about was Bradley..."

"I thought I'd made you forget Bradley."

"You have," I said. "Mostly."

"Need a refresher?"

He looked like he might be inclined to give me one if I said yes. He also didn't look upset anymore.

"Um..." I said.

His lips curved. "I'll take that as a yes. C'mere, darlin'."

He hooked his hand over the top of the sheet I was clutching and tugged. When the sheet dropped, his eyes did too, and he smiled. And when he reached for me, I slid into his arms without demur.

"I love you," he said against my cheek.

"I love you too." His skin was warm and smooth against my lips when I lingered.

"Next time I'll let you know what's going on." He pulled me a little closer.

"Please," I said, and then I lost my breath when his hands started wandering south.

Five

"So tell me about your weekend," Rafe said again an hour later. We were still in bed, but considering getting up and going out for something to eat. Or at least I was. I hadn't had any lunch, and it was a long time since breakfast, and besides, the strenuous exercise we'd just undertaken had further depleted my energy.

"How about we talk over dinner? My treat?"

He grinned and drew a suggestive finger down my arm. "You sure you wouldn't rather stay in?"

Of course I'd rather stay in. The reaction of my body to just that one finger made it blatantly obvious to both of us. But if I stayed where I was, we wouldn't eat. And besides, it was difficult to concentrate with so much nakedness staring me in the face.

"I'm hungry," I said.

"I can fix that." He winked.

"I know you can. But I haven't eaten since breakfast. And if you look at me like that—if you look like that—I won't be able to concentrate on the story."

That got his attention. "What story?"

"When we get to the restaurant," I said, sliding out of bed. That would give him some incentive to move that gorgeous posterior. And anyway— "You haven't told me what you were actually doing all weekend."

"At the restaurant," Rafe said and headed for the bathroom.

A HALF HOUR LATER WE WERE seated on opposite sides of a table in a dark corner of the FinBar, a sports bar just down the street from the real estate office, and not too terribly far from my apartment. Rafe was tucking into a cheeseburger with onion rings, while I was trying to show a little more restraint and had ordered a salad instead. It tasted pretty good, as salads go, although that didn't stop me from gazing enviously at his burger.

"I wish you'd stop ordering food you think you should eat," he told me around a bite of beef and bun, "and order what you want instead."

"If I ate the way you do, I'd weigh as much as you do, too." I forked up a dainty shred of lettuce and conveyed it to my mouth.

"I'd still be able to carry you to bed." He snagged an onion ring from his plate and held it out. "Open up."

I opened up, obediently, and took a bite. And went almost cross-eyed as the flavors burst on my tongue. "Mmm."

"Yep. That's what you're missing." He popped the rest in his own mouth. "Your mama ain't here, darlin'. It's just you and me, and I don't care what you eat. You might as well make it something you enjoy."

"Habit," I said. Mother taught me to always eat like a bird in front of a potential husband. We wouldn't want him to think I was A) unconcerned with my looks or B) going to be expensive to maintain.

"You want I should get you something different? The waitress is right over there." He glanced over my shoulder.

"That's not necessary," I said, but it was too late. The waitress must have noticed him looking at her—she had probably been looking at him—because she materialized next to the table, all long legs and tight jeans and a low cut T-shirt. When she stopped beside us, she leaned forward, oh so casually, to make sure he got a good look into her cleavage. "Can I help you, sir?"

Her voice was Marilyn Monroe breathy, and I had to focus hard so I wouldn't roll my eyes. My mother raised a lady, but there are limits.

Rafe grinned. "I'm gonna need an order of French fries, sugar, when you have a chance."

He winked at me. He gets a kick out of watching women react to him. Not because he needs the ego boost—he has a pretty healthy ego to begin with—but because he thinks it's funny how we forget our names and walk into walls whenever he turns on the charm.

The waitress stumbled off, and I shook my head. "You shouldn't do that. It isn't fair."

"Ain't like I plan to take it beyond dinner, darlin'."

"That's why it isn't fair," I said.

He shrugged. "You gonna tell me about your weekend now?"

"After you tell me about yours," I was chasing a Kalamata olive over and under the pieces of lettuce on my plate.

"Nothing much to tell. I helped Wendell move a witness."

"Really?" I had seen scenarios like that in movies and on television, of special agents from one letter agency or another transporting witnesses from the airport to the courthouse to the safe hotel and back. "Anyone I'd know?"

"Can't tell you that. But no, prob'ly not."

I nodded. "What about the gun?"

He hesitated, or maybe it was just that he saw the waitress coming. When he smiled, I was afraid that the plate of French fries would end up in his lap. It was only quick reflexes that saved him. "Thank you, sugar."

He waited for her to walk away again before he pushed the plate of fries across the table toward me. "Here. Eat."

"After you tell me about the gun."

"It's nothing. Standard operating procedure. Most of the time it's there, you don't ever need to draw it." He reached over to grab a couple of fries, dredged them in ketchup, and popped them in his mouth. "Now tell me how you spent the weekend. Eat your fries. And talk."

"I spent Saturday morning in the office," I said, carefully selecting a single fry and dipping it in the ketchup. "Nothing exciting happened, other than that I caught Tim rinsing blood off his hands in the bathroom when I walked in." I popped the fry in my mouth. *Mmmm.*

"Did he cut himself on his tongue?" Rafe picked up his burger again.

"He said he had a nosebleed. It might even be true."

"Sure," Rafe said. "Why not?"

"I called Grimaldi."

"About Tim's nosebleed?"

I shook my head. "To ask her whether she knew where you were. She said no."

He nodded, his mouth full. So at least he hadn't confided in Tamara Grimaldi, and she hadn't lied when she told me she didn't know anything. And if that sounds paranoid, I can assure you, it's happened before.

"She was working a case," I said. "Dead man found in Shelby Park, stabbed and rolled in a sheet, left by the side of the road. His name was Brian Armstrong."

"Never heard of him," Rafe said, around another bite of burger.

"Me either. Until this afternoon."

He swallowed. "What happened this afternoon?"

I told him about the open house, the wake I'd accidentally crashed, and the realization that the Armstrongs were Tim's clients. I also mentioned that bloody handprint I thought I'd seen on the back of Tim's car the other morning.

Rafe, being Rafe, took less than two seconds to see where I was going with the information I had. He leaned back in the booth and folded his arms across his chest. "Did you talk to Tim?"

"I tried," I said. "He wasn't home. His voice mailbox is full. I left a note on his door, but he hasn't called back."

"Did you call Tammy?"

"Do you think I should?"

"Yes," Rafe said. "I think you should."

"You don't think he could just be out with a friend? Or in bed with a friend? Too busy to answer the phone?"

He hesitated. "Is that something he'd do?"

It was my turn to hesitate. "I don't really know him well enough to say. But it could happen, I guess. I mean, if he ever got the chance to spend the night with you, I'm sure he could be persuaded to turn the phone off."

"I'll keep that in mind," Rafe said. "So it's possible he found somebody like me, someone who swings his way, and he's in bed."

"It's possible. Or he could he halfway to California by now. I thought I'd wait until tomorrow morning to start fretting. If he doesn't show up for the staff meeting at nine, and he hasn't been in touch with Brittany, then I was going to call Grimaldi."

Rafe nodded. We sat in silence for a few seconds until I broke it.

"You don't really think he killed that guy, do you? Mr. Armstrong?"

"I don't know," Rafe said. "I don't know either of them well enough. Do *you* think he killed the guy?"

"You've met Tim. Can you imagine him killing someone?"

"I can imagine anyone killing someone," Rafe said, "if the stakes were high enough. Even you."

True. I never have, but there have been times when I've wanted to.

"Any evidence that this Armstrong guy lived a double life?" Rafe wanted to know. "Nice little wife at home, gay lover across town?"

I wouldn't call Erin Armstrong a nice little wife, myself, but beyond that— "I have no idea," I said. "You'd have to ask Grimaldi. And she probably won't tell you."

He nodded. "You gonna eat those fries?"

I glanced at his plate. While we'd been talking, he'd polished off his burger and onion rings. Now he was eyeing the plate of fries the same way he sometimes looks at me.

I pushed it toward him. "Knock yourself out."

"You don't want any?"

"I've had some," I said. And the reminder that my boss might be a murderer had made me lose my appetite. "Let's go home."

"Works for me," Rafe said and gestured for the check. While we waited, he ate the rest of the fries.

Six

He was there when I woke up the next morning, his skin warm against my back and one muscular arm wrapped around my waist as if to make sure I couldn't go anywhere. We spent a bit of time sharing various parts of ourselves with the other, and then I rolled out of bed and headed for the shower. While I got ready for the sales meeting at the office, in skirt, blouse, and pumps, Rafe hit the shower too and then pulled on a pair of jeans.

"You sure you don't want me to go with you?" he wanted to know.

"I'd love for you to come with me." I perched on the edge of the bed and watched with regret as he yanked a white T-shirt down to cover all that smooth skin and hard muscles I'd just finished playing with. "But I don't know what good it would do. You'd be bored. And it isn't like Tim's going to come in looking like Lady Macbeth, scrubbing at his hands."

"Prob'ly not," Rafe admitted.

"He definitely won't come in looking to stab anyone else. I won't need protection."

He nodded.

"You're just looking for an excuse not to work on the house."

"I don't mind working on the house," Rafe said, running a hand over his head. There wasn't enough hair there to run his fingers through. "We agreed the best thing was to put it on the market. My grandma won't be back to live there. I don't want you living there. If nobody's gonna live there, we may as well sell it."

I nodded, even as my heart skipped a happy little beat at that mention of 'we.' It was Mrs. Jenkins's house. He was her grandson. I was nobody in the scheme of things, other than the woman he was shacking up with and claimed to love. Yet he talked about it as if it was both of our decision what to do with the house. As if we were one.

"The sooner I finish, the sooner you can put it on the market. I don't mind working on the house."

"But?"

"I wanna know what happens," Rafe said. "I've met Tim a couple times. I'd hate to think of him going to prison. It wouldn't be a good place for him."

Probably not. And as someone who'd spent a few years there, I figured Rafe should know.

"I'll call you," I said.

"Yeah?"

"Sure. If he doesn't show up, I'll call both you and Grimaldi. I promise."

He nodded, seemingly satisfied. "I'm gonna go." He leaned in to kiss me goodbye. The kiss turned into a little more than a quick peck, and I was breathless by the time he straightened. If it hadn't been for the sales meeting, I would have gone over backwards and dragged him down on top of me. He knew it too, judging from the unholy gleam in his eyes. "Hold that thought."

"No need," I informed him. "It'll be back the next time I see you. Like clockwork."

He grinned. "Call me."

"I will. Be careful."

"It's home renovation," Rafe said. "What could happen?"

A whole lot of things could happen, but he walked away before I could list them. It was probably better that way. Considering the dangers he'd lived with every day for ten years, the threat of accidentally hitting his thumb with a hammer probably wouldn't loom large, and I couldn't blame him.

I MADE IT TO THE OFFICE with a few minutes to spare, and dropped my coat and bag in my office—actually a converted coat closet off the lobby—before heading into the conference room, where a half dozen people were ranged around the big table.

We're not a big company. We've only got about two dozen agents, all told, and more than half of those do real estate part time, in the evenings and on weekends. A lot of real estate happens then anyway, since a lot of people work 9-to-5 during the week, and evenings and weekends is when they have time to go looking for property. And then there were the ones who had taken on steady jobs to supplement the real estate income. It's not an easy business to get ahead in, as I had learned to my detriment. I'd had my real estate license for six or seven months by now, and I'd only pulled a half dozen closings out of my hat. I wasn't getting rich. I wasn't even making ends meet. If Rafe hadn't moved in, I might have had to beg my brother for a handout to pay my bills. (I couldn't have asked mother, because she would have told me to marry Todd so I wouldn't have to worry.)

Anyway, the handful of people seated around the table were the full-timers, the ones who weren't bagging groceries or pouring coffee or cutting grass at nine on a Monday morning.

I gave everyone a friendly wave, and took a seat on one side of the table. "Is Tim not here?"

"I haven't seen him," one of the women said.

"Probably just running late," one of the men added.

Sure. I settled back to wait. No sense in making waves until I knew anything for sure.

By 9:10 Tim still hadn't shown up. Someone else had started the meeting 'while we wait,' and we'd gone around the table and shared good news and new listings and the like. Since Tim wasn't there to give sales stats for the business as a whole, it turned into a short meeting. By twenty after, we had broken up and everyone had flown the coop, heading back to work. I stopped in front of Brittany's desk in the lobby. "No word from Tim?"

She didn't even look up from the latest issue of Cosmo, just shook her head.

"Doesn't that bother you?"

She tossed her ponytail. "Why would it?"

"He's the broker. He missed the sales meeting. It isn't like him."

"So?" Brittany said. "What do you want me to do about it?"

I sighed. "Nothing. I'm going to go check his office."

She giggled. "Do you think he's hiding under his desk?"

"Maybe his desk calendar says something about a weekend trip, or something." Before I called Detective Grimaldi and accused Tim of murder, I should probably make sure there wasn't some innocent explanation for everything.

"Sure," Brittany said and waved her hand. "Knock yourself out."

That made it easier, anyway. Not that I needed her permission, but I also didn't need her running after me, screaming that I had no right to snoop in Tim's inner sanctum.

Tim's office used to belong to Walker Lamont, founder of LB&A and our previous broker. Walker left us in August, and is now cooling his heels in medium security prison. It's a long story, and although he tried to kill me at one point, we've always gotten along fairly well. I'll always be grateful to Walker for unknowingly reintroducing me to

Rafe. If he hadn't killed Brenda Puckett, Rafe wouldn't have called the office the first Saturday in August, and I wouldn't have gone out to meet him, and we wouldn't have found Brenda's body, and so on and so forth.

When Walker went to prison, Tim took over as broker, and moved his stuff into Walker's corner office. It has a nice mahogany desk and an expensive ergonomically correct chair, not to mention a whole lot of filing cabinets and folders everywhere.

I stopped just inside the door and looked around. Tim had removed Walker's tasteful landscapes and had livened up the walls with a handful of framed Playbills—he spent a few years in New York trying to get on Broadway before coming back to Nashville and becoming a realtor—and also a panoramic view of Manhattan above one of the filing cabinets. A framed photograph on the desk piqued my interest, but when I walked around to look at it, it turned out to be Tim's own face smiling out at me from a silver frame. An old headshot, maybe, all bright eyes and bright teeth.

The rest of the desk was pretty clean. There was no big flat desk calendar taking up space in the middle of the blotter, but when I opened the desk drawer, I found a smaller, sheet-a-day calendar tucked away there. For good reason: Tim occasionally brings clients to the office, and they might not appreciate seeing a calendar of scantily clad men on their (male) realtor's desk. East Nashville is diverse, but I'm not sure it's quite that diverse. I was frankly surprised he'd brought the calendar to the office at all, but maybe he amused himself by looking at it during downtimes.

I lifted it out and put it on the desk. The sheet on top of the stack was Saturday's, and there were no notations of meetings or appointments on it. No early visit to a construction site, for instance. On Sunday, the open house at the Armstrongs was penciled in, below a picture of a dusky-skinned hunk not too dissimilar to Rafe, who made me blush.

I'd seen Tim very early on Saturday morning. Brian Armstrong had died overnight, sometime late Friday or in the early hours of Saturday. Grimaldi would know more definitely, but she hadn't seen fit to share that information with me. Either way, if Tim had scheduled a meeting with Armstrong—or with someone else—it would probably have been for Friday night, not Saturday morning.

The small trashcan under the desk was empty save for a used breath mint strip. Tim must have emptied it before he left on Friday.

Getting up from the chair—a lot more comfortable than mine—I tucked the X-rated desk calendar back into the drawer and closed it, before heading to the kitchen. The trashcan there is the biggest in the office. If Tim hadn't taken his trash outside to the dumpster at the back of the lot—and I was hoping the cold weather might have prevented him—he'd have emptied his stuff in it.

Digging through was an unpleasant task. We recycle anything recyclable, and shred anything sensitive, but that still leaves a lot of nasty garbage to go into the kitchen trashcan. I picked through sticky candy wrappers and empty TV-dinner trays, used paper plates and wadded-up paper towels. It would have been worth it if I'd found the Friday sheet from Tim's calendar, but I didn't. All I got for my trouble was sticky hands and a pain in my lower back from bending over.

While I was in the middle of it, my phone rang, and I ended up smearing sticky nastiness all over that, as well. And it wasn't even Rafe calling. It was my mother, so I couldn't very well ignore it. You never know; something might be wrong.

"Hello, darling," she said when I'd identified myself. Her 'darling' sounds very different from Rafe's. My mother is Southern to the bone—born and bred in Savannah, my namesake—but she doesn't drawl. At least not sexily.

"Mother. What can I do for you?"

"I just wanted to see how you were, darling," my mother said.

"I'm fine. Why wouldn't I be?"

"No reason," mother said smoothly. "There's no cause to be defensive, Savannah."

Sure.

"We're fine," I said again, with the emphasis on 'we' this time. Yes, there was cause for me to be defensive. My mother hated my boyfriend. She was probably hoping I'd tell her he'd hit me or cheated on me or something, so she could feel vindicated and I could be free to marry Todd Satterfield.

There was a slight pause while mother regrouped and reconsidered her mode of attack. "Will we see you at Abigail's birthday party this weekend, darling?"

"I don't know," I said.

"Dixon invited you, didn't he?"

Of course he did.

Abigail is my brother Dix's oldest daughter. She was turning six, and he was planning a big party for her. Abigail and Hannah, her two years younger sister, had lost their mother in November. Christmas had been tough without her, and I guess maybe Dix was going all out to take Abigail's mind off the fact that Sheila wouldn't be there to celebrate her birthday this year. There would be a huge little-girl party on Saturday afternoon, with bouncy castles and balloon animals and all of Abigail's little friends from school, along with Hannah and Annie, my sister Catherine's daughter. I'm sure Dix had invited Catherine's boys too, but Cole and Robert had probably declined the pleasures of the Cinderella bouncy castle. They're not yet old enough to think that girls are anything but icky.

The family party was scheduled for Friday night, the evening before the big day, since Dix had told me he expected to be beat after the Saturday shindig and was looking forward to a bottle of scotch and a quiet evening at home to recover.

"Do you have other plans?" mother asked.

I didn't. "I'm just not sure I'll be able to make it."

I could almost hear my mother's eyes narrow. "I don't like the way he's keeping you away from your family, darling. We haven't seen you since Christmas."

"He's not keeping me away," I said. "I just don't like to choose between my family and my boyfriend."

There was a pause while mother struggled with what to say. She could tell me that of course Rafe was welcome in Sweetwater too, but we both knew better. He makes my mother uncomfortable. She makes him a bit uncomfortable too, I think, even if he doesn't readily admit it.

"He has bad memories of Sweetwater," I added when I couldn't handle the silence anymore. Mother brought me up to put people at their ease, to diffuse difficult situations, and although part of me really wanted her to feel bad for not welcoming the man I loved to the family, the other part bowed to conditioning and good manners.

Rafe and I grew up in the same hometown: Sweetwater, Tennessee, just over an hour south of Nashville, between Columbia and Pulaski. But while I spent my formative years in what Rafe calls the 'mausoleum on the hill,' the Martin Mansion, he grew up in the Bog, the trailer park on the other side of town. While my family can trace their antecedents back to the War Between the States and beyond, Rafe only recently discovered who his father was. And while I'm as close to antebellum aristocracy as it's possible to come, the Colliers were—not to put too fine a point on it—white trash, and then LaDonna compounded that offense by getting herself in the family way at fourteen by a colored boy. A colored boy her daddy, Big Jim Collier, promptly shot to death.

It wasn't what you'd call an auspicious beginning, and Rafe was in trouble almost from the time he was old enough to talk. He didn't stop until he landed himself in prison at eighteen for assault and battery.

To all of Sweetwater, including my mother, he'll always be LaDonna Collier's good-for-nothing colored boy. And since everyone knows about his prison sentence, but very few people know that he's spent the past ten years doing undercover work for the TBI, risking his own life to put bad guys behind bars, most everyone also thinks he's a danger to himself and others. People stare at him sideways and talk in whispers when he shows up Sweetwater. Why would I want to subject him to that?

There was nothing mother could say, of course, and she wasn't about to tell me I was wrong and that she really wanted to see Rafe. If she never saw him again, I'm quite sure it wouldn't be soon enough. And to be honest, I could never quite make up my mind which was the lesser evil: dragging him to Sweetwater with me, making everyone (including him) uncomfortable just so I could make my point, or leaving him in Nashville while going to Sweetwater myself, thereby letting my mother win. So far, I had refused to make the decision one way or the other, and had stayed in Nashville with Rafe rather than going to Sweetwater to see my family. But that was a temporary fix at best; the only reason I'd gotten away with it for the past two months, was because there had been no birthdays or major holidays since Christmas.

Until now.

"I'll talk to him," I said. "If he ends up coming with me, I want you to promise to be nice to him."

"When am I not nice?" mother asked, offended.

"When my boyfriend walks into the room. You're cold enough to freeze his testicles off."

"Savannah!" mother exclaimed, shocked.

"I'm sorry. But it's the truth. You're perfectly correct, but you make it clear you think he's beneath you." And me. "And I don't appreciate it."

Mother was silent. I guess she couldn't very well deny feeling that way, but at the same time, she wasn't about to apologize for it, not when it was her opinion that he damn well was.

"I love you," I said. "And I love Dix and Catherine and Jonathan and the kids. I hate missing out on family occasions. But I won't have my boyfriend insulted and made to feel unwelcome. I love him too, and until you can learn to be nice to him, I think it's probably better that we both just stay away."

There was a pause.

"I'll talk to Dix," I said when mother didn't speak. "And now I have to go. I'm in the office. Thanks for calling."

Mother pulled herself together. "Take care of yourself, darling."

I said I would and hung up, while I reflected that it might have been nicer if she'd told me to take care of Rafe and trusted him to take care of me.

There was no calendar page in the kitchen trash. I washed my hands—and the phone—in the sink, and wondered whether I ought to put an out-of-order sign on the bathroom faucet and turn off the water to the sink in there, just in case there were blood traces to be found in the drain.

I really should call Detective Grimaldi. I just wanted to find that calendar page first, if I could.

Tim might have shredded it. We have several shredders: one in the lobby for Brittany to use, and a huge one in the copy room for everyone else. A few of the agents have individual ones in their offices, as well.

I went back to Tim's office and looked around. He did have a small shredder tucked away between two of the filing cabinets. It was full of thin strips of paper, like black and white confetti. Most were long strips, legal or letter size paper. But some were shorter, and brightly colored. When I saw what I thought was half a nipple on one of them, it convinced me to gather as many of the colored strips as I could.

Tim had envelopes on his desk, and I snagged one and filled it up with all the naked men shreds I could find. There were a lot. He must have been in the habit of shredding calendar pages. Maybe he didn't want anyone to know that he had pictures of scantily clad men in his office. Maybe he was afraid someone would think it was dirty magazines instead of a perfectly—mostly—innocent calendar.

Whatever. Once my envelope was full to bulging point, I headed back to my own office. It was time to make phone calls. If I waited until I had matched the thousands of shreds and managed to recreate Friday's calendar page, it would be the end of the day. If I were going to call Grimaldi, I had to call her now.

But first I had to call Rafe.

It took him a couple of rings to pick up. When he did, his voice echoed hollowly, the way it does when you're standing in an empty, high-ceilinged room with no furniture and no rugs to absorb the sound. "Morning, darlin'."

"Hi," I said, as his voice, as usual, sent pleasurable shivers down my spine.

When I didn't say anything else, he added, "Something wrong?"

I pulled myself together. "No. Or maybe. My mother called."

"Everything OK?"

"Everything is fine," I said. "It's my niece's birthday this weekend. Dix is having a big party for her. To take her mind off Sheila, I guess."

Rafe made a sort of auditory nod. It wasn't quite a word, nor a grunt or anything so base, but it was an encouragement to go on.

"Mother called to ask whether I... whether we were planning to be there."

"You should go," Rafe said. I could hear from his voice, and from the sounds behind him, that he was continuing to work while we talked. I couldn't tell what he was doing, but I could hear that he was doing something.

"I know I should. I just wanted to know if you'd like to come with me."

"Your mama hates me, darlin'," Rafe said.

"She doesn't. She just..."

"Wanted you to marry Satterfield instead."

Well, yes. "She'll get used to you. If she ever gets to know you, that is."

There was a beat. And another. When he didn't tell me he'd go with me, just let the silence hang, I relented. "I really called to tell you that Tim didn't show up for the meeting."

"Have you called Tammy?" Rafe asked.

"Not yet. I've been looking for his calendar, to see if he had any appointments scheduled Friday night. Grimaldi will want to know that, too. This way I'll have saved her the trouble."

"Did he?"

"Not sure yet. He shredded his calendar pages. They have dirty pictures on them."

"Ah." I couldn't see him, but I could hear the grin in his voice. "You gonna play puzzles, darlin'?"

"I'm going to try," I said. "It'll give me something to do while I wait for Grimaldi to get here." Or not. It was possible she wouldn't be interested in the information I had. "You still think I should call her, right?"

He hesitated. "Don't you?"

"I think... probably, yes. It seems like too much of a coincidence. If he'd been here for the meeting and everything had seemed like normal this morning, maybe I wouldn't think so, but the fact that he's gone..."

"Let me know how it goes," Rafe said.

I promised I would. "I'll talk to you later. Love you."

"Love you too," Rafe said, and hung up.

Seven

Tamara Grimaldi answered on the first ring. "Ms. Martin."

"Detective."

"Your boyfriend gone again?"

"No," I said, with dignity, "he's at Mrs. Jenkins's house, painting."

"So what can I do for you?"

I meant to tell her about Tim, I swear I did. Instead, the words that fell out of my mouth were very different. "It's my niece's birthday this weekend."

"Yes?"

"Did you already know that?"

"I may have heard something about it," Grimaldi said.

"Did Dix invite you to come down?"

"In my job, it's hard to make plans." It wasn't a straight answer, but it sounded like he might have. "Is there a problem?"

"Just the usual. My mother hates my boyfriend. My boyfriend doesn't want to upset my mother. And either way, I fail someone."

"I'm sorry."

"It's OK. I'll figure it out." I mentally shook myself. "I actually called to talk to you about something else. The Armstrong case."

"I told you—"

"You did. This is different." However, I was rethinking my plan of telling her about Tim's bloody hands and sinister disappearance while I was sitting here, just across the lobby from Brittany's desk. Brittany is vacant, but that might be pushing it. "Are you in your office?"

"No," Grimaldi said, without elaborating.

"Could we meet somewhere?"

She sighed. "Why don't I just come to you? Where are you?"

I told her I was in my office, and she said she'd be here in a half hour. We both hung up, and I opened the envelope and shook the shreds of Tim's calendar pages across my desk and went to work.

By the time the detective walked in, I had managed to piece together approximately half of Friday's calendar page. I was starting to get a feel for what the guy looked like: fair skinned and seriously built, with long, blond hair falling over his extra-broad shoulders. Some form of Norse god, at a guess, or at least that general type. It made it easier to sift through the various strips of male skin: I could eliminate the ones that were darker-skinned and the ones with darker hair.

When the door opened, I looked up and into the lobby, and as soon as I recognized the detective's dark curls and businesslike overcoat, I raised my voice. "Over here."

She stopped in the doorway and arched her brows. "Puzzles?"

"Something like that." I left the mess on the desk and got to my feet. "Let's talk somewhere else."

"Sure," Grimaldi said. "Coffee shop?"

"Conference room." Once she heard what I had to say, she'd probably want to take a look at Tim's office, and it was just as well if it were within easy reach.

Brittany eyed us curiously as we headed across the lobby, but she didn't say anything. I ushered the detective into the conference room and made sure the door was closed behind us. She watched with her eyebrows elevated as I gave the room a once-over to make sure no one was hiding in the corners. "What's this about, Ms. Martin?"

"Tim Briggs," I said and sat down.

Detective Tamara Grimaldi is a few years older than me, and looks like a cop. Her name is Italian, and so is she, I imagine. She has black hair, brown eyes, straight brows, and an olive complexion. She's not unattractive; in fact, she'd probably be quite the looker with some makeup, and dressed in something other than her usual severe business suit and low heels.

She took a seat across the table from me. "Your colleague?"

"My broker," I said. "Since Walker left."

"What about him?"

"Remember when I told you that the name Brian Armstrong didn't ring a bell? Well, yesterday afternoon..."

I told her about the open house that didn't happen, how Tim hadn't called me, how I had found him in the bathroom on Saturday morning rinsing blood from his hands, and how I'd stopped by his house yesterday afternoon to look for him but he hadn't been there.

"He's not answering his phone. His voice mailbox is full. He didn't show up to the sales meeting this morning, and no one's heard from him."

About halfway through my retelling, Grimaldi had pulled out a notebook and started taking notes. "So you think he had something to do with Brian Armstrong's death."

"I have no idea what I think," I said. "But he was here at the office, a mile or two from Shelby Park, the morning the body was found. He doesn't live on this side of town. He had blood on his hands and there was a bloody handprint on the trunk of his car. If Brian was taken to the park by car, chances are someone kept him in the trunk, since having him sit upright in the passenger seat might mean that someone would recognize him, or at least notice that he wasn't breathing."

Grimaldi nodded. "So Tim was the Armstrongs' real estate agent."

"So it seems. I haven't looked at the contract, but his sign is in their yard."

"The contract would be in his office?"

"I assume it is," I said, kicking myself for not looking for it. "If it isn't, it's either at Tim's house or in his car. Brittany should have a copy, though."

Grimaldi made a note on her pad. "When you saw him on Saturday morning, did anything strike you in particular? Anything out of the ordinary?"

"Other than the blood, you mean?" I thought back. "He was dressed very casually. More so than I've ever seen. Jeans and a sweatshirt."

"A lot of people wear jeans and sweatshirts on weekends," Grimaldi said.

I shook my head. "Not Tim. He wears designer jeans and Ralph Lauren Polo shirts to participate in the annual Habitat for Humanity home build."

"So you think he was deliberately dressed in old clothes because of the blood."

"He told me he was going to a new construction site. Those can be dirty. But I've seen him take clients to new construction homes before, and he's never looked that casual. And there was no Saturday morning appointment written on his calendar. So yes, I think there's a chance it was because of the blood. Because he didn't want to get blood on his nice clothes."

"Did you ask him about the blood?"

"He said he had a nosebleed," I said, "but I saw no signs of one. Not on his face and not on his clothes. That doesn't mean he couldn't have had one. But..."

She nodded.

"And he did seem a bit startled when I walked in. But that could have been just because it was early and he didn't expect anyone else to be here."

"I'm sure he didn't expect anyone else to be here," Grimaldi said dryly. "And then he asked you to fill in for him at an open house yesterday afternoon. Was that unusual?"

I shook my head. "I sit open houses for him all the time. He has a lot of listings; I don't have any. But he usually gives me more notice than that. If I hadn't accidentally walked in on him, I don't know if he would have asked at all. He hadn't said anything about it before."

"And you'd seen him recently?"

I'd seen him practically every day the previous week, including Friday afternoon just before the office closed. I told her so and added, "He never said a word about it. He was probably planning to do it himself. But if he'd killed Brian, he'd want to distance himself from anything to do with the Armstrongs, don't you think?"

"Quite possibly," Grimaldi said, making notes. "So you didn't see him again for the rest of the day on Saturday."

I hadn't. I'd gone home, read my romance novel, and waited for Rafe.

"Speaking of your boyfriend, did you figure out what he did this weekend?"

"Helped Wendell Craig transport a witness," I said.

"For the TBI?"

So I assumed. He hadn't actually said so, but surely that was implied.

"I thought Mr. Collier was done with the TBI."

"So did I." And I don't mind admitting the fact that he might not be made me nervous. "You know, it would be OK if you called him Rafe. He calls you Tammy."

"I know he does," Grimaldi said, her voice grim. She looked back down at her pad. "So you didn't speak to Mr. Briggs again on Saturday, or on Sunday morning. Tell me again what happened when you went to the Armstrongs' house yesterday afternoon."

I told her again, using different words this time. I've been on the receiving end of the detective's interviews before, so I know she always asks the same question a couple a times, in a couple different ways.

"And then you went to Mr. Briggs' home."

"After I tried to call him, yes. He wasn't there."

"How do you know?"

"I knocked on the door," I said. "He didn't answer. And his car was gone."

"And this morning he didn't show up for the office meeting."

"I asked if anyone had heard from him, and they said no. No one's seen him or spoken to him since Friday."

Grimaldi nodded. "Anything else you can think of?"

I thought about it. "Nothing comes to mind. What are you going to do?"

"Verify some of this with your receptionist," Grimaldi said. "Take a look at the Armstrong contract and make sure of the connection. Then head over to his house and see if anyone's home."

I opened my mouth, but before I'd managed to say anything, she sighed. "I can't stop you from driving over there, can I?"

I closed my mouth again. No, she couldn't. Obviously she wasn't about to offer me a ride—likely that would be unprofessional, since we didn't, after all, work together—but she couldn't keep me from, accidentally-like, being outside Tim's house at the same time she was there.

"I'll call Rafe," I said.

"Give him my regards," the detective retorted. "Introduce me to your receptionist, if you don't mind. And for now, let's keep the information about Mr. Briggs between us. The fact that a client of the company has been murdered is reason enough for me to want to look at the file."

Indeed.

So I took her back to the lobby and did as directed. Brittany immediately got a deer-in-the-headlights look in her eyes, that didn't fade even when Detective Grimaldi told her she just wanted a look at the Armstrong file.

She didn't demur, though, just fished it out of the file drawer and handed it over.

"Thank you." Grimaldi picked it from her shaking hand. "Come with me, Ms. Martin." She strode back toward the conference room. I scurried after, with a grimace at Brittany over my shoulder.

"What was that about?" I asked when we were once again safely ensconced behind the closed door.

Grimaldi glanced up at me. "What?"

"You scared her."

She glanced at the door, and through it to Brittany. "Guilty conscience?"

"You think she's involved in this?"

She shrugged. "More likely, she and her boyfriend indulge in some recreational weed in their time off, and she's afraid I know about it."

"You know her boyfriend?" His name was Devon and he was a musician, of the lank haired, tattooed and pierced variety. I wouldn't be surprised at all to learn he engaged in recreational marijuana.

"No," Grimaldi said, "but I know the type." She pushed the file in my direction. "Have a look at this and tell me if anything strikes you."

I sat down, obediently, and pulled the file toward me. Three minutes later I pushed it back. "Everything looks normal."

"Nothing illegal? Nothing like that..." she hesitated, "net deal we came across in Mrs. Puckett's file back in August?"

I shook my head. "Nothing like that. Everything looks just the way it should. It's a straight-forward listing agreement. No red flags at all."

"Good to know. At least we don't have to worry about that." She closed the manila folder and got to her feet. "While you take this back to Brittany, I think I'll stop by the powder room."

"Knock yourself out," I said, lifting the manila folder.

"Mr. Briggs's office is located in the back as well, if I recall?" She'd been here before, first when Brenda died, and then after Clarice did.

"Last door on the right. He took over Walker's office in August. The bathroom is on the left before you get there. Let me know if you need a plastic baggie or anything. We have some in the kitchen. I may even be able to rustle up a Q-tip, if you need one." For swabbing the drain.

"Thank you," Grimaldi said, "but I brought my own. I'll stop by on my way out."

"I'll be in my office."

The detective nodded. I opened the door, and we went our separate ways, me with another out-loud pointer toward the bathroom, so Brittany wouldn't wonder what the detective was doing in the back of the office for so long. Grimaldi headed that way, and I gave Brittany the folder back.

"Is everything all right?" she whispered.

"Of course. She just wanted to see the file because Mr. Armstrong died."

Brittany nodded, tucking it away in a drawer. "When is she leaving?"

"She went to the bathroom," I said. "I'm sure she'll go when she's finished."

Brittany glanced down the hallway.

"Is there some reason you don't want her around?"

Brittany shook her head but looked worried, her teeth sunk into her bottom lip.

"Have you heard anything from Tim?"

"No," Brittany said.

"Would you tell me if you had?"

"Of course." She looked offended.

"I'll be in my office," I said, and went there. And returned to pushing shreds of paper around.

Grimaldi came back into the lobby after ten minutes or so. If Brittany wondered what she'd been doing for all that time, she didn't ask.

Grimaldi leaned a shoulder on my doorjamb for a second and watch me sift through shreds. "I'm going to head out."

"Still to the same place?" It was just as well to make sure she hadn't changed her mind and was still planning to hit Tim's house. And better if Brittany didn't realize it.

She nodded.

"I haven't called Rafe," I said.

"Don't let me stop you. I'll see you later."

She turned and headed out. I scrambled to shove all my paper shreds into the envelope and pull on my coat before I followed.

By the time I got outside, she was already in her car with the engine running. I hustled across the parking lot to the Volvo and slid behind the wheel. Then I cranked the key over with one hand while I dialed Rafe with the other. "Want to take a break?" I asked when he answered.

I could hear the smile in his voice. "Depends on what you have in mind, darlin'."

"Not what you're thinking." I explained that I had called Grimaldi and that she was on her way to Tim's house as we spoke.

"I'll pass," Rafe said, his voice echoing. "I'm in the middle of painting."

"You'd rather paint than spend time with Grimaldi and me?"

"If there was any chance the two of you would get naked and mud wrestle," Rafe said, "I'd consider it."

"You're kidding."

"Yes, darlin'. I like Tammy, but not that way."

Good to know. "Hopefully we won't find Tim dead on the floor of his house."

"If you do, Tammy'll take care of you."

"I'd rather have you take care of me."

"I'd rather take care of you too," Rafe said, "but you don't need me for this."

Probably not. And much as I wanted him, I also wanted him to finish painting the house so I could sell it. I was looking forward to my very own first listing. "I'll see you at home later, then?"

"Yes, darlin'," Rafe said, "you will."

Good. I put the car in gear and slid out of the parking lot into traffic.

Eight

The detective was already parked in Tim's driveway when I pulled up to the curb. I got out of the car and slammed the door behind me, and she did the same. "Nice place," she told me when I reached her.

I nodded. "Very. If you like the old, anyway."

She glanced at me. "Don't you?"

"Of course I do. I grew up in an 1839 antebellum mansion."

"But you live in a new condo."

"Apartment," I said. "I don't own it. Not enough income after the divorce to get a mortgage. If I could afford it, I would buy a house. An old house."

"Yet Mr. Collier is working to put the house on Potsdam Street on the market." What she didn't say, but which was certainly true, was that if I wanted old and historic, Mrs. Jenkins's house fit the bill to a T. An 1880s Italianate Victorian with gingerbread trim on the porch, a round tower on one corner, and a ballroom that takes up the entire third floor.

"He doesn't think it's safe for me to live there," I said. "And you know if Rafe doesn't think it's safe, it's got to be pretty bad."

Grimaldi nodded. "That area doesn't have the lowest crime rates in town, certainly."

"I do like old houses, though. That's why I went into real estate in the first place." After dropping out of law school, getting married, getting divorced, and spending a couple of years selling makeup at the mall to make ends meet. "Where do you live?"

She looked at me. Maybe it was too personal a question. Or maybe, as a cop, she just wasn't supposed to share that kind of information. "I can ask Dix instead," I said. More to be informative than as a threat.

She sighed. "I own a house near Charlotte Park."

"Really?" Middle-class neighborhood on the west side of town, across Charlotte Avenue from the much more upscale neighborhood of West Meade, where Rafe's son David lives with his adopted parents.

The detective nodded. "Yes, really. I like historic houses too, but there are limits to what someone can afford, on a cop's salary."

"Can I see it sometime?" I love looking at other people's houses. As a little girl, whenever I went home with a friend after school, I was always nosing around their place. You can learn a lot about someone by looking at the space they inhabit.

"Sure," Grimaldi said, in a tone of one humoring a pest, and changed the subject back to where we'd started.. "Mr. Briggs must be doing all right financially."

He certainly wasn't suffering. "With Brenda gone, he's the biggest producer in the office. From what I know about it, just from watching his closings, he makes at least ten thousand a month. Sometimes a lot more."

Grimaldi nodded. "Let's knock."

We headed up the steps to the porch. My business card was still stuck in the crack between the door and the jamb, but we rang the bell anyway, and when that didn't work, we knocked. No one answered. I refrained from saying, "I told you so," but just barely.

"Let's go around back," Grimaldi said.

I followed her down the steps and around the house. "There's a side door to the garage." I pointed. "It has a window. You can see in. The garage was empty yesterday."

Grimaldi headed there. I stayed where I was and waited. She was wearing pants and low-heeled boots. I was wearing a skirt and heels. If anyone ought to traipse through the grass to the side door, it was her. Besides, it was her job.

"It's empty today too," she told me when she came back.

My second business card still adorned the back door. "Looks like he hasn't been here since yesterday. Or maybe even Saturday." Whenever he'd decided to go away.

Grimaldi nodded. "Was the door locked when you were here yesterday afternoon?"

I hesitated. Did I want to admit that I'd tried the door? Would she be shocked that I'd considered breaking and entering?

Nah. She'd be more shocked if I told her I hadn't checked. "Yes."

"Are you concerned about him?" Grimaldi asked.

"Of course."

"That's good enough for me." She covered her hand with her sleeve and hit one of the glass panes in the door, hard. Glass tinkled onto the floor inside. After knocking out the leftover shards, she stuck her hand through and unlocked the door, the same way I'd thought to myself that I'd do it just yesterday afternoon.

Grimaldi pushed the door open and put a hand on her gun before stepping through. "Mr. Briggs?"

I followed her into the laundry room. "Tim? Are you here? It's Savannah."

There was no answer. Grimaldi entered the kitchen. The refrigerator hummed softly; otherwise there was nothing to be heard.

I kept behind her as we walked from room to room, her low boots mostly silent and my heels clicking on the hardwood floors. Everything looked normal, and pristine. Tim has exquisite taste, and his house looked like a—slightly gay—magazine spread. There were touches of his favorite baby blue in almost every room, in throw pillows or pictures or tchotchkes, and rather more zebra print than I liked.

The downstairs consisted of the kitchen and laundry room, a formal dining room, a living room, a parlor or library, a hall bath, and two guest bedrooms, one of which Tim used as a home office. Grimaldi pulled the covers back on the guest bed—perhaps to inspect the sheets for blood—but found nothing. It was fully outfitted with comforter and a full sheet set, anyway. The sheet Brian Armstrong had been wrapped in hadn't come from this bed.

"He must sleep upstairs," I told Grimaldi, gesturing up the stairs. "There's probably a master suite up there."

She nodded. "Stay behind me."

I did. I didn't really think we'd find Tim in a puddle of gore in the master bedroom, but if we did, Grimaldi could find him first and tell me not to look. I'm not proud.

The stairs opened directly into a big and beautiful bedroom. Not surprisingly, the watered silk comforter on the king-sized bed was in Tim's trademark baby blue. The bed was immaculately made up, wrinkle-free, with a ton of little throw pillows and a stuffed elephant, also blue.

"If he killed Brian Armstrong here," Grimaldi commented, "he took the time to make the bed afterwards."

She folded up the corner of the comforter. The bed was in apple-pie order, with corners tucked in and everything accounted for: fitted sheet, flat sheet, and pillowcases. Blue.

"What was the color of the sheet Brian Armstrong was wrapped in?" I wanted to know.

Grimaldi hesitated, but in the end she told me. "White with navy stripes."

"Ticking?"

"If you say so." She folded the comforter back down again and smoothed it. "Nothing like these. Good quality Egyptian cotton, though. High thread count. Queen size."

"I suppose you've checked whether they came off his own bed?"

"First thing," Grimaldi said. "Or first thing once we found the body, anyway. Eight or ten hours after he was killed. They didn't match his sheets. Or his wife's."

"They have different sheets?"

"They're separated," Grimaldi said. "She's still in the house. He's in a furnished rental near his office."

"So that's what—" I trailed off.

"What?"

"When I saw her yesterday, she said something about needing to see Tim this week. About the house. That there were issues. That now that Brian was gone..."

"Now that Brian was gone, what?"

"She didn't say. Just trailed off like that. But maybe she's thinking of taking the house off the market. If they were divorcing and splitting assets, and that's why they had to sell the house, maybe she'll decide to keep it now. She won't have to sell. All the assets will be hers."

"Hmm," Grimaldi said.

I shrugged. "You must have thought about it. You told me the spouse is always the first person you look at."

"Usually. Spouse or significant other. Next of kin. Heirs. Business partners or rivals. It goes from there." She looked around. "I don't see anything particularly interesting here."

I shook my head. Me either. "If the sheet Brian was wrapped in came off a queen bed, it didn't come from here."

"The bed downstairs is a queen," Grimaldi said.

"But if Tim took Brian to bed, why wouldn't he take him to his own bed? Why use the guest bed?"

She glanced at me. "Do you have any reason to think Tim took Brian to bed?"

Well... "He was naked when you found him. I guess I assumed he was naked when he was stabbed, too."

She nodded. "No fibers in the wounds."

"And I thought, since he and his wife were separated, that maybe he was getting it on with someone else."

"Maybe," Grimaldi agreed, "but do you have any reason to think he was gay?"

I shook my head. "Do you?"

"His wife didn't mention it."

"Would she have known?"

"If they separated because of it, she must have."

Yes, although that didn't necessarily mean she'd say so. Then again, if Brian had been gay, why marry Erin in the first place? These days, it isn't as if gay men have to try to look straight. It's perfectly acceptable to be gay now.

"How long were they married?"

"Six years," Grimaldi said. "They married when she was twenty three and he was forty."

"That's a big age difference." Although at forty, he certainly ought to have known whether he was gay or not.

"Hollywood," Grimaldi said, as if that was explanation enough. "I'm going to take a look at the master bath before we leave."

She headed for it with me trailing behind.

The entire attic of Tim's Victorian had been converted to one giant master suite. The bedroom was easily twenty five feet long, and beyond it was a short hallway with closet doors on either side, that gave way to a bathroom. I stopped in the doorway, struck by envy.

As I'd already told Tamara Grimaldi, I didn't own my apartment. It was a rental, and although it's not a bad place to live, it's nothing fabulous. Convenient location, nice, clean and new, but nothing special.

All of it would fit into Tim's second floor. And his bathroom blew mine out of the water. It had skylights, a marble floor, a freestanding pedestal tub for soaking, and a double—or maybe triple—marble shower stall bristling with rainwater heads from every conceivable angle. It was the kind of bathroom you'd see on Lifestyles of the Rich and Famous, twenty first century edition. All of the Kardashians would fit in this bathroom, with space left over, and they'd look like they belonged, too.

"Wow," I said.

"Nice," Grimaldi agreed and turned on her heel. There was nothing here to interest her, obviously. I followed, after another quick and envious look around the room.

Outside in the hall between the bedroom and bath, Grimaldi pulled open one of the sliding closet doors. The space beyond was full of Tim's clothes, and he has a lot. Suits and ties for work, silk and satin for playtime. All colors of the rainbow, from staid and conservative navy pinstripe to eye-searing lime, aubergine, and royal blue. Looking at it, I was struck again by just how unusual Tim's choice of dress had been on Saturday morning.

Grimaldi closed the closet without comment and opened the matching door. Same thing there. More clothes. There were no obvious gaps, or empty hangers, so it didn't seem as if Tim had packed to go anywhere.

Grimaldi shook her head when I said as much. "Did you happen to notice a linen closet in the bathroom?"

"I didn't." I'd noticed everything else, but not that. "Maybe downstairs?"

"Maybe." We traipsed down the stairs again, after a last look at Tim's boudoir.

Down on the first floor, the detective got busy looking for the linen closet while I wandered into Tim's home office and looked around. It was pristine. At a guess, he used the elegant desk to write bills but not much more. This had none of the busy disarray of the desk at the office.

The single file drawer held bank statements and paid bills. I wanted to check and see how much his loan payment was for the house he lived in, but I resisted the temptation.

I closed that drawer and opened the other one, the wide, shallow one running underneath the writing surface, just as Grimaldi's voice sounded from the hallway. "Ms. Martin?"

"Detective?"

"Could you come here a moment?"

"Sure," I said, and closed the drawer again. It was full of the usual disarray: scattered rubber bands and paperclips, business cards and pencils. "What's up?"

She was standing in the hallway, outside the door to the bathroom.

"Check the linen closet, if you don't mind. You have to go inside and close the hall door in order to open the closet door."

Sure. I entered the bathroom and closed the door behind me. Opened the closet door and peered in.

Like the desk drawer, it contained the usual stuff. A few rolls of toilet paper wrapped in plastic on the floor. A plunger, in case of stoppage. Bottles of ammonia, Clorox bleach, and drain cleaner. A shelf of wrapped soaps and shampoo bottles, shaving cream, lotions, cotton balls, and Q-tips. Above that, a shelf with stacked towels: white, black, gray and baby blue, and replacement sheets. At the bottom of the stack, almost as if someone had attempted to hide them, was a neatly folded sheet and a few pillowcases with navy stripes on a white background.

"I see them," I told Grimaldi.

"Good. I used my phone to take a picture. Bring them out here, please."

No problem. I removed the sheets from the bottom of the stack, without allowing the rest of the stack to topple over on top of me, and brought them out into the hallway. The detective was already prepared with an open plastic bag for me to slide the sheets into.

"You think they're the rest of the set?" I scrubbed my palms against the outside of my thighs. I have no idea why, since the sheets felt and smelled clean.

"They look like they are," Grimaldi said, closing the bag. "I'll have to compare them to the sheet in the evidence room, but the pattern is the same. And there's a flat sheet missing."

The flat sheet that had been wrapped around Brian Armstrong's naked body. "What happens now?"

"I put out an APB on Tim Briggs," Grimaldi said, as we made our way through the kitchen into the laundry room again.

Wanted, in connection with murder...

"Gosh," I said, "I know he's always happy to get his name on TV, but I don't know if he'll like that."

"We'll do an internal bulletin first, and try to find him through those channels. Get a court order to pull his phone and credit card records, that kind of thing. In a day or two, if we can't find him that way, we may have to go to the media."

"Is there anything I can do to help?" I watched Grimaldi secure the back door.

"I'll let you know. I will need you to sign an affidavit saying we entered Mr. Briggs's house because you were in fear for his safety, and also that you saw me remove the sheets from his closet."

"Just let me know when."

"First I have to get these to the lab," Grimaldi said, hefting the bag with the sheets.

"Will you let me know if you find him?"

She hesitated, but eventually she nodded. "I assume I can trust you to do the same?"

Probably. I nodded back.

"What are you planning to do now?" Grimaldi wanted to know.

I glanced at my watch. It was past lunch time. "I guess I'll find something to eat. You want to come?"

"Some other time. I have work."

"I guess I'll pick something up and drive over to see Rafe. He's probably ready for a break, too."

"Tell him I said hello," Grimaldi said and opened the door to her car. I said I would and headed for mine.

Thirty minutes later I pulled the Volvo up outside the house on Potsdam, with a bag of steak sandwiches on the seat next to me. My stomach was rumbling, and the entire car smelled of meat and onions. It was wonderful, and I couldn't wait to dig in.

What wasn't so wonderful, was getting there and finding that Rafe's mode of transportation was missing from the front of the house.

He drives a big, black Harley-Davidson, muscular and shiny with metal and chrome. The sight of him astride the beast, with his thighs gripping the seat and the muscles in his arms flexing under the sleeves of a tight T-shirt, never fails to give me a thrill.

Of course, it was winter now, so that short-sleeved T-shirt was usually hidden under a black leather jacket, but you get my drift.

But now the beast was gone.

I got out of the car anyway, and made my way up to the front door. Leaving the sandwiches in the car, since I figured it'd be a waste of effort to take them with me. I didn't expect him to be there. I expected to knock on the door and have no one answer.

I knocked on the door. No one answered.

I didn't have a key, so I couldn't go inside. I'd had one once, because I spent a few days with Mrs. J last autumn, after someone broke into my apartment and left a threatening message scrawled in lipstick on my bedroom wall, but I'd long since given it back. All I could do was knock, and press my nose against the glass in the door, fogging it up.

Everything looked normal inside. There were the usual couple of paint cans lined up in the hallway, along with a long-handled brush and a folded up drop-cloth. Nothing unusual there. If I pushed the mail slot open and stuck my nose in the crack, I could even smell fresh paint. Obviously he'd been here. He'd painted. He just wasn't here now.

I trundled back to the car, fuming. The first thing I did was call him, and if it occurred to me that I was acting like the stereotypical jealous girlfriend, I ignored it. I'd left him alone all weekend. I'd trusted him. It hadn't even crossed my mind that he wouldn't be here now.

I'd spoken to him just over an hour ago. He hadn't mentioned anything about going out. So where the hell—heck—was he?

Nine

There was no answer, of course. I hadn't expected one. And because I did realize I was acting like a jealous girlfriend, and I wanted above all to avoid sounding like one, I hung up without leaving a message.

If I could have eaten his cheese steak sandwich in addition to my own, I would have, just so I could have told him later that I did. I couldn't, and I'd lost the appetite for my own too, so I pulled the car up alongside two homeless men lounging on a bus bench on Dresden Avenue and handed them the bag. "Enjoy."

They looked at me like I were crazy, but by the time I'd reached the next corner, they had opened the bag and were digging in. I felt maliciously good about that.

The office was quiet when I got back to it. Brittany must be out to lunch, because the front door was locked and the reception area unoccupied. I unlocked the door, since you never know when someone might walk in off the street looking for a real estate agent, and then I went into my own office—I'd hear the door open from there—and went back to work arranging Tim's shreds of calendar page.

An hour passed in blissful silence before Brittany came back. By then, I had most of Friday's page assembled. It was missing a few strips here and there, that I must have missed when I dug through the confetti in the shredder, but I had what I needed. Tim had had an appointment on Friday night. Or at least he'd had plans.

Chaps, 9:00.

Did he have a fitting for a cowboy costume? Or did he have a bunch of British friends he was planning to hang out with? Or maybe Chaps was a place?

I booted up the computer and did an internet search. And bingo: Chaps was located on Church Street, on the opposite side of downtown from where I lived, near the hospitals and universities. Opening hours, 7 PM to 4 AM. Not just a place then, but a nightclub.

They weren't open on Mondays. Bummer. I made a mental note to visit tomorrow. Maybe Tim would be there. Or maybe I'd find someone who'd seen him on Friday and could tell me whether he'd been alone.

"Any word from Tim?" I asked Brittany on my way through the lobby.

She shook her head. "That Mrs. Armstrong called, though. The widow."

I slowed my steps. "What did she want?"

Brittany shrugged, her huge earrings—big enough to fit around my upper arm—jingling. "She just said she needed to talk to Tim. But his voicemail is full. I said I'd give him the message."

"When?"

"When he comes in," Brittany said, as if it were obvious.

"When do you think that might be?"

But Brittany had no idea. Of course not. Unlike me, however, that didn't seem to bother her.

"Why didn't you give the call to Heidi?" Heidi is by way of being Tim's assistant. She was Brenda's dogsbody before Brenda was killed, and then Tim more or less took her over. Or so I'd thought, anyway.

"She wasn't here," Brittany said.

She hadn't been here for the meeting, either. I'd been so focused on Tim that it was only now that I realized that Heidi had been missing, as well. Did that mean something?

"Did you call her?"

Brittany shrugged.

I sighed and put out a hand. "Give me the number."

"Why?"

"Because someone has to call Mrs. Armstrong. Tim can't, since he's not here and probably won't call to get the message. Heidi won't be back until tomorrow, if then. And Mrs. Armstrong shouldn't have to worry about her house right now. She just lost her husband."

Brittany hesitated.

"You can call her back yourself," I said. "Find out what she wants. Take care of it. Or you can get one of the other agents to do it. Just as long as someone does. But I'm standing right here, offering. And I spoke to her yesterday. You may as well let me take care of it."

"Fine," Brittany said and handed me the message slip.

I thanked her as graciously as I could and headed for the back door and the parking lot.

Once in the car, I pulled out my phone. There'd been no call or text from Rafe, of course, and I was damned if I was going to call him again. And if he thought he could come home tonight and attempt to snuggle up to me without telling me exactly where he'd been and what he'd been doing this afternoon, he had another think coming.

I thought I might get a voice message, but Mrs. Armstrong answered on what was almost the first ring. "This is Erin."

"This is Savannah Martin," I said. "From LB&A? We spoke yesterday. At the... at your house."

There was a beat of silence. I figured she must have expected someone else.

Then her voice came back. "Of course. What can I do for you?"

"I understand you called the office looking for Tim," I said. "I thought maybe I'd be able to help you instead."

There was another pause while she, apparently, thought about it. "Where's Tim?"

"We're not sure," I admitted. "He didn't come to work today, and he's not answering his phone or his door. We're not sure what's going on."

"I see," Erin said. After another second she added, "I guess you could help me."

"I'll do my best. What do you need help with?"

"It's the house," Erin said, just as a call-waiting buzz echoed down the line. I took the phone away from my ear—what if it was Rafe?—but I saw nothing. By the time I'd put it back, Erin was excusing herself. "...been waiting for this call from my brother. I'll call you back in a few minutes."

She'd disconnected before I could offer to hold.

"Of course," I told the silent phone and put the car in gear.

PART OF ME DIDN'T EXPECT her to call back, but she did. And picked up the conversation where we'd left off, just as if it had been a minute or two instead of thirty.

"Sorry about that."

"No problem," I said. By now I'd gotten home, and was on my way up the stairs to the apartment. I'd parked on the street, since I thought I might be required to go back out again, and I wanted to be prepared. I hadn't seen any sign of Rafe's Harley, which only served to make me more annoyed.

"I'd like to talk to someone about the house. Now that Brian is... I mean, after what happened..." She trailed off, took another breath, and started again. "With everything else that's going on, I think maybe it would be best if I didn't try to sell the house right now."

"Of course." It was totally understandable, in fact. She certainly had plenty of other things to think about. "I'd be happy to meet with you and discuss the options."

"Oh." She sounded a bit taken aback. Maybe she'd thought it would be a more difficult task to accomplish. "Now?"

"If you want. Or later."

"I'm at work," Erin said. "Can we put it off until tonight?"

Sure. I'm a realtor; I work 24/7, whenever someone wants me. Usually that's evenings and weekends. On the flipside, I wasn't sure I'd be working if my husband had been murdered two days ago, but to each their own, I guess. Maybe she found it helped her keep her mind off things. "What time works for you?"

She hesitated. "Six thirty?"

"That's fine." We arranged to meet at her house rather than my office to make it easy for her—and because I hadn't had a chance to see much of it the other day, and I was curious—and then I slipped the phone into my pocket and the key in the lock of the apartment door and let myself in.

The apartment was empty, of course. I had assumed it would be, but that didn't make it any less annoying.

Where the hell—heck—was he?

I'd missed lunch, and by now I was hungry, so I made myself a snack of Brie and crackers. Then I called Tamara Grimaldi. "Do you know where Rafe is?"

"No," the detective said, "why?"

"He isn't where he's supposed to be. He isn't answering his phone and he didn't tell me he was planning to leave."

"Maybe he's visiting his grandmother," Grimaldi said.

Maybe. I hadn't thought about that. If he were, he probably wouldn't interrupt the visit to talk to me. Mrs. Jenkins is a bit touched in the head. Some of the time she has no idea who he is. Sometimes she thinks he's his father Tyrell, whom Old Jim Collier killed more than thirty years ago, and that I'm LaDonna, pregnant with Rafe. Other times she's perfectly lucid and knows exactly who we both are and what's going on. If this was one of those times, it was no wonder he'd want to talk to her while she actually recognized him.

"Any news on the sheets?"

"It's too soon," Grimaldi said. "I dropped them off at the lab. They do match the sheet in question in appearance and scent."

"Scent?"

"Laundry detergent. As if they were washed together."

Ah. I wouldn't have thought of that, which is why she's the detective and I'm the real estate agent, I guess. "I'm meeting Mrs. Armstrong at six thirty," I said. "She wants to talk about taking her house off the market."

"Hmm."

"You can't blame her. With everything that's going on, I'm sure she has more important things to worry about than making sure the house looks neat and tidy for showings."

"Who said anything about blaming her?" the detective asked blandly. "I'm sure she has more important things to think about, too."

"Do you suspect her?"

"I suspect everyone."

I huffed. "Give me a break. I'm going over to this woman's house tonight. Alone, since my boyfriend is nowhere to be found. If I'm going to meet someone who might decide to stab me if I say the wrong thing, I'd like to know about it."

"Even if she killed her husband," Grimaldi answered, "and I'm not saying she did, she probably wouldn't kill you."

Probably? "That's not very encouraging."

Grimaldi sighed. "According to the M.E.'s findings, Mr. Armstrong was killed sometime between midnight and 2AM on Friday night, or more accurately, early Saturday. Mrs. Armstrong says she was in bed at that time. She can't prove it, but most people can't when they sleep alone. If she had an alibi for that time, it would actually be more suspicious."

"Because it would mean she'd made sure not to be alone. At one in the morning." When most people were alone, unless they were married or involved.

"That's right. The security system was armed at 11:30 and wasn't disarmed until the next morning. She might have gotten around that—the attic windows aren't connected—but it's difficult to imagine that she climbed out and down."

Indeed it was. I had met Erin Armstrong, and she hadn't struck me as a gymnast. A tennis player, yes, but not a gymnast.

"And she spoke to her brother just before 1AM," Grimaldi added,"which shows on her call log. She was on her cell phone, so it doesn't prove she was at home when she took the call, but he confirms that he spoke to her."

"That's rather late to be talking to someone, isn't it?"

"The brother lives in Los Angeles," Grimaldi said. "Where Mr. and Mrs. Armstrong lived until two years ago, as well."

"An actor?"

She made a confirming sort of sound.

That explained it, then. Midnight here is only ten o'clock there. "Any idea where Brian was murdered?"

"Not at the house in East Nashville," Grimaldi said. "CSI went over it. There was no blood. And as many times as Mr. Armstrong was stabbed, there would have been something."

"Urk," I said, but I didn't argue.

"Nor was he killed at his own apartment. CSI have been over both. He was in someone else's bed when he was killed, and he was wrapped in someone else's sheet."

A sheet that matched the set we found in Tim's house. A set with the flat sheet missing. "Have you sent CSI over to Tim's house yet?"

"I'm waiting for court approval," Grimaldi said. "Just because I need it done, doesn't mean I'm free to invade people's privacy. Mr.

Briggs's house is private property. I can't just send a forensic team into it without permission, no matter how much I may want to."

"Can you just walk into someone's house without permission?"

"Of course not," Grimaldi said, offended. "That's why I asked you whether you were afraid for Mr. Briggs's safety. If there's concern about someone's safety and well-being, there's probable cause."

"We checked the bedroom, though. There was no sign of blood. And I'm sure it would have been hard to get out of that baby blue shag carpet."

"The downstairs bedroom had hardwood floors. No carpet at all. Not even an area rug. I don't know about you, but that struck me as interesting."

It hadn't struck me as interesting. It hadn't struck me at all. It had escaped my notice. "Oops," I said.

"You were busy in the office," Grimaldi answered magnanimously. "And I don't expect you to notice things like that."

"Because I'm stupid?"

"Because it isn't your job. Not because you're stupid."

"I feel stupid," I said. "I can't believe Rafe's gone again. Why is he doing this to me?"

"I don't think he's doing anything to you, Ms. Martin. He's probably just visiting his grandmother. Or a friend. His life is different from what it used to be. It's understandable that he'd be bored."

"I don't want him to be bored," I said.

"I know that. So does he. But that doesn't change the fact that he is."

"I'm afraid he'll get bored with me."

"It isn't you," Grimaldi said. "He loves you."

He did. He'd told me so. He might even have told her so. And I believed him. I just doubted it at times. It helped to hear someone else tell me. "Thank you."

"Don't mention it. Let me know if anything happens tonight you think I should know about."

I said I would, and we hung up. And because I had the phone in my hand anyway, I dialed my brother's number in Sweetwater.

"Savannah?" he said when he answered. "Something wrong?"

"Nothing. Everything's fine."

I heard him switch the phone to his other ear. "Collier treating you OK?"

"Why?" Did he know something I didn't?

"No reason," Dix said. "Just checking. Are you sure nothing's wrong?"

I sighed. "I don't think anything's wrong. The problem is, he's not talking to me."

"At all?"

"Of course not 'at all.' Don't be ridiculous."

I told him what had happened this weekend, and what was going on now. "I'm not sure I can trust what he told me. What if the TBI thing was just something he made up so I wouldn't worry?"

"Where do you think he is?"

"I don't know. That's the problem." I waited for him to say something, and when he didn't, I added, "He hasn't told you anything, has he?"

"No," Dix said. "We're not on those terms."

"Speaking terms?"

"We speak when we meet. But he doesn't tell me his secrets."

"But you get along, right?"

"Better than I thought we would," Dix admitted. "Why do you ask?"

"Mother called me this morning. To ask whether I'm coming to Abigail's birthday."

"Oh," Dix said. "It's OK if you can't make it, sis. I know you're in a tough situation."

"But I shouldn't be!" My voice was shrill, and I had to stop and take a breath before I could continue. "We're all adults, and I have the right to live my own life. It's unfair that I should have choose between my family and my boyfriend!"

"You don't have to choose between your family and your boyfriend," Dix said.

"How do you figure that? Mother hates him!"

"I wouldn't put it quite that strongly," Dix said judiciously. I would, but I kept quiet. "She just thinks you could have done better."

"I think I couldn't."

"That's because you know him. She doesn't."

Obviously. "That's not going to change, though, Dix. She doesn't want to get to know him, and she makes it very clear."

"That's her loss," Dix said, "but it doesn't mean you have to miss out. You can come to Abigail's party."

"I know I can. I talked to him about it, and he said it would be fine if I went."

"You can come to Abigail's party," Dix repeated, "and bring him. If mother doesn't like it, that's mother's problem."

"It's *your* problem, if she refuses to be under the same roof with him."

"She won't," Dix said. "She allowed him under her own roof at Christmas. The two of you were upstairs in your room all night, and probably not sleeping either. She didn't object."

"It was Christmas. And I'm sure she knew that if she asked him to leave, I would leave too."

"No doubt," Dix agreed. "But you're both welcome at Abigail's party."

"I appreciate that. I just don't think he wants to come."

"Afraid mother's going to eat him?"

I shrugged, not that he could see me. "I think he just doesn't want the hassle. And he wants me to be happy. Things get tense when he's around my family. So he stays away to make things easier."

"He'll have to stop doing that," Dix said. "Or things are never going to get better."

"I'm aware of that. But it isn't comfortable for him either. Mother is rude to him. In the politest way possible. And I don't want to make him feel bad."

"He's a big boy," Dix said. "He can take care of himself."

He was. He could. And he was choosing to stay away from my mother. Maybe that was his way of accomplishing the task. Maybe I should just leave well enough alone until he was ready. Assuming he got back. But I didn't want to think about that. So I said, "I saw Grimaldi today."

There was a beat. "Did you?" Dix said.

"What's going on with the two of you?"

The response was quick. "Nothing." Maybe a touch *too* quick.

"She bought your daughters Police Barbies for Christmas."

"We're friends," Dix said.

"That's something."

He didn't answer, and I added, "When was the last time you saw her?"

"In person?"

"Yes, in person. Unless you see her in your dreams."

"No," Dix said. "We had lunch a couple of weeks ago."

My eyebrows crept up my forehead. "You came to Nashville and you didn't call me?"

"I was busy," my brother said.

"Is she coming to the party?"

"No," Dix said. "She's working."

"How do you know? Did you invite her?"

"No."

"Afraid mother's going to eat her?"

He didn't answer. "She had a new case. Something about a naked guy in a park."

I knew all about the naked guy in the park, but it was probably better if I didn't say so. But it did remind me— "I should go. I have an appointment."

"Sure," Dix said. "Thanks for calling."

"I'll talk to Rafe about the party. If he doesn't want to come, I'll drive down by myself." Abigail was my niece, after all, and Dix my brother. I shouldn't miss her birthday, especially now that Sheila was gone. And if Rafe didn't want to come with me... well, as Dix had said about mother, that was his loss.

"I'll let Abigail know you'll be there," Dix said. "See you Friday."

He hung up and I did the same. And then I finished my crackers and Brie before it was time to head out to Erin Armstrong's house.

Ten

The place was a lot quieter today than yesterday. No cars were parked at the curb when I drove up, and there were no other signs of life. When I rang the doorbell, no one answered.

My mother brought me up properly, so it was 6:30 right on the nose. Obviously Erin's mother hadn't been as conscientious as mine, or maybe Erin just wasn't as much a slave to her upbringing as I was. Either way, she breezed up ten minutes late, in a dark blue Lexus SUV, without so much as an apology. "Have you been waiting long?" was all she said as she unlocked the door.

Since it would be impolite to tell her I'd been waiting since the time we'd agreed to meet, I just smiled. "A few minutes."

Inside the house, it looked like a cyclone had been through. The place was empty, of course. The dining room table, which had been groaning under the amount of food piled on it yesterday, was bare but for an ostentatious flower arrangement in funereal white. Lilies, carnations, and baby's breath. But everything else was in disarray. There were dirty footmarks all over the hardwoods from people traipsing in and out yesterday, dragging rainwater and mud inside. Sofa pillows were on the floor, picture frames were askew on the walls, and there were crumbs and splotches of food everywhere.

"I can recommend a cleaning service," I said, "if you'd like."

"I have one," Erin answered with a glance around. She grimaced. "They can't come any too soon."

There was no arguing with that.

My apartment is small, so I don't really need help keeping it clean—nor can I afford it—but I grew up with a cleaning service that came in on a weekly basis to keep the mansion spic and span. My mother doesn't get her own hands dirty. Obviously Erin didn't, either.

"Let's sit in the kitchen," Erin said. "It's friendlier."

Sure. I followed her down the hallway to the back of the house, where I hadn't been yesterday.

The kitchen was a bright and sunny room, bigger than it appeared in the internet pictures I'd seen. It was a painted a pale green, with tile floors, granite counters, and the standard stainless steel appliance package, including the obligatory gas-fed stove. Everything was messy, with the same dirty footprints, crumbs, and splotches from the party, and a sink full of dirty dishes.

Erin looked around. "Sorry."

"It's no problem. You have more important things on your mind."

"Can I get you something to drink?" She made a beeline for the fridge, and pulled out a bottle of Chardonnay.

I shook my head regretfully. I love white wine, but— "I'm working." And I wanted my wits about me, both because she was Tim's client and I wanted to do right by her and by the company, and because I wanted to be sure to notice and remember anything interesting she might say, so I could tell Detective Grimaldi later. Not that a few sips of Chardonnay would impair my abilities, but this wasn't a social occasion and we weren't friends.

Erin filled her own glass and stuck the bottle back into the refrigerator. Then she leaned her back against the fridge and downed half the contents of the glass in one swallow. "That's better." She put her head back and closed her eyes.

"Rough day?" I took stock of her, while she couldn't see me looking.

She wasn't much older than me, but the California tan made her skin look leathery and tough.

"You can't imagine. Although Saturday was worse."

"I'm sure it was." That would have been when she got the news that her husband had been murdered. "I'm sorry for your loss. How can I help you?"

"I think," Erin said, straightening, "that it might be best if I take the house off the market for the time being."

"Of course."

"With everything that's going on, it's hard to keep up with everything. And I'm not sure I'm up for making the place look nice every time there's a showing."

"Of course."

"And because of the way Brian died, people are coming to gawk at the place. I'm afraid there'll be a stigma."

Most people probably had no idea there was a connection between Brian Armstrong—who had featured in the news only as an unidentified naked male found in Shelby Park on Saturday morning—and this house, but I didn't say so. Stigmas, unfortunately, are only too real. Someone dies in a house, and immediately it becomes a hundred times harder to sell, as well as irresistible to a certain segment of the population. The ghost hunters, the para-psychological, the ghouls.

"Of course," I said again.

Every time I said it, it seemed Erin felt compelled to come up with yet one more reason why taking the house off the market was a good idea. "There are probably issues with selling, too, now that Brian's gone."

"Possibly." I've never had a client die on me in the middle of a transaction—though one or two have come close—and I hadn't taken the time to look it up, since I'd come here with the impression that she didn't want to work things out, she just wanted to withdraw the listing. But chances were that yes, when one of the parties to a transaction dies, there are probably issues with signatures and survivorship and the likes. What's a pretty straight-forward situation when everyone's alive and kicking, becomes infinitely more complicated when one party croaks right in the middle of the transaction.

"I really think it would be better for everyone if we just took the house off the market."

"Of course."

"I won't have to worry about packing up and moving..."

She trailed off, as if realizing she'd said too much. I pounced. "Did you guys have another place picked out?"

Erin hesitated. Looked at her glass and the wine swirling at the bottom of it. "We were separated."

"I'm sorry."

"He called me the day he died." Her eyes were filling up with tears. She was either a very good actress, or sincere. "He asked if we could talk on Saturday. I think maybe he was thinking about changing his mind."

"Was splitting up his idea?"

But she must have said too much and realized it, because she clammed up again. "I'm sorry. This isn't something you need to worry about. Just... let me know what I have to do to take the house off the market for now."

"Of course." It wouldn't do me any good to push, I figured, so I didn't. Instead, I fished a piece of paper out of my briefcase. "This is a withdrawal form. If you'll sign it, I'll fill out the address and dates and take it to the office tomorrow and get the listing taken down. There may be other paperwork that's necessary too, to close the file, but I'll let Tim deal with that when he comes back."

She nodded, scrawling her name on the dotted line. "Where is Tim?"

"I don't know." I slipped the signed sheet back into the briefcase. "I haven't spoken to him since Saturday morning."

"Saturday?"

"I ran into him in the office."

"Did he say where he was going?"

I shook my head. "He didn't say anything at all. Just asked me if I could take over his open house yesterday."

Erin looked worried. "You don't think anything's happened to him, do you?"

"Like what?"

"I don't know," Erin said. "Do you think he could be dead too?"

I thought it much more likely that he was on the run after killing Brian, but of course I didn't say so. She didn't need to hear it, and besides, I had no proof. And to be honest, I did have a hard time imagining Tim killing anyone. Too fastidious. Like my mother, he doesn't like to get his hands dirty.

Then again, I'd had the same impression of Walker Lamont—a well-dressed, well-spoken, sophisticated, gay-as-a-meadow-lark businessman—until he'd revealed that he'd killed several people, a couple of them up close and personal.

"I'm not sure," I said honestly. "I've tried to get hold of him, but he's not answering his phone or his door. Do you have any reason to think that whoever killed your husband would have killed Tim too?"

Erin shrugged.

"Well, was there something going on between them?" She looked like she might be taking offense to the suggestion, so I added, quickly, "Were they friends? Is that why you're using Tim as your real estate agent?"

"Brian did that," Erin said. "I'm not sure how he knew Tim. Or how well they knew each other."

Right. And I couldn't really ask Erin whether she and her husband were splitting up because Brian had a hidden gay streak. It just isn't done.

So I let it go, and prepared to leave, closing the snaps on my briefcase and getting to my feet. "I'll have Tim get in touch with you as soon as I talk to him. In the meantime, I'll get the house taken off the market for you."

"Thank you," Erin said.

"Would you like me to remove Tim's sign from the yard while I'm here?"

"That would be great," Erin said.

I put my briefcase on the front seat of the Volvo and made my careful way through the dead wet grass of the yard, my high heels sinking into the moist ground, to haul the LB&A sign out of the dirt and drag it back to the car. Clumps of dirt fell off the spiky metal legs and into the clean interior of my trunk. Wonderful.

Erin stood on the front step and watched me, wine glass in hand, so after it was done, I traipsed back up to her. "Anything else I can do for you right now?"

She shook her head and glanced down the road. Maybe she was waiting for someone.

"Let me know if there's anything more I can do for you."

She said she would, and I headed back to my car, while Erin went inside the house and closed the door behind her. I pulled away from the curb and headed for home.

I was three blocks away, going along at my usual sedate pace, when a car passed me, zipping in the other direction. It was a small bright blue Mini Cooper with white stripes.

I knew someone who drove that kind of car. I'd met him about six months ago, outside another of Tim's listings. His name was Beau Riggins, and he was a house cleaner. He'd been on his way into the house when I'd been on my way out, and we had gotten to talking. He had pulled down his zipper right there on the porch, to show me his 'uniform'—a pair of Wonderjocks™. I'd found out later that he'd slept with one of his clients, who had ended up dead. For a while, I'd suspected him of being a murderer.

Now that I thought about it, I'd noticed his business card in Tim's desk drawer this afternoon, when I'd been at Tim's house with Tamara Grimaldi. It hadn't really registered at the time—I'd opened the drawer just when she'd called me to come into the bathroom to look in the linen closet—but now I remembered. The slogan on Beau's business card was, *Feeling dirty? Call the house boy!* and that kind of thing is hard to forget.

What was Beau doing here?

If indeed it was Beau in the car, and not some other owner of a blue Mini Cooper. That certainly wasn't impossible; there are plenty of Mini Coopers around, and I shouldn't jump to conclusions.

But even so, I turned at the next corner, and then backtracked until I could go down Erin's street again.

There was no sign of the car I'd seen. Not outside Erin's house, and not anywhere else on the street. But when I peered at Erin's house, and at the lighted windows, I swear I saw the outline of two silhouettes behind the curtains.

I pulled up to the curb and stopped, but it had only been a glimpse. Now there was nothing to see. So I got out of the car and stood for a second on the slick pavement, staring at the house and thinking.

There was no way I could skulk around in the yard trying to peer in through the windows. It was latish and dark, but someone might see me. Erin might see me.

Much better to go knock on the door and pretend I'd left or lost something. If nothing else, I might get a look at whoever had arrived, to determine whether it was Beau Riggins or not. They probably hadn't quite made it to bed yet.

If anyone was here at all, that was.

So I walked up to the front door and rang the bell. And waited. It took a minute or two—and another ding of the bell—before Erin answered.

"Yes?"

Impatient. And out of the severe business suit and into a... was that a robe?

It was. Not revealing in any way, but a soft, purple velveteen that covered her from shoulders to floor, with a belt tied around the waist. All someone would have to do would be tug on the knot and it would open.

"Hi again." I smiled winsomely. "Sorry to bother you. I wondered whether I left my cell phone here? I got halfway home and realized I didn't have it."

She hesitated. "I'll look."

I had my mouth open to tell her I could look myself, but she'd already shut the door, leaving me standing there on the stoop.

Rude. But it did make me think she had something to hide, something she didn't want me to see. Why else would she care if I came back inside?

I peered through one of the sidelights as Erin made her way down the hallway to the kitchen. No one else was in sight.

She came back just a few seconds later, without the cell phone. Obviously, since it was in my pocket. I fumbled the ringer off; that way, if it rang while she had the door open, at least she wouldn't be able to hear it.

"I'm sorry," she said when the door was open a crack. "I didn't see it."

"That's OK." I gave her another smile. "Maybe I left it somewhere else, and just didn't realize it until now. Keep an eye out for it, would you?"

"Of course."

I hesitated, but when she didn't say anything more, and I couldn't think of anything else to say, I conceded defeat. "Have a good night."

She thanked me and closed the door, but when I looked over my shoulder before getting into the Volvo, I could still see her silhouette outlined against the wavy glass of the sidelight. She clearly wasn't going to leave the front hall until I had driven away.

So I did. But although I made another trip around the block, in hopes I'd get lucky, there was nothing to see when I came back around in front of the house. Erin's silhouette was gone, and so was the other silhouette I had—or thought I had—seen.

Eleven

smelled spaghetti sauce before I even put the key in the door. Rafe's not much of a cook, but he does know how to boil pasta and heat sauce out of a can.

He must be feeling guilty, I figured. Cooking isn't something he usually does. For ten years, he didn't have anything resembling a home life, and I have a feeling he ate in restaurants and bars, and ordered takeout whenever he needed a meal. Since he moved in with me, we've eaten at home a bit more. Often because we couldn't drag ourselves out of bed until it was too late to go anywhere, true, but also because I was doing my damndest to show him the charms of domesticity.

He'd had a miserable childhood and youth, then spent two years in prison, and after that, he'd gone undercover. During all that time, as far as I knew, he'd never had a normal romantic relationship. There'd been women, sure. Lots of women. He couldn't have gotten as good as he is without considerable practice. But they hadn't been what I'd call normal relationships. He'd told me once that he'd never thought about the future because he'd never dared to trust that he'd have one. Now he did. He had a chance at a normal life again, and I was bound and determined to keep him happy so he'd stay with me.

Sometimes it scared me just how crazy I was about him, especially as he wasn't someone I was supposed to have those kinds of feelings for. "Not our people," as mother would say. Yet the idea that something could happen to him and I could lose him, kept me in a state of constant terror. That part of it had gotten a little better now that he'd stopped working for the TBI and stopped risking his life every day. Nowadays, I was more worried that he might get tired of me and leave. So for the past two months, I'd done everything in my power to make simple domestic life seem as appealing as possible. Home cooked food, clothes, lots of sex whenever he wanted it—not that I didn't benefit greatly from that, as well.

Anyway, he was home. He was cooking. I smelled the spicy sauce in the hallway, and by the time I'd unlocked the door and let myself into the narrow hallway, it was all around me.

The scent, not the sauce. The sauce was in a pan on the stove, simmering and popping, probably making a mess I'd have to clean up later. The spaghetti was already drained and sitting in a colander in the sink under a lid, and I thought I detected the underlying hint of garlic bread toasting in the oven. From where I stood, I could see that the dining room table was set with plates and stemmed glasses, napkins and silverware. He'd forgotten the coasters.

I raised my voice. "Rafe?"

There was a sound in the back of the apartment, and then he appeared in the bedroom doorway on bare feet, with faded jeans slung low on his hips and a blue T-shirt stretched tight across his chest and shoulders. His hair—the little bit he has—was still wet from what must have been a recent shower.

My mouth watered. Or maybe that was the scent of the food.

Either way, there was warmth in his eyes. Not heat, although there might have been a hint of that too, but warmth, like he was happy to see me. "You're out late, darlin'."

"Business meeting," I said.

"I made dinner."

I nodded. "I see that."

"You wanna change into something comfortable while I get the food on the table?"

I tilted my head, considering. What I wanted to do, was push him backwards through the doorway into the bedroom, and keep going until the backs of his knees hit the bed and he tumbled... but that's not something a properly brought up Southern Belle admits to wanting, let alone does.

Unless...

He was grinning at me, as if he knew just what I was thinking. When I walked toward him, he didn't move out of the way, just watched me come closer. When I put out my hand and gave him a push, he took a step backwards. And another. Just before he fell backwards onto the bed, he grabbed me and pulled me down on top of him.

As usual when he kissed me, my mind went fuzzy. It could have been a few minutes later, or more than a few, that he tipped me over on my back and got to his feet. "Food first."

I pouted and he chuckled. "I'll get the food on the table. You get changed. Into something that it'll be easy for me to take off you later."

He winked. It was a personal joke: once upon a time he'd asked me to dinner and told me to wear something comfortable. Because I was obsessively reading sexual innuendo into everything he said to me, my mind had made the connection between the request and the movies, where 'something comfortable' usually means a negligee. But since I wasn't about to go to dinner in a restaurant in my nightgown, I'd ended up in a wrap dress, and if he'd wanted to, he could have untied the knot and spread the dress out like a picnic blanket. He didn't. Instead he wined and dined me, took me home, kissed me goodnight—the memory of that kiss still had the power to curl my toes—and left for Memphis. I hadn't seen him for weeks after that, and I'd spent all that time wishing he'd chosen to take advantage of me before he left. I fell into bed with him almost as soon as he came back. There's a lot to be said for that old adage about absence making the heart grow fonder, or at least more amorous.

There's also a lot to be said for wrap dresses.

He walked out into the living room and I got myself upright and over to the closet, where I exchanged the skirt and business blouse for the same dress I'd worn in September, before I headed into the dining room for dinner.

His lips curved with appreciation when he saw me. "I've always liked that dress."

"Good memories."

"You had it on the night I went to Memphis, right?"

I nodded.

He gave me another appreciative up-and-down. "Took all I had to get on that bike and leave. What I wanted was to haul you up over my shoulder and carry you upstairs."

"I wanted you to."

He shook his head. "No, you didn't. I saved your life and you thought you owed me, but you were still afraid of me. You needed that time while I was gone to get your head straight."

Maybe so. Part of me had definitely been disappointed that he hadn't chosen to take advantage of me before he left. The other part had been relieved, but there was that part that had wanted him to carry me upstairs and overcome my maidenly scruples. A part that was getting more and more vocal every day. "Feel free to haul me up over your shoulder and carry me anywhere you want from now on. If you can."

An eyebrow quirked. "You worried about my back or your weight, darlin'?"

"My weight." There was nothing wrong with his back.

"You look just the way I like." He pulled out one of the chairs and gestured.

I seated myself, and let him bring the food, since he seemed to want to wait on me. And since he'd told me he liked the way I look, I didn't say a word about the heaping helping of spaghetti he piled on my plate, nor did I mention the fact that the garlic bread was likely adhering itself directly to my hips as I chewed. I just enjoyed the food and the company.

For a while. Until Rafe asked me where I'd been so late.

I swallowed. "Mrs. Armstrong's house. Tim isn't back yet, and she wanted to take it off the market. I think maybe selling it was her husband's idea. Or maybe they had to, to divide the assets."

"Divorce?" He bit into a piece of garlic bread. It crunched, and a few crumbs hit the table.

"They're separated," I said. "She lives at the house, he had an apartment."

"So he wasn't in bed with her when he was stabbed."

I shook my head. "Grimaldi's CSI crew went over the house as well as the apartment. There was no blood, and she said there would have been."

He took another bite of bread. "How's Tammy?"

"Fine," I said. "She said to give you her love."

"Surely not."

Fine. "She said to tell you hi."

Rafe nodded. I took a breath. "I stopped by your grandmother's house with a steak sandwich this afternoon. You weren't there."

I watched him closely. If I had expected to see a reaction, I was disappointed. Since I hadn't—I know better than to expect him to give away anything he doesn't want to—I wasn't. He just quirked a brow and kept eating. "Yeah?"

"Where were you?"

"I imagine I was out getting a burger," Rafe said calmly.

"Oh."

"Lunchtime. I got hungry."

Of course. I flushed, feeling stupid.

"So what did you wanna tell me over steak sandwiches?"

"How do you know that I didn't just want to see you?"

"I'm sure you did wanna see me," Rafe said, "but you had something you wanted to talk about, too. I know you. You ain't the type to come find me because you want sex up against the wall in the afternoon."

I wasn't? "Grimaldi and I found a sheet set in Tim's house that matches the sheet Brian Armstrong was wrapped in. The flat sheet was missing."

"No kidding."

I shook my head.

"Blood anywhere?"

"None we could see. Grimaldi was going to send in a CSI team to make sure."

Rafe nodded. "You stab somebody that many times, there's gonna be a lot of blood. Hard to get rid of all of it."

I didn't even want to know how he knew that. "Remember back in September, just after Lila died? I met this guy named Beau Riggins. A housecleaner." Of sorts.

He looked puzzled for a second, before his face cleared. "The guy who slept with Perry's wife?"

"That's him. I saw his business card in Tim's office drawer."

"So?" Rafe said. "Tim's a realtor, right? He probably recommends housecleaners all the time."

Probably. "Beau drove a blue Mini Cooper with speed stripes."

"So?"

"I passed a car like that just after I left Mrs. Armstrong's house tonight."

Rafe tilted his head. "You think it was him?"

I shrugged. "By the time I got around the block, the car was gone. I knocked on the door and asked if I'd left my cell phone there, but Mrs. Armstrong didn't let me in. She left me on the front step while she went to look."

"How rude," Rafe said, grinning.

"It was!"

"I know, darlin'. But most people ain't been as well brought up as you."

That was true. I'd had proper manners ground into me from a very early age. "Do you think she didn't want me to see who was there?"

"Maybe," Rafe said. "If somebody was."

"Do you think it was Beau?"

He shrugged. "Coulda been. Coulda been someone else. Coulda been nobody."

Could have. "Do you think I should tell Grimaldi?"

"Can't hurt."

"Now?"

"Later." He pushed his chair back and came around the table. "C'mon."

"Where?"

"It's later. Time for me to take the dress off."

I glanced at the table. "But the dishes..."

"Can wait," Rafe said firmly and pulled me toward the bedroom door.

THE NEXT MORNING WAS A replay of the one before. He got up and showered and headed out to Mrs. Jenkins's house to paint. I got dressed and went to work. There was no sales meeting this morning, and the place was dead, pardon the expression. Brittany was late, so it was just me in the office. I took advantage of the opportunity to call Tamara Grimaldi while I thought no one would hear me.

"Ms. Martin." As usual when she's in the middle of a case she sounded tired. "What can I do for you?"

"You can tell me whether your crew found any bloodstains in Tim's house."

She hesitated, and for a second I thought maybe she'd tell me it was none of my business. Then she sighed. "No."

"So Brian Armstrong wasn't killed there?"

"We don't know that. He could have cleaned extremely well."

"Is that likely?"

"No," Grimaldi admitted. "Most people, after they've committed a bloody murder, wipe up what they see, but they're not usually cool enough to go to town with cleaners and bleaches and brushes and everything else."

"Well, then?"

"But we can't rule it out. The rest of the sheet set was found in his closet. And there's that missing carpet from the guest bedroom."

And the Chlorox bleach and ammonia I'd seen in the upstairs bathroom.

"So Tim killed Brian, and wrapped him in the sheet that was on the bed. He took the body to East Nashville and dumped it in the park. He went to the office and washed his hands. He went back home and tossed the rest of the sheets in the washer and dryer while he cleaned the bedroom to within an inch of its life. He discarded—somehow—the carpet that had been on the floor. And then he folded the sheets—with the flat sheet missing—and put them back in the closet before he left town? Does that make any sense?"

"Maybe they weren't the sheets that were on the bed," Grimaldi said. "Maybe that was a different sheet set, that he took with him and threw in a dumpster somewhere, along with the carpet, because there was too much blood on them to get out. Maybe the sheet the body was wrapped in came from the closet, and he forgot that the rest of the set was there. He was probably rattled after it happened. Most people don't think straight after committing a murder."

"But you just said he thought straight enough to clean his bedroom so well that there was no sign of blood there."

She was quiet.

"I saw a business card in his desk yesterday," I said, and went on to explain about Beau Riggins and his houseboy business. "You remember him, don't you? Didn't you talk to him after Lila Vaughn was murdered?"

"I did." She paused for a second, probably to bring the information into focus. "He worked for all three of the houses where the open house robberies took place. One of them was Timothy Briggs's listing."

I nodded, although she couldn't see me. "The two gay guys. One of them took off work every week to come home early and watch Beau swing his feather duster." And his fanny.

"It was a coincidence," Grimaldi said, and continued before I could tell her that no, it hadn't been; not at all. "He had nothing to do with the robberies or the murders, but I talked to him before we knew better."

"He slept with Connie Fortunato."

There was a second's pause. "The second victim? Did I know that?"

"I think I probably told you," I said. "But maybe not. It wasn't important to what happened. Anyway, Tim had Beau's card in his desk."

"You think Mr. Riggins was the one who came in and cleaned up?"

It was possible. I didn't know Beau well, and had no idea whether he'd be willing to keep quiet about murder. That would depend on how he felt about Tim, I guess. His own morals had always struck me as a bit elastic. But he might not even have known what he was doing. Tim could have done the basic mopping up himself, and could have called Beau and asked him to do a more thorough cleaning.

Then again, I hadn't ever gotten the impression that Beau actually did much heavy lifting. He was more like sexual entertainment: a dishy guy in Wonderjocks™ bouncing around the house, flexing and bending, with a dust rag and mop.

"I saw his car yesterday," I told Grimaldi, and qualified it, "or rather, I saw the kind of car that he drove last fall. When I was leaving Mrs. Armstrong's house."

There was a beat. "Maybe she uses him, too," Grimaldi said.

Maybe she did. In some fashion. I declined the bait, as befitted a well-brought-up Southern Belle. "It was late-ish. Seven o'clock. Past business hours. She had changed into a robe."

"Ah." Grimaldi paused for a second before she asked, "And you say he slept with Mrs. Fortunato last year?"

"That's what he said. Did Brian and Erin separate because she was sleeping with someone else?"

"Irreconcilable differences," Grimaldi said.

"Is that what she told you? Or what you're telling me?"

"It's what I'm telling you. It's none of your business why they separated. Thank you for the information. I'll look into it."

Fine. Be that way. And since she was, I decided not to tell her about my second piece of information: the fact that Tim had had an appointment at Chaps on Friday night. I'd just go there myself instead. And if I found him—or more likely found out what he'd been up to on Friday, or who he'd been with—I'd tell her later. And gloat.

"You're welcome. Have a nice day."

I was just about to hang up when I heard her voice again. "Ms. Martin?"

I put the phone back up to my ear. "Yes, detective?"

"Did Mr. Collier come home last night?"

"Of course he came home," I said. "He even cooked dinner."

"Did you forgive him?"

"There was nothing to forgive. He was out getting something to eat when I stopped by the house in the afternoon. It was my fault. I should have tried calling him first."

"Of course." She was silent. "Have a good day, Ms. Martin."

"You too, detective. Let me know if there's anything more I can do for you." *Or anything more you can share with me.*

I didn't say it, but I knew she'd heard it in my voice.

Since the office was still empty, I dug the folder for the Armstrongs' house out of Brittany's filing cabinet, added the withdrawal form I had gotten signed yesterday, and set to work removing the listing from the Multiple Listing Service. It had to be done electronically on Brittany's computer, since she was the one with the company passwords, and I didn't want to leave it any longer than I had to, since I didn't want poor Erin Armstrong to have to deal with any more showings. It was a nice house in a desirable neighborhood, and the price wasn't bad either, and she'd probably had a run on the doors ever since the house went on the market.

I was in the process of getting the job done when Brittany's—or rather, the company's—mailbox signaled an incoming email with a little trill of sound.

Twelve

Normally I wouldn't have bothered with it. It's supremely bad form to look at someone else's email correspondence. It may even be illegal. Opening other people's snail mail certainly is. But just in case it was Tim, or something else pertinent to what was going on, I opened the email program and peered at the message.

And... bingo.

The message was from TBriggs @ LBA, which is short for Lamont, Briggs and Associates. In other words, the company we both work for. The message itself was short and sweet: *Anything for me?*

I flipped through the little stack of messages on Brittany's desk and found nothing. So I wrote back saying no, and added that, *Mrs. Armstrong requested that her house be taken off the market after the death of her husband. Did you hear about that?*

I waited for a response, and just when I started to worry that one wouldn't be coming, he sent one back. *On the news. Did you withdraw the listing?*

I told him I had, just this morning, and added, *The police were here yesterday.*

This time the response was much quicker. *Why?*

They were at your house too, I told him. *Where are you?*

Friend's house.

We should meet and talk.

There was another longish pause, then finally: *Who are you?*

Savannah, I wrote back. And imagined the consternation on Tim's face when he realized he'd been corresponding not with Brittany, but with me.

I didn't hear from him after that, nor had I expected to. But at least I knew he was alive and well, and checking his email. So I sent one last message his way. *The police found sheets in your house that matched the sheet Brian Armstrong was wrapped in. I really hope you have a good alibi for Friday night.*

That done, I deleted—and double-deleted—the conversation, since there was no point in leaving it for Brittany to find. That done, I retired to my own office to work on a postcard mailing I had planned in an attempt to scare up a few clients.

By eleven, I was bored and peckish—and still alone in the office— so I called Rafe to see if he wanted to go to lunch.

"Sure," he said readily. I could hear his voice echo, so he was still at Mrs. Jenkins's house. (Not that I was calling to check on him or anything.)

"What are you in the mood for?"

There was a pause, and I imagined the slow smile on his face and the way his eyebrow tilted. I blushed, of course. He's got me trained so that he doesn't even have to be there anymore; I know what he's thinking, and that's enough.

"I could go for a burger," he said eventually, predictably, after he'd enjoyed listening to me squirm.

"That's fine." I'm more of the Cordon Bleu type myself, but wherever there are burgers, I can usually count on finding some sort of salad too. "Where do you want to meet?"

He named a place, not too far from Mrs. J's house, on the border between the hideously expensive and the not-quite-gentrified parts of the neighborhood.

"Are you ready now?"

"Thirty minutes," Rafe answered, and hung up.

I made myself busy for another fifteen, and then I locked the still-empty office and got in my car.

The joint he'd picked—I won't honor it by calling it a restaurant—wasn't too far away, but he was there before me. When I walked in, he was sitting in a booth in the rear, with his back to the wall—the better to see any threats coming his way—and the phone to his ear. He saw me coming, though, and finished up the conversation by the time I stopped beside the table. He even got up to greet me. He slipped a hand around my waist under the winter coat I was wearing and leaned in to—I thought—give me a polite and gentlemanly peck on the cheek. Instead, the kiss landed on my mouth and lasted a bit longer than a peck. By the time he pulled back, my knees were weak, and I was clutching handfuls of his T-shirt. That was probably why he'd slipped that arm around me in the first place.

He grinned, of course, since the knowledge that he has that effect on me never fails to amuse him. "Careful, darlin'."

"I was being careful," I said, and managed to drop down on the bench almost gracefully, instead of as if my knees gave out. "Until I got involved with you."

"Too late now." He slid into the booth opposite, and added, "I ordered you a cheeseburger and fries."

So much for the demure salad I'd planned to eat.

"You're going to make me fat," I said.

"Just trying to keep your strength up," Rafe answered, his voice innocent but his eyes laughing. "I have plans for tonight."

"So do I, actually." I took a sip of the dark brown liquid in front of me, and grimaced. Real Coke. Not Diet. Tastier, yes, but I could feel the sugar and carbs buzzing through my veins as I drank, headed directly for my hips.

He quirked a brow. "Something you're not telling me?"

"Not at all." We just hadn't had time to talk. "I found out where Tim spent Friday night. I was going to go there and see whether I could find anyone who remembered him, and who could tell me whether he was alone when he left."

"Left where?"

"It's a place called Chaps," I said. "Some kind of nightclub, I think. On Church Street."

"Chaps." He had a funny look on his face.

I tilted my head. "Have you been there?" Had it been part of some undercover operation at some point or another?

He shook his head. "I think I should come with you, though."

"Why? It doesn't sound like a particularly rough place." Church Street is in a decent part of the midtown business district, and Chaps sounded like it was some sort of cowboy bar, maybe, like Coyote Ugly or the Wildhorse Saloon. There are plenty of those kinds of establishments around Nashville, with the country music industry. Lots of people in cowboy hats and boots, if not many actually wearing chaps. But I sincerely doubted that I'd need personal protection.

"I don't imagine so," Rafe said, his face amused, "but once you get there, I think you'll probably be happy to have me along."

I squinted at him. "Do you know something I don't?"

"I know lots of things you don't," Rafe said, "and I'll be happy to show you some of 'em as soon as we're alone together." He winked.

"You know that's not what I meant." But I blushed anyway.

He grinned. "Just deal with it, darlin'. Unless you've got some guy on the side you don't want me to know about, that you're meeting tonight?"

"Of course not." What would I want with another man when I had him? "You're welcome to come along. I just didn't want to assume you wanted to."

"Oh," Rafe said, "if you're going to a place called Chaps, I think I'd better."

Fine. He had nothing to worry about from other men, British or not, but I certainly wasn't about to turn down the offer of company. I'd so much rather be with him than apart from him.

"He emailed this morning," I added, after the waitress had dropped two cheeseburgers and fries on the table and had taken herself off, not without a lingering glance at Rafe.

"Tim?" He reached for the ketchup bottle, the muscles in his arm moving smoothly under the short sleeve of the white T-shirt.

"Uh-huh," I said, distracted.

He grinned and lifted the bottle. "Want some?"

"Please." I watched as he reached across to my plate and deposited a load of ketchup there, and then did the same on his own. And then I watched as he put the bottle away. Lovely arms. Lovely muscles. Lovely... everything.

He chuckled. "Eat your food, darlin'."

I nodded and reached for a fry. "I'm crazy about you."

"I know." He dragged a fry of his own through the ketchup and popped it in his mouth. "I keep waiting for you to wake up and wonder what the hell you were thinking."

Surely not?

It wasn't like I'd fallen in love with him overnight, after all. It had taken months, and quite a lot of soul-searching, at least on my part. I'd known him a long time, even if I couldn't say I'd had much to do with him back when we'd gone to school together. He'd brushed past me in the hallway once in a while, with a bold grin and a wink—"Looking good, sugar!"—whereupon I'd stuck my nose in the air and pretended I hadn't heard him, all the while blushing furiously.

He'd told me recently he'd liked me in high school, but he'd stayed clear because he figured my brother and Todd Satterfield would gang up on him if he did more than look at me sideways. Also, I was fourteen and jailbait, and he had enough problems with the law as it was. Besides, it wasn't like I'd want anything to do with him anyway, he reasoned. Which was unfortunately true. I'd been afraid of him back then. He was three years older than me, and from the wrong side of the tracks, with a bad reputation and a blatant sexuality, even at seventeen, that had set my nerves to jangling.

But I'd been aware of him. Very much aware. And back then, the story about fourteen-year-old LaDonna Collier getting herself in the family way by someone we'd never seen, someone from outside our small community, and having a mixed race baby... well, it all sounded sort of romantic, rather than sordid, the way my mother made it out to be. Shades of Romeo and Juliet.

As I got older, I realized it couldn't have been much fun for LaDonna, literally left holding the baby at such a young age. And when I got pregnant myself—at twenty seven, but out of wedlock and by LaDonna Collier's good-for-nothing colored boy—I got a crash course in just what it was like.

Losing that baby, and then losing Rafe, is the hardest thing I've ever had to go through. And when he came back, I was ready. I had admitted—to myself and anyone else who would listen—that I loved him. Not just liked him, not just got weak in the knees when he smiled at me—but loved him. Couldn't imagine being without him anymore.

The fact that he still wanted me, after everything I'd put him through, was a source of constant amazement to me, and there was no way on God's green earth I'd change my mind. As far as I was concerned, he was perfection incarnate, and anyone who said differently got an instant earful of all the reasons they were wrong.

"Not going to happen," I said.

He shrugged. "So he emailed this morning."

"Who?"

"Tim," Rafe said. "Isn't that what you were telling me?"

Oh. Right. "While I was sitting at Brittany's desk, withdrawing the Armstrongs' house from the market. The email program dinged, and

I thought I'd better make sure it wasn't something important. Since Brittany wasn't there yet."

"In other words," Rafe translated, "you snooped."

"Someone had to. Brittany still hadn't shown up when I left for lunch. I hope nothing's wrong."

"Prob'ly just taking the day of since the boss is gone," Rafe said. "So what did the email say?"

"At first he just wanted to know whether there was anything he needed to take care of. I told him about the Armstrongs' house and that I'd taken it off the market. Then I told him that the police had been to the office. That seemed to worry him."

"It'd worry most people," Rafe said.

Perhaps. More likely to worry someone who'd done something he was afraid they'd discover, I imagined.

"I also told him the police had been to his house and that they'd found a sheet set that matched the one Mr. Armstrong had been wrapped in when he was dumped in the park. That's when he figured out I wasn't Brittany."

"Imagine that," Rafe said dryly. "I don't suppose you know where he's holed up?"

I shook my head. "I asked. He said he was at a friend's house. But then he figured out he was talking to me and not Brittany, so he disappeared."

Rafe nodded. "I don't suppose you know any of his friends?"

"I'm afraid not," I said. "I've seen him a couple of times with a few other gay guys—once at Fidelio's, remember?—but I don't know who any of them are. We don't really move in the same circles."

"Course." But his lips quirked.

"What?" I said.

"Nothing. Eat your food." He took a bite of his own burger, chewed, swallowed, and added, "So when d'you wanna leave tonight?"

Chaps opened at seven, or so the website had said.

"That prob'ly means things start getting underway at nine," Rafe said, and sounded like he knew what he was talking about. He certainly knew better than me, since bars are not within my area of expertise. My ex-husband was a lawyer, and when he took me out, it was to the opera or the ballet. Those I'm familiar with. Bars, not so much.

"We can wait until nine." I glanced at him across the table. "Do you have something else you have to do?"

"Earlier. I'll be home in plenty of time." He bit into his burger. I was so gratified to hear him describe my apartment as home that I forgot to ask where he was going and with whom.

It wasn't until much later, after we'd finished lunch and gone our separate ways—me back to the office and he to Mrs. Jenkins's house—that it occurred to me to wonder about his plans.

I debated back and forth for a minute whether calling and asking would be too clingy, too much like I was checking up on him—and then I decided to hell with it. We were in a committed relationship, and he called my apartment his home; I had a right to ask.

But when I dialed his number, he didn't pick up.

I was still alone in the office, although in the interim I had taken it upon myself to contact Brittany and ask why she wasn't here, when she was supposed to be. She'd given me a lousy excuse about a cold, one I could see right through, since her nose wasn't even stuffy. I informed her that I had used her computer to withdraw the Armstrongs' listing so she wouldn't have to, and then I hung up so she could go back to bed and to Devon, the grungy boyfriend.

There was nothing more for me to do, so I headed out. And— yes, I admit it—I drove in the direction of Potsdam Street and Mrs. Jenkins's house.

It wasn't that I didn't trust Rafe. It isn't that I don't. I have no reason not to. So I wasn't really worried. I just wanted to see him. To make sure that nothing was wrong.

Getting there and finding the place empty was... annoying.

Something was obviously going on. And since he'd told me about helping Wendell the other day, but he wasn't telling me about this, it was probably something personal.

Naturally, the first thing that came to mind was another woman.

As I drove back down Potsdam Street, I reminded myself that he'd never cheated.

Other than with Carmen Arroyo, but that was in the line of duty and while we were broken up.

He'd never indicated that he wasn't happy with me.

Our sex life wasn't suffering.

He wasn't displaying any evidence of guilt.

Not that he would. He's had years to perfect his lying. If he was cheating on me, I'd never know it. Not until he told me.

Could he be cheating?

As I turned onto Dresden, I took the thought out and tried to look at it dispassionately.

He was a man, and men do occasionally cheat. Not all of them, I suppose, but my ex-husband did. Maybe that's predisposed me to think all men do. Maybe men don't cheat any more than women, really.

Anyway, other than the fact that he was gone and I didn't know where, I had no reason to suspect that Rafe was cheating. There'd been no strange perfume smell, no lipstick on his collar or neck; none of the usual telltale signs of an affair.

Then again, that was how it had started with Bradley, too. The perfume and lipstick had come later. At first it had just been late hours at the office and a waning in his desire for me. He was getting his needs met elsewhere, and I'm sure he felt guilty, so he developed a habit of falling asleep on the couch, or of working so late that I'd be sleeping by the time he came to bed. That way he wouldn't have to deal with me in any intimate manner.

I'd been asleep the other night when Rafe came home. He could have slipped in beside me with no fanfare. Instead, he'd woken me up to make love to me.

Did that mean he wasn't cheating? Or just that he wasn't as guilt-ridden as Bradley about it?

We weren't married, so he might not be feeling as guilty. Cheating on a girlfriend isn't as bad as cheating on a wife.

Or maybe he simply realized that sex was one surefire way of keeping me quiet and unworried. He'd been able to sneak out again the next morning without waking me—and without having to answer any awkward questions—so obviously the vigorous round of lovemaking had done the trick. But was that the intention, or just a side benefit?

Had he gotten tired of me already? Maybe it was a case of the forbidden fruit: for as long as he couldn't have me, he'd wanted me, but once I was available, suddenly I wasn't very exciting anymore.

Or maybe my attempts to sell him on the charms of domestic life—the folded laundry and home-cooked dinners—were doing the opposite of what I hoped. Was I smothering him in domesticity, and now he was out there looking for sex with no strings attached?

I drove all the way home in such unpleasant contemplation, and once I got there, fell facedown on the bed with a groan, running over and over in my head the reasons why—and why not—Rafe was surely getting some on the side.

The more I thought about it, the more reasonable the explanation became. All the signs were there. He wasn't where he was supposed to be. He wasn't answering his phone, nor telling me where he was.

On the contrary, he was lying. That story about going out for a hamburger at lunchtime yesterday... it made sense, and there was no way I could disprove it, but I was willing to bet it wasn't what he'd been doing. It had been a story to throw me off. If I asked him later where he'd been this afternoon, he'd probably tell me he'd had to run to the hardware store for another paint roller.

And the thing was, he might have gone to the hardware store for another paint roller. There was no way I could disprove it. There was no reason to doubt it, even. It made perfect sense. Sometimes he did need new paint rollers. No reason why he wouldn't have needed one today.

If I went to the hardware store right now, he probably wouldn't be there. But he could have been and gone before I arrived. That's what he'd tell me if I asked.

Not that I'd ask. Because asking would make me sound like a worried, nagging, distrustful girlfriend, and nobody wants one of those.

And the realization that I'd be willing to keep my mouth shut, to put up with what might be infidelity because I was too afraid to kick up a fuss and perhaps lose him, was both eye-opening and shameful.

Did I love him enough—did I want to hang onto him badly enough?—that I'd put up with sharing him?

The thought was nauseating—and instantly rejected. The idea that he'd come from someone else's bed to mine was abhorrent. And when I narrowed it down to those terms, I couldn't see him doing it, either. In spite of who he was—his past, his less-than-high-class family, his ten years of dealing with the dregs of society—he was honorable in his own way. When I'd asked him about Carmen Arroyo, he hadn't denied sleeping with her. He could have prevaricated or lied, but he didn't. He could have refused to answer, but instead he'd told me the truth, and had made sure I knew it was only in the line of duty, not because he'd wanted to. That it hadn't had anything to do with him and me.

Would he really sleep with someone else now? Would he sneak around like this, instead of just telling me the truth? Would he keep telling me he loved me if he were bedding someone else?

Or was it another case of "in the line of duty"? Was something else going on, something he didn't want me to know?

Something that would cause me worry if I knew about it?

He hadn't gone back into undercover work. That much I knew. His cover had been blown sky high a few months ago, and trying to go back to what he'd been doing before would make him an instant target for all the people he'd dealt with in the past ten years. He wouldn't be stupid enough to try.

Those people could equally well find him now, though. He'd been using his own name, after all, except for the last few months when he pretended to be Jorge Pena. Maybe someone had found him. Maybe someone was threatening him, and he was trying to take care of the situation without involving me.

Or maybe Wendell and the TBI had pulled him in to tie off loose threads in the investigation. Maybe that's all it was, and he just didn't want me to worry about it. Maybe he didn't tell me because there really wasn't anything to tell. Nothing of any consequence.

Or maybe he was with someone else right now, in her bed, while I was alone in mine.

The dizzying swirl of my thoughts got to be too much after a while, and I shook off the self-pity and the worry to enough of a degree that I was able to make dinner. Grilled chicken salad, light on the chicken, to make up for the burger and fries for lunch. I made enough for Rafe too, since he'd said he'd be back in plenty of time before we had to go to Chaps.

But he didn't come home, and the food was getting cold and soggy, so I ate by myself. And when I was finished, and I'd cleaned up, he still hadn't come home, so I sat down and waited, skipping from channel to channel on the television. The news were on, along with assorted reruns. The canned laughter of the sitcoms set my teeth on edge, so I focused on the news shows, hoping—dreading—possibly hearing something about a shootout in East Nashville, leaving a man dead and another on the run.

But it didn't happen. Nobody had gotten shot, there was no update on the Brian Armstrong murder—at least not for public consumption—and the headline news of the evening was an Eye-5 investigation into misconduct and neglect in local nursing homes. I watched that, getting increasingly disturbed. It ended with the news that the Milton House Nursing Home would be fined and expected to clean up their act within a month, or they'd be closed down for good. I wanted to applaud, since the Milton House was where Rafe's grandmother Tondalia Jenkins had been living when I first met her, and it was one of the more horrible places it's ever been my misfortune to visit. I'd thought at the time that I'd rather shoot one of my loved ones than leaving them to rot at the Milton House, and I hadn't wasted any time in ordering Rafe to get Mrs. J out of there. He hadn't wasted any time in obeying either, once he could prove that he was her grandson and had the right to make that decision.

Of course, that brought me full circle, back to thinking about Rafe again, and about where he was and what he might be doing. After thirty minutes, I was ready to start clawing holes in the furniture. That's when I decided to hell with it: if he wasn't here, I'd go to Chaps without him. It was barely past seven o'clock. It wasn't even full dark outside. And I was traveling at most twenty minutes from home. The place I was going to was a legitimate business in a decent neighborhood. I didn't need his protection. I was a grown woman and I could take care of myself. I didn't need him.

So I marched downstairs and got into the car and headed for the other side of town, and imagined the look on his face when I walked back in at home later with the information that I'd found Tim and talked him into turning himself in to Detective Grimaldi.

Thirteen

I knew the address already, and Chaps turned out to be just about where I expected. A block or two closer to where interstate 40 bisected town, separating downtown from midtown, than I'd thought, maybe, but in the same general area.

It was a big warehouse-looking building: one story tall, all brick, with no windows, catty-corner from the Hustler store on the corner of Church and Interstate Drive. For a nightclub, it was pretty big. For a bar, it was enormous. It was clearly the right place, though. The name was written on a discreet sign high on one wall, illuminated by a spotlight from above. Best as I could make out, the script was supposed to look like a rope, or I guess maybe a lariat or lasso.

The entrance turned out to be around the corner, on the side street, directly opposite from a big parking lot where I left my car.

The lot was less than half full, and the vehicles that were there, were a mixture of old and new, expensive and economy priced. There were no small blue Mini Coopers with white stripes in evidence.

What there were, were a couple of Harley Davidsons parked in one corner, and for a second my heart skipped a beat. Maybe Rafe had beaten me here. Maybe he was already inside. Maybe he'd been thinking to spare me the trouble, and the discomfort, of investigating the place myself.

But as I walked closer, I noticed subtle differences. One bike was red, while Rafe's is black. One had tall handlebars, while his are normal. And one had big saddlebags, which his doesn't.

I'd never thought I'd see the day when I'd be able to differentiate one motorcycle from another, but I guess you live and learn.

At any rate, he wasn't here. Nor was Beau Riggins, it seemed. Nor Tim, unless he was driving something other than his usual baby blue confection.

My heels clicked on the pavement as I hustled across the street, my shoulder bag bumping against my hip. The entrance to Chaps was a single heavy door under a small awning, with a single spotlight shining down. I'd driven around the block looking for another way in, otherwise I might have suspected that this was the back door, not the front. But there'd been no other way into the building, so this had to be it, no matter how unassuming it looked.

There was no guard or bouncer on duty, and no entrance or cover fee. I could just push the door open and walk in.

I did, into a long, narrow corridor with doors on either side. Music was thumping loud enough to make the floor vibrate. It seemed to come from the room at the end of the hall. It looked big, and it was dark and a bit smoky and I could see shadows moving back and forth through the gloom. The place smelled weird too; a little bit antiseptic in the same institutional way as the old Milton House, where the smell of heavy duty cleaning supplies tried and failed to mask other, less pleasant odors.

Not that there's anything pleasant about industrial strength Pine Sol in enough quantities to make your stomach lurch.

Mine did, and I swallowed hard. Between the smell and the vibrations from the music, not to mention the flashing of the strobe lights in the other room, I'd be working up a migraine if I were prone to such things.

Part of me wanted to turn around and leave. Just give up. Go outside and wait for Rafe to call, which he surely would when he came home and found the apartment empty.

But the other part, the proud and stubborn one, refused to accept defeat. So what if the place made me feel uncomfortable? What if it wasn't what I had expected? I was a big girl. I could take care of myself. And someone here might know where to find Tim.

So I squared my shoulders and crept forward, toward the music and the moving shadows.

About halfway down the hall, I passed a niche, and jumped when I saw the outline of a figure out of the corner of my eye. Tall, dark, menacing, with a raised arm.

It was only a couple of seconds before I realized I was looking at a statue, but by then my heart was beating doubletime all the way up in my throat, and it took a while to get it back down where it belonged. Long enough for me to get a good look at the thing, and to realize that it was naked except for a leather vest and a pair of chaps. The latter perfectly framed the statue's larger-than-life-sized personal package.

I averted my eyes, of course, as soon as I realized what I was looking at. But by then it was too late, and I was blushing furiously. It was also dawning on me that perhaps I wasn't in a country and western joint, after all. The music certainly didn't have the steel guitar twang I'd come to associate with the style, and it was a lot heavier on the bass.

But I was here, so I made myself go forward, leaving the niche and the statue behind.

Another couple of yards took me to the doorway to the big room, and I peered in, cautiously.

It was, as I had expected, a bar-cum-nightclub. The dance floor was mostly empty now, although a handful of people were gyrating to the beat. Between the darkness and the flashing of the strobe lights, it took me a few moments to realize that they were all men. And they were dressed in leather pants. Some of them had shirts on, some didn't. One guy wore some sort of harness and another wore a leather cap.

And it wasn't because they'd all ridden motorcycles. There'd only been three Harleys in the parking lot. There were a lot more than three guys on the floor. The others must have gotten here by car. Staid Volvos, zippy little Neons, and big, black trucks, to name a few of the vehicles I remembered from the lot across the street.

Some of what they were doing on the dance floor didn't look much like dancing, either. They were dressed, to enough of a degree that they couldn't really be doing what it looked like they were doing, I realized that... but it still looked like they were doing it. And the fact that they were all men made it even more shocking.

I'm not a prude. In spite of my upbringing and my numerous well-bred hang-ups, I've never had a problem with Tim or his lifestyle. It isn't for everyone—specifically, it isn't for me—but it's his life and he can choose to live it any way he wants to. I've worked with gay people, on both sides of a transaction. It was just a few weeks ago that my clients Aislynn and Kylie had closed on the house I'd helped them find in early December.

So I don't have homophobia. Or any other kind of phobia, unless we're talking about cockroaches or giant spiders.

Most of the time, though, when I've found myself around gay people, they've acted just like straight people. Tim has swooned as ardently over Rafe as any number of women I've introduced him to, and Aislynn and Kylie don't French kiss in front of me any more than mother and Bob Satterfield do. (Supposing they kiss at all, of course, but I assume they do, in private. My mother and her gentleman friend,

I mean. I'm sure Aislynn and Kylie do. Mother and the sheriff probably
do too. The point is that they don't do it in public, any more than
Aislynn and Kylie.)

Such was not the case here. These guys were rubbing against each
other like they were in the privacy of their own bedrooms, and nobody
seemed to think anything of it. Nobody except me, who blushed to the
roots of my hair and didn't know where to look.

"First time here?" a voice like audible honey asked, and I spun to
face the speaker, almost tripping over my own feet.

He was close enough that I could get quite a good look at him,
even in the semi-dark, and part of me wished he wasn't.

Not that he was hard on the eyes. Not at all. Just a bit taller than
me, and barely out of his teens, with big eyes with long lashes, a buzz
cut, and smooth, baby-soft skin. Lots of it. As it turned out, that statue
I'd encountered in the hallway outside? It was modeling the Chaps
employee uniform. The guy in front of me wore the same black leather
vest and black leather chaps belted around his waist. I'm sure he had
something on his feet, as well, but after the first automatic glance
down, I kept my eyes firmly anchored above the neck.

He grinned. "Think maybe you took a wrong turn somewhere, doll?"

I wish.

"I'm looking for a friend," I said. Or yelled, rather, over the music
that was still thumping.

He tilted his head. "We're kind of empty. It's a Tuesday, and early."

Sure. I hadn't really expected Tim to be here. Hoped, maybe, but
not expected.

"Do you know Timothy Briggs?"

My new friend giggled. "No. Should I?"

"He was here last Friday night."

"So were a few hundred other people," my companion said with a
graceful shrug that set into motion a chain reaction of muscles under
the black leather.

"He's about six feet tall, thirty-some years old, with blond hair. Real estate agent. Drives a blue Jaguar. And I wouldn't think he's a regular." I had a hard time imagining Tim in a place like this at all. He wore tailored suits and brightly colored shirts—aubergine silk and lavender cotton—and the idea of him decked out in leather pants and a dog collar boggled the mind.

And anyway, if he came here every weekend, he wouldn't have had a need to write the appointment on his calendar, would he?

My new friend shook his head, and the little stud in his ear sparkled in the strobe lights. "Can't help you."

"Did you work on Friday night?"

He hadn't.

"Is there anyone here tonight who did?"

He shot a glance over his shoulder in the direction of the bar. "Earle. But I don't think he's gonna wanna talk to you."

"I'm just looking for my friend," I said. "He's been missing for four days."

Not strictly true, since I'd spoken to him—sort of—this morning. But it did the trick. My companion got pale under the tan. "Missing?"

"Since the early hours of Saturday. After he washed off the blood."

"Blood?" At this point he looked ready to pass out.

"I probably shouldn't talk about it," I said apologetically. No joke, either; I knew I shouldn't. But it served as a handy excuse for why I couldn't say more. "I'm just hoping that someone saw him Friday night. And maybe noticed who he left with."

He swayed. Literally, back and forth. "Are you... from the police?"

I stared at him. "No." Did I look like I was from the police?

When he didn't say anything else, I added, "I'm just a concerned friend. Who's Earle?"

"The bartender." He turned to watch me as I walked away, in the direction of the bar. It seemed to take him a moment to realize what I was doing, and then he trotted after, equipment bobbing. "But you can't..."

On the contrary. I skirted the dance floor and slid up to the bar, where Earle was busy filling glasses with beer.

He was an older guy—mid-fifties, maybe?—with a shaved head and a full beard, and a pirate ring in one ear. He was dressed in the same leather vest as my young friend, but the effect was quite different. Where the young man had smooth, hairless skin—maybe he waxed—Earle had a furry pelt covering his chest and stomach, and beefy arms with tattoos running from his wrists all the way up to his shoulders. Snakes or maybe vines twined. The lower half of him was mercifully hidden behind the bar, and I was glad, since I didn't want to know whether he also wore chaps and nothing else below the waist.

My tentative smile was met with a scowl. Obviously Earle wasn't as happy to see me as his young friend. They probably didn't get a lot of female visitors. Maybe he was afraid of me.

"Hi," I said. "I'm Savannah."

He grunted something.

"She's looking for a friend," the young man said over my shoulder, almost apologetically, "sir."

Earle glared at him too, and I could almost feel him wilt.

I turned back to the bartender. "Tim Briggs. Do you know him?"

He shook his head without meeting my eyes.

"He was here Friday night. To meet someone. Nine o'clock."

I thought something might have flickered in his eyes, but it was hard to say for certain when he wouldn't look at me. Instead he pushed the two tankards of beer across the bar and grunted to the young man beside me, "Table five."

"Right away, sir." My new friend took the drinks and scurried off, leaving me to the mercies of Earle. I had hoped that maybe, with just the two of us, he might be more forthcoming, but he didn't say anything more. Just grabbed a rag and proceeded to mop the counter where the drinks had stood.

"He's been missing for a few days," I said, since it had worked last time.

The wiping checked for a second, albeit not quite long enough for me to be sure it was in response to what I'd said. Could have been a coincidence.

"His calendar said he was meeting someone here Friday night."

Nothing.

"You were working then."

He looked up, finally. Met my eyes for a second. "Don't know him."

"How do you know? You haven't even asked me what he looks like."

No answer. I felt movement behind me, and glanced over my shoulder. Another couple of men had come up to flank me. They didn't say anything, just stood there and looked menacing.

Funny, but up until now, I'd always thought of gay guys as soft. Like Tim. Glossily handsome, with bleached teeth, perfectly coiffed hair, and elegant clothes.

There was nothing elegant about these guys, and certainly nothing soft. They were big, they were butch, and they wore leather. They looked like they could break me into a couple of pieces with their bare hands, and they also looked like they wouldn't mind trying. It was like having a wall of bikers at my back, closing in.

My heart was beating uncomfortably hard when I turned back to Earle. "I'm not looking for any trouble. Just my friend." My voice even hitched a little, and that was in spite of still having to talk over the loud beat of the music.

He glanced up again, and opened his mouth. And then his eyes flickered to the side, over my shoulder. His expression changed, and that was the only warning I had before an arm slipped around my waist. I felt the heat of a hard male body at my back, and a hand splayed possessively over my stomach.

I think my heart stopped for a beat or two before it picked up the rhythm again, staggering along at a much more rapid pace.

"Don't ever," a voice murmured in my ear, "do that again."

I sagged, and he'd probably figured I would, and that's why he stood so close with his arm around me, so he could take some of the weight and my collapse wouldn't seem so much like what it was.

The atmosphere had changed. Nobody moved, visibly, but there was a sort of emotional backing off I could feel. A cessation—or maybe just readjustment—of hostility. Maybe they realized they couldn't intimidate Rafe as easily as they intimidated me, or maybe they just recognized another alpha male and withdrew from what was clearly staked territory.

Or maybe they were simply too busy staring. I've had occasion to watch Rafe work a (small) gay crowd before—Tim and a handful of his friends—and he's just as effective there as he is with straight women. The fact that Tim imagines him naked doesn't seem to bother him any more than the fact that I do... along with any number of other females.

He didn't seem uncomfortable now either, in the midst of this crowd of aggressively masculine gay men who were probably wishing they could rip his clothes off. He just kept an arm around me, and his focus on Earle. "Thanks for your time. We'll be leaving now."

I drew breath to protest—I hadn't learned what I came here for—and had it squeezed back out of my lungs again when his arm tightened. He practically lifted me off my feet to turn me around. We faced a wall of leather and bare skin, and rather more erect penises than I was comfortable with. Truth be told, I was barely beginning to become friendly with Rafe's, and to see a half-dozen others saluting me—or more likely him—was beyond disconcerting and well into mortifying.

I had no idea where to keep my eyes as the moment lengthened. Then finally someone moved. The ranks drew apart, leaving a pathway to the door. "Go," Rafe said in my ear.

I went, and although I hoped it looked like an ordered retreat, I'm afraid it came across more like I was running for my life. I just hoped they weren't laughing at me behind my back. Although if they were, I wasn't about to say anything about it.

Rafe followed, but not immediately. I ended up scurrying all the way to the back door before I realized I was alone, and then I ended up standing there for a minute, waiting for him, dithering between braving the outside on my own or staying where I was.

When he came down the hall, it was unhurried, and nobody was following him. He didn't linger at the door, though, just gave me a push. "Go."

I went, out the door and across the street to the parking lot with him right behind. My heart had settled down into more of a normal rhythm now, and I didn't feel like I was running away, or like the chances of pursuit were imminent, but my pulse was still jittery. This time it wasn't the leather-clad gay guys that worried me, though. It was Rafe. I knew what was coming, and I wasn't looking forward to it.

When I stopped beside the Volvo to unlock the door, he grabbed my arm and spun me around. My back hit the side of the car and his body hit my front and kept me there.

I assumed he was going to yell at me. He didn't. Instead, he just asked, "What the hell were you doing?"

I didn't even have time to answer before he kissed me, but the fact that my mouth was open made things easier.

The kiss went from zero to sixty in no time flat, blistering with heat and anger and—I didn't doubt it for a moment—worry. I held onto him, because it was all I could do, and kissed him back, because it was impossible not to. He wouldn't have accepted anything less, and anyway, I was grateful for my rescue as well as happy to see him.

The status quo went on until a throat clearing broke through the dizziness that accompanies one of Rafe's kisses. I clawed my way back to the surface.

"Sorry to interrupt," a pack-a-day voice said.

I halfway expected it to be patrol officers Spicer and Truman, Tamara Grimaldi's pet minions at the MNPD, who had interrupted us in this kind of endeavor a few times before. It wasn't.

I blinked. "Sally?" And Rafe, who had spun on his heel to stand protectively in front of me, relaxed his stance.

"Evening, princess." Sally's voice is as deep and gravelly as a man's, and the mohawk on her head was as fire-engine red as the last time I'd seen her, last autumn.

"What are you doing here?" I asked.

She didn't answer. She didn't have to, since the answer was self-evident. She was coming from, or going to, Chaps. Coming from, based on the next question. "You OK?"

"Fine," I said, with a glance at Rafe. "Now."

"I was just about to get involved when I realized I didn't have to." She turned to him. "You must be Collier."

He nodded.

Sally runs a small shop on Franklin Road, on the south side of town, that sells police gear and self-protective stuff. I'd been told of it by Tamara Grimaldi, back when I was snooping around looking for Lila Vaughn's killer. Sally had sold me a tiny lipstick cylinder with an even smaller serrated blade inside, as well as another lipstick cylinder with a nozzle, full of pepper spray. And while I'd been at her store, I'd seen Wendell Craig, Rafe's handler from the TBI, arrive. So Sally knew Grimaldi, and she also knew Wendell. And she knew me. It was sort of obvious that she'd know about Rafe. I had even talked to her about him once, I think.

"I'm sorry," I said automatically. "Sally Harmon, Rafael Collier. Rafe, Sally."

They exchanged a sort of amused look, probably at my excessive concern with good manners in the midst of this situation.

"What can we do for you?" Rafe asked.

Sally nodded toward the warehouse. Her cock's comb waved. "Just wanted to make sure Miss Priss here was OK."

"I'm fine," I said again.

"They wouldn't really have hurt you."

I wasn't so sure, and I don't think Rafe was either, because he didn't say anything.

"I heard you were looking for someone?" She glanced from me to him and back.

"Tim Briggs," I said. "A colleague of mine. He was here Friday night. Had an appointment to meet someone at nine, according to his calendar."

"Did something happen to him?"

"We're not sure," Rafe said. "We're just trying to discover whether anyone saw him and who he was with."

Sally nodded. "I mighta seen him. There was a new guy sitting at the bar on Friday night, got a lot of attention. Nice-looking boy. Blond hair, green shirt."

That sounded like Tim. With the caveat that he wasn't a boy, he was a thirty-something man. But to Sally, he might have looked like a boy. He was a good ten or fifteen years younger than she was, and he looks younger than he is.

"Do you have any idea who he left with?"

She shook her head. "Didn't see him leave. He was there, and the next time I looked he was gone. Wasn't like I was keeping an eye on him, you know. Not my type. And I figured he was just broadening his horizons. Experimenting."

"Who was he talking to?" Rafe asked.

Sally shrugged. "Nobody I knew. Nobody I noticed. The place gets pretty busy on weekends."

"Tamara Grimaldi is looking for him," I said, "in connection with a murder. So if you remember anything more..."

"I'll be sure to let her know."

That wasn't what I wanted to hear, and it must have shown on my face, because she grinned. "Sorry, princess. But if Tamara is looking for him, that's official business. Trumps your desire to know."

It did. I just didn't want to be out of the loop. But there wasn't much I could do about it. So I thanked her, and she headed back across the street into the club. It wasn't until she was gone, back inside the building, that Rafe turned to me. "Keys."

I handed them to him. He unlocked my car and opened the door. "In."

"What about...?"

He tossed the keys in my lap. "I'll follow you. Don't even think about driving anyplace but straight home."

"No, sir."

The words were out before I'd thought about them, and I saw something flash in his eyes. His lips tightened. "Don't call me that."

I had my mouth open to ask why not—I hadn't meant anything by it, after all, other than to tweak him a little over his high-handed tone—when I remembered that that's how the young waiter inside the club had addressed Earle the bartender. Maybe it meant something I didn't realize it meant.

So I closed my mouth again and nodded. "I'm sorry."

"Not as sorry as you're gonna be when I'm done with you," Rafe said and slammed my door. I watched as he stalked to his bike, parked with the others, and then I waited for him to fire it up before I pulled out of the parking lot and headed home.

Fourteen

I didn't really think I had anything to worry about. He wasn't really angry with me. He couldn't be. I hadn't done anything wrong. Nothing serious enough to really make him upset.

But because I wasn't a hundred percent certain, I drove carefully straight home, and made sure I didn't lose him along the way. If there was a yellow light up ahead, I slowed down and waited rather than making it look like I was trying to ditch him.

It wasn't a long drive. One block from Church Street to Charlotte Avenue, then straight east through downtown onto the James Robertson Bridge, and from there across the Cumberland River to the corner of Fifth and East Main. It took less than fifteen minutes, with barely any cars on the road.

I drove into a spot in the underground parking garage and waited for him to pull the bike to a stop beside me before I opened my door. And then I waited while he took the helmet off and hung it on the handle.

"C'mon." He took my arm and headed for the stairs. I didn't ask any questions, just concentrated on keeping up, since he was motivated enough not to bother adjusting his stride to mine.

By the time we'd navigated two flights of stairs—basement to first floor, first floor to second—at two steps at a time, I was out of breath and my heart was slamming against my ribs. Not all of it was exertion. Maybe he really was angry. Maybe I did have to worry.

"Keys." He held out a hand, and I dropped my keychain into it. He unlocked the door to the apartment and pushed it open. "In."

I crossed the threshold and dropped my bag on the floor in the hallway. The door slammed into the frame behind me, quivering, and I heard the sound of the deadbolt hit home. And I guess I should have run as soon as I was able, because I'd only managed two steps before he grabbed me and spun me around again. "Dammit, Savannah!"

"I'm not sure what you're so upset about," I said a little breathlessly. "Nothing happened."

"No thanks to you." But he didn't object when I slipped my hands under the leather jacket he had on. Maybe that's what had made the leather-clad men back off. He had his own leather armor, and he looked like he belonged in a place like Chaps in a way that I—in my cashmere coat—never could.

"I just wanted to talk to them." I slid my hands up his torso and chest, feeling soft cotton against my palms, and the heat of his skin underneath.

"They didn't wanna talk to you."

"I figured that out." I pushed the jacket off his shoulders. He dropped his hands from my arms for long enough to let it hit the floor. When the hands came back, it was to brace himself against the wall on either side of my head so he could lean down into my face.

I looked back up at him while my hands continued to explore.

His lips curved. "You trying to distract me, darlin'?"

"Not at all." I crossed my fingers and slid my hands back down his chest and around to his back to pull him closer.

"Sure." But he didn't stop me. Not until one of my questing hands found the handle of the gun tucked into his waistband at the middle of his back, and then he moved, quickly as a snake, to snag my wrist. "Careful."

"I wasn't going to shoot you," I protested, but I let him take the gun out of my hand and make sure the safety was on before he hung it on one of the coat hooks a few feet to my right.

He turned back to me. "I ain't worried about you shooting me."

"What, then? You think I'm stupid enough to shoot myself?"

He didn't answer, and I added, a little miffed, "Why were you carrying your gun in the first place?"

"Thought I might need it," Rafe said.

"You're joking."

He shrugged. "Things coulda gone wrong back there."

"They were a bunch of gay guys!" Butch, leather-clad gay guys, but it wasn't like my virtue had been in danger. And shooting them would surely have been overkill.

"Gay men'll kill you just as soon as straight men," Rafe told me.

"Don't be ridiculous. Why would they kill me?"

"Let me think," Rafe said, glancing up at the ceiling for a second before drilling his eyes into mine again. "Oh, yeah. Now I remember. You walked into their place—their safe haven—and accused them of killing one of your friends."

"I did not!"

He mimicked my voice, quite accurately too. "He was here Friday night. And no one's seen him since."

Oops. Yes, when he put it like that, maybe someone could have taken that statement to mean that I was accusing them of murder. "But Tim isn't dead!"

"You know that," Rafe said, "and I know that, but they don't. Why'd you go there on your own? Why didn't you wait for me?"

I squirmed and looked away. "I was upset."

"Why?"

"I went by Mrs. Jenkins's house this afternoon, and you weren't there."

He sighed. "I told you I'd be home in time to go with you."

He had. I'd just let my jealousy and worry get the better of me. "I'm sorry," I said.

"Sure."

"I am!"

He quirked a brow. "How sorry?"

"Excuse me?"

"Just how sorry are you?"

Oh. Um... "Very sorry?"

The corner of his mouth lifted. "How sorry's that?"

"Sorry enough that I might be induced to make it up to you?"

The smile widened. "How d'you figure you're gonna do that?"

"I'm sure I can think of something you might like," I said, skimming my hands back around his waist, under the T-shirt this time. Hot skin and hard muscles quivered under my touch.

His eyelids drooped and he lowered his forehead to mine. "I like that."

"I thought you might." I tugged on the shirt, and he stepped away for long enough to peel it up over his head and drop it on the floor. As usual, the sight took my breath away, and so did the feel of him against me when he stepped back in. By then, he wasn't satisfied with being touched, either, but slipped his hands around my waist and began working my blouse up. His hands were hot and hard against my lower back when he pressed me closer to him.

"You scared me," he murmured against the side of my neck as he nuzzled my hair to the side. "When I came home and you weren't here."

I tilted my head to give him better access. "I'm sorry."

"Don't do that again." His breath was hot against my skin and made a shiver run down my spine. Or maybe that was the tone of his voice, halfway between warning and appeal.

"I won't." The last thing I wanted to do, was make him worry about me. I'd spent so much time worrying about him that I knew the feeling only too well, and I wouldn't wish it on my own worst enemy, let alone the man I loved.

Although there was no denying that tonight's events had put him in an especially amorous mood. Most of the time we made it to the bedroom, at least. This time he didn't seem to care. He simply worked my skirt up, lifted one of my legs to his hip, and stepped in, pushing me up on my toes.

"Here?" I squeaked, my cheeks hot.

"You owe me."

"Yes, but... I thought maybe you'd want me to... you know..." Get down on my knees or something?

"No," Rafe said. "Not tonight. I want us to be together."

We were together. We'd be together even if I were on my knees in front of him.

But he shook his head. "Later. Right now I just wanna..."

Right. I wanted that too. So I held on to his shoulders and gave him what he wanted, and got what I wanted in the process, as well.

It wasn't until an hour later, when we'd finally made it to the bed and were basking in what the romance novels call 'the afterglow,' that he continued the conversation. "It ain't that I don't enjoy having you on your knees, darlin'."

"I know."

"It's just... not tonight. Not after that place."

"Chaps?"

He nodded.

"What about it?"

"I don't like the lifestyle."

I blinked. Of all people, Rafe knows that prejudice is wrong. He's lived with enough of it. And if he has an intolerant bone in his body, I had yet to notice.

I scrambled for something to say. Something that might make sense of what he'd just told me. "You mean... gay?"

He shook his head. "Course not. The leather thing."

"You wear a leather jacket," I pointed out.

He shook his head. "Darlin'..."

"What?"

"It's a lifestyle. The leather crowd. BDSM. Sadism and masochism. Whips and chains and handcuffs and humiliation."

Oh.

He glanced over at me, and shook his head again, unwilling amusement in his eyes. "And you wonder why I worry about you."

"I'm sorry," I said. "It's just... how do you know that all gay clubs aren't like that?"

"Not cause I spend a lot of time in'em. But I've been in enough to know the difference. That wasn't your ordinary pick-up joint. It was a leather club. They probably had a dungeon in the back."

"Surely not?"

He turned on his side to run the tip of a finger down my arm. "Yes, darlin'. And some of those guys mighta swung your way."

"They were gay."

"Sure," Rafe said, "but there are always some outliers. And the ones who get off on making someone else bleed ain't always that particular about whose blood it is. Most play by the rules, and they only hurt the people who like to be hurt—"

"There are people who like to be hurt?"

He nodded. "—but some take it where they can get it, too. And not always willingly."

A shadow crossed his face. His grandfather had rather enjoyed making him bleed, although of course there hadn't been any sexual component to it. Old Jim had just been a mean old bastard who hated his daughter's 'colored' offspring. But as a result, Rafe knew a little bit about people who hurt other people for pleasure.

I thought for a moment. "Is that why you didn't like it when I called you sir?"

He nodded.

"I was joking. I just did it because you were ordering me around."

"I was ordering you around for your own good," Rafe said. "To get you outta there before something happened."

"Sure."

But maybe I didn't sound convincing enough, because he rolled over on top of me, pushing me into the mattress, and framed my face with his hands. "I love you, Savannah."

"I love you too," I said, just a little bit overcome, both by the nearness and the words. He often said them back to me, but usually I had to say them first. Not that it mattered—I'm sure he meant what he said, either way—but it was especially nice to hear him tell me first.

"I'm just trying to protect you." His thumbs stroked my cheeks.

"I know." I ran my hands over his back under the blankets and felt him stir against my thigh.

"I'll never hurt you."

"I know you won't."

"I was only—"

"I know, Rafe." I reached up and put my hands on his cheeks, too. There's something quite intimate and possessive about it, and at the moment I wanted to make sure he knew that not only did I belong to him, but he belonged to me too. "I know you were worried for me. I know you'll never hurt me. I trust you."

He kissed me. And that, as the saying goes, was all she wrote.

HE WAS GONE WHEN I WOKE up in the morning.

I hadn't expected that. Don't ask me why, because I probably should have.

But there I was, alone in the bed when the alarm rang. There was no sign of him. His toothbrush was wet, and so was the towel on the shower rod, so he'd both showered and brushed, and I hadn't heard him do either.

Yesterday's clothes were still strewn where we'd dropped them—his and mine both—and I contemplated leaving his where they were, to register my displeasure with the way he'd snuck out on me. But by the time he came back I'd probably be so happy to see him that I'd feel guilty about not picking them up in the first place, so I just went ahead and did it. And then I showered and brushed my own teeth, and by then my phone signaled a text message.

Sorry, it said. *Had to go.*

I resisted the urge to make a snide comment. *Everything OK?*

Fine. Tell you later. Love U.

I melted a little, and texted back, *Love U 2*, instead of what I wanted to type.

And then, since the conversation seemed to be over, I got dressed and headed out. To the office, where everything was exactly as it had been when I left yesterday afternoon. No Heidi Hoppenfeldt, no Brittany at the front desk. No Tim.

I sat at Brittany's desk for a while again, but there was no email from Tim today. No messages from anyone else, either. Not even an excuse from Brittany as for why she wasn't at her post. I didn't bother to call; I just assumed the cold she'd told me she had yesterday would serve as her excuse today too.

At the rate we were going, LB&A would soon fizzle into obscurity.

I thought about calling Tamara Grimaldi, but then I'd have to tell her about last night and listen to her yell at me for trying to do her job, and I was annoyed enough. It'd be different if I had something to tell her, but I didn't. Only that Tim had—supposedly—had an appointment at Chaps the night before he showed up here with blood on his hands; the same night Brian Armstrong ended up dead. I had no real proof that he'd even been there—Tim, or for that matter Brian. Just because Sally said she'd seen a blond in a green shirt sitting at the bar, didn't mean she'd seen Tim.

If nothing else, I should make sure of that bit of info before I called Grimaldi. And luckily, there was an easy way to do it.

I wandered down the hall to Tim's office and snagged his headshot in the frame on his desk. It was a good likeness, if half a dozen years out of date. But Sally ought to be able to recognize him from that, if I showed it to her.

Then I went back to the reception and logged onto Brittany's computer to look for images of Beau Riggins.

He wasn't difficult to find. He had a Facebook page. There was even a picture of him in the Wonderjocks™ prominently featured on the main page. I imagined he got quite a lot of business from that.

I copied it and printed it out, as big as I could make it. However, the focus of the picture was the Wonderjocks™ and not Beau's face, so I thought there was a chance that people might not recognize him. So I found a picture of him with a friend, an angelic looking blond, uploaded just a few days ago—Friday night, as a matter of fact; they were both bare-chested and grinning into the camera—and printed that too. And then I went back to Google and typed in Brian Armstrong's name in the search bar.

I had expected the late Mr. Armstrong to be harder to find, being older and less of an exhibitionist, but I underestimated the power of the internet. He had a website, with what looked like a professional headshot on it.

I hadn't seen a picture of him before. Erin hadn't had any at her house, or not that I'd noticed.

He looked like he might be in his early-to-mid forties, with lots of straight, blindingly white teeth in a tanned face with bright blue eyes, surrounded by slightly too-long dirty blond hair.

He looked like an aging surfer dude, or maybe that was just because Tamara Grimaldi had told me he'd moved to Nashville from

California. But he had that look: tan and healthy, like he was used to spending a lot of time outdoors.

And now he was dead.

I printed that photo too, and put it with the others. And since I couldn't think of anyone else whose photo might come in handy, I gathered what I had and headed out.

SALLY'S PLACE IS DOWN ON Franklin Road, on the south side of downtown, in the antique store district. It's a cute little yellow bungalow set back from the street, with Sally's name in curly script above the door. The place looks as if Sally ought to sell seashells by the seashore, or at least something more girly than pepper spray and Chinese stars.

The bright red Harley Davidson parked beside the house ruined the effect a little bit, and once I got inside the yellow bungalow, there wasn't anything girly about the interior, either.

I wended my way between racks of body armor and shelves full of hand- and ankle-cuffs over to the display case in the back where Sally was waiting. "Good morning, princess," she boomed. "You all right?"

I nodded. "Fine."

"Your boyfriend take good care of you?" She winked.

I blushed, of course. "Yes, thank you."

"Whatcha got there?" She nodded to the picture frame under my arm.

"I just wanted to ask you whether this was the man you saw at Chaps on Friday." I held Tim's picture up in front of her.

She contemplated him for a moment. "Looks like. Him or his elder brother."

"This is a few years old." I put it down on the counter, face up. Tim continued to grin at us from out of the silver frame. "Are you sure you don't know who you saw him with?"

She shrugged. She's as muscular as any man, and her biceps bulged beneath the sleeves of the T-shirt. "Can't rightly say I do, princess. He was just a guy sitting at the bar, you know? Not my type, so I stayed away. A lot of the guys didn't, but I don't know that he settled on anyone in particular. Looked more like he gave'em all the brush-off."

"Like he was waiting for someone?"

She nodded, and the red cock's comb bobbed.

"But you don't know who?"

"It's like I told you, princess. Lots of people come to Chaps on a Friday night. Leather's gotten popular lately."

As far as I was concerned, leather was a classic, but I figured she was talking about the lifestyle and not the material.

"Used to be, only the insiders would show up. These days, we get tourists."

"No kidding."

She shook her head. "Friday and Saturday nights, half the people in the place are looky-loos. I blame that damn book."

I had a feeling I knew which book she was talking about. I hadn't read it—a nice steamy romance novel is good enough for me—but I had heard talk.

"Damn thing got it all wrong," Sally said with disgust, "and suddenly we're overrun with people wanting to experiment. Stupid idiots."

I couldn't have agreed more. "So there were people wanting to experiment there on Friday night?"

"There were strangers there," Sally said. "Your friend. Other men. A couple girls hoping for God knows what. They didn't get it."

Obviously not, if said girls were straight and hoping for a tall, dark, heterosexual dominant male to discover them.

"Can I ask you to look at a few more pictures?"

"Sure," Sally said. So I brought out the picture of Brian Armstrong and put it in front of her.

She nodded.

"He was at Chaps Friday night?" The well-to-do married—presumably heterosexual—orthodontist?

"Dunno about Friday," Sally said, "but he's been coming around for a few months. Not every night, but enough."

"Doing... what?"

The look she sent me was jaundiced. "Whatcha think, Miss Priss?"

"Um..." I cast about for a euphemism, "looking for company?"

"Yeah," Sally said, with a snort that sounded suspiciously like a laugh.

"So he was... gay?"

"I've no idea what he was," Sally said. "All I know is, I've seen him around."

She glanced at the other piece of paper in my hand, and I put it on the counter. Her lips curved. "Twinkies."

"Excuse me?"

"Didn't you ever hear of Hostess Twinkies, princess?"

Of course I had. Golden snack cakes filled with cream. Great taste but no nutritional value.

And then I realized... "Oh."

"Yep," Sally said. "That's a twinkie."

"Do you know them?"

"I've seen 'em around lately. This one more than the other." She put the tip of a beefy index finger on Beau's companion.

"Did you see either of them on Friday? Talking to my friend?"

But she hadn't, or said she hadn't. "That don't mean they weren't there, princess. Like I said, the place gets busy. *You* coulda been there, and I might not have noticed."

"But you're sure you saw Tim?"

She was.

And since that was the best I figured I'd get out of her, I thanked her and took my leave.

Fifteen

I called Grimaldi from the car and told her everything. About Tim's calendar page, about Chaps, and about Sally and her identification of Brian Armstrong as someone who spent time at the leather club. I didn't say anything about Beau and his friend, since I'd already pointed out to her that Beau and Tim knew one another. And I was lucky and got her machine, so I didn't have to tell her any of it in person—or listen to her tell me I should stay out of her business. I just rattled it all off before the time could run out, and hung up.

And then I drove to the house on Potsdam Street so I could tell Rafe everything... and so he could tell me what had been so important that he had to leave our bed so early this morning.

I was half a block away when the Harley came out of the driveway, spurting gravel. And lucky for me, I was behind a bus that was idling at the bus stop down the street. I'd been thinking about pulling out and around the bus, which was disgorging and taking on passengers, but now I was glad I hadn't. Because of the bus, I was hidden, and he hadn't seen me. And that gave me the opportunity to figure out where he was going.

Except I was stuck behind the bus. A bus which moved a lot slower than the Harley. Rafe has a lead foot under the best of circumstances, and when he has a reason to, he has no problem pushing the speed limits until they break. We were in a residential neighborhood, so he had to keep himself under control to a certain degree, but as the bus lumbered back into motion, and creaked up the street with me breathing exhaust behind it, Rafe and the Harley pulled further away with every second that passed.

When he disappeared over the knoll at the top of the hill, while the bus slowed down to make another stop, I decided I'd been good for long enough. I made sure there were no cars coming toward me in the other lane, and then I stomped on the gas pedal and squealed out and around the bus. The driver laid on the horn as I flashed by, a deep, angry honk like a mutant goose, and then I was past and on my way up Potsdam, driving hell for leather to try to catch Rafe before he turned onto Trinity Lane and I wouldn't know which way he'd gone.

I crested the hill just in time to see the taillight of the bike disappear down the road to the left. By the time I hit the light on Trinity, it had turned red, and I had to wait for it to turn back to green again before I could cross the intersection and follow. By then, there was no sign of him up ahead. A half dozen cars had driven by while the light was red, and I was at the back of the line where the bike was at the front. And on a busy two-lane street, there was no way to pass anyone, either.

But I got lucky. A few blocks later, as the line of cars crested another hill, I saw the red traffic light at the intersection of Dickerson Road, and the bike waiting there.

He was still a block and a half away, and the light changed to green while I was on my way down the hill. The bike took off like a shot, but at least I had him in my sights again. I kept an eye on him while I did my best to keep up.

Not surprisingly, he headed for the interstate. I crossed the Dickerson Road intersection, just a few blocks north of where we'd broken into Brenda Puckett's storage locker back in August, as he zoomed past the entrance to I-65 north. He was either going straight, or taking the entrance for I-65 south on the other side of the underpass.

I made my foot a little heavier on the gas and gained a few yards.

He took the entrance for I-65 south. By the time he hit the top of the ramp and started merging with traffic, I zipped through the underpass and started climbing. Then it was my turn to merge, and once that was done and I was integrated into the traffic flowing south toward downtown, I started looking around for him again. And spied him two lanes over, in the exit-lane for the I-24 east bypass.

I followed suit, and made sure to keep a few cars behind us so he wouldn't notice me there.

I did realize that my chances of going undetected were slim, just to make that clear. After all those years undercover he was adept at picking up a tail. I'd seen him do it before. I'd also seen him outrun one. I was fairly certain he could outrun me. The bike was much smaller and easier to navigate than the Volvo, and it had more pick-up-and-go. It also had—might as well admit it—a better, less cautious driver.

Although maybe he wouldn't bother. If he saw me back here, maybe he'd just let me tag along until he could stop me to find out what I thought I was doing.

Nonetheless, I did my best to stay back as far as possible on the off-chance that I might escape his notice, at least for a while.

We skirted the east side of downtown and he merged into one of the two lanes for I-40 west. I followed suit. Not immediately, because if I did, he might notice that I was mimicking his moves. That was something he'd told me once, about tailing someone. Make it as unobtrusive as possible. Change lanes before them, if you know where they're going, or wait as long as possible after they do, so they may not notice. The worst thing you can do, is do it right away.

So I waited. And as he zoomed into the underpass, I squeezed between two SUVs in the exit lane. The one behind me honked angrily.

I just hoped Rafe was far enough away by then that he wouldn't bother to check his mirrors for the reason why.

He got off at the exit immediately after merging onto I-40, and took a left at the light at the bottom of the ramp. I got caught at that same light, and had to wait a minute or two before I could turn. As I headed down Fourth Avenue South, I peered out the windshield for a glimpse of the motorcycle.

Like most modern cities, Nashville is set up in a grid pattern, with streets running east to west and avenues running north to south. Fourth Avenue is a straight shot out of downtown in both directions for a couple of miles, at least. I could see ten or twelve blocks in front of me, until the road crested the hill by the fairgrounds and turned into Nolensville Pike just beyond. But there was no sign of Rafe or the Harley.

My heart dropped like a rock. After all that effort, how could I have lost him now?

Had he seen me after all, and ducked out of sight? If I kept traveling south, would he pop up on my tail in a block or two? Or had he simply vanished, ditching me and going on to wherever he was headed?

And then I saw, out of the corner of my eye, movement in a parking lot on my left.

And there he was, behind a building, in the process of getting off the bike.

I couldn't stop, of course. I was in the middle of moving traffic, with cars in front of and behind me. And I couldn't turn around, because Fourth Avenue is a one-way street, running south. The only thing I could do was take a left at the next cross-street, another left on the next northbound street, which happened to be Second Avenue—Third dead-ended at the interstate—and then I had to go back under the interstate, take another left, and yet another left, to end up where I'd started.

It took a couple of minutes, but the bike was still there when I came back around the block. I found an empty spot in a parking lot across the street, as far away from the bike as I could get while still keeping it in sight, and settled in to wait.

It didn't take long. He came back out just a minute or two later. And he wasn't alone. But before that happened, I'd had time to examine the building he'd gone into, and I'd realized something.

The building across from it, where I was parked, was a commercial print shop. The area on the south side of downtown has a lot of businesses like that. Print, merchandizing, that sort of thing.

However, the building Rafe had gone into was what is euphemistically known as a gentlemen's club. The kind of place that features—from what little I know about it—naked women swinging around poles.

It was called Benny's Booby Bungalow, which killed the whole 'gentleman' concept right there, if you ask me. No real gentleman would be caught dead in a booby bungalow. No real gentleman would visit a gentlemen's club at all, but certainly not one with a name like that.

I was floored at the realization that my boyfriend had just done so.

Part of me wanted to leave. Just drive away and find something else to do, something to take my mind off what I'd just discovered. He could be in there for hours. I'd heard stories about men who blew all their money in places like this, while their wives and children starved. I should leave.

But the other part couldn't tear myself away. My boyfriend was inside that building, with a bunch of naked women and—judging from the number of cars in the parking lot—a few dozen sweaty, horny men. How could I leave?

And then I was glad I didn't because it was just a couple minutes after I parked, that he came back out, followed by a woman.

Considering the location, I assumed she was one of the strippers. She looked like a stripper. Long legs in tight jeans, lots of long, blonde hair. I didn't get a good look at her, though. Rafe handed her his helmet and got on the bike without it himself. While she stuffed her hair up under it, he glanced around. I ducked down below the dashboard so he wouldn't see me, and then I lay there, curled up with my heart beating hard in my throat, until I heard the bike start up. He must not have noticed me, and I wouldn't have to explain—in front of her—what I was doing there.

They roared out of the parking lot and down the street.

I followed, of course. I knew I was acting stupidly, pathetically, like the worst kind of stalkery girlfriend, but I couldn't help it. I wanted to know where they were going. I wanted to know who she was, and what he was doing with her, and why he kept telling me he loved me, while he kept seeing a girl in a strip club.

As we traveled down Fourth Avenue at a pretty good clip, I reflected that this must be where he had spent so much of his time recently. Hanging out with a stripper. It was too much of a coincidence otherwise. He'd spent most of the weekend with her—while he'd told me he'd been helping Wendell move a witness; hah!—and for the past three days, he'd left the house on Potsdam Street in the afternoon, presumably to go pick her up. And go God knew where with her.

The where was answered just a few minutes later, when the bike rolled up in front of a small brick building in the Wedgewood/ Houston neighborhood. Technically it was a house, a smallish early mid-century ranch with a gambrel roof, but someone had turned it into a daycare facility at some point. It had a fenced backyard full of big wheel tricycles and a jungle gym, and a sign in front that said *Tot Spot* in big, brightly colored letters on a white background.

I parked half a block away, in a church parking lot down on the corner. My chances of going unnoticed in this neighborhood, with no other traffic, were slim to none, so I didn't dare venture any closer. I could see well enough from where I was, anyway. Better than I wanted to, to be honest.

The bike pulled into the small lot in front of the daycare and parked beside a white Toyota that looked like it had seen better days. The girl got off the bike and shook out her hair. She handed the helmet to Rafe and said something. I have no idea what, but he nodded. When she walked into the building, I thought he might drive away—maybe he'd simply given her a ride—but he didn't. Instead he got off the bike and hung the helmet on the handlebar, just like last night. I watched as he circled the white car, peered inside, got down on his hands and knees to look underneath the chassis before opening the door.

He waited a moment before getting behind the wheel and shutting the door behind him. After a second, I heard the engine catch. Nothing happened, and I let out a breath I hadn't been aware I was holding.

Maybe it was watching too many action movies lately, but from where I was sitting, it looked like he'd been checking the car for bombs.

That was ridiculous, though. He'd probably been looking for rust spots or something.

I was so intent on peering out the window that I jumped when my phone started up with the Hallelujah chorus. And although I was too far away, with the car windows closed against the February chill, so there was no way he could hear it, I still scrambled to fish it out of my purse as quickly as possible. Damn Grimaldi; what a terribly inconvenient time to return my call!

Only it wasn't Tamara Grimaldi's number on my screen.

"Damn." I bit my lip. "I mean... darn." And yes, I was fully aware of the idiocy of changing my swear word to a less objectionable one when I was the only one listening to myself.

I thought about not answering, but if I didn't, he'd guess why. He was probably sitting in the white car watching me. I'd only be postponing the inevitable by letting voicemail pick up. And embarrassing though it was to be caught stalking my boyfriend—by my boyfriend—I had less reason to be embarrassed than he did. At least I hadn't been picking up anybody from a strip club.

Or maybe I'd get lucky and he was just returning my call from earlier. Maybe he didn't realize I was here. Maybe it was just a coincidence that he happened to call just now.

Nonetheless, my heart was beating uncomfortably fast when I put the phone to my ear.

"What are you doing?" Rafe's voice inquired in my ear. While he didn't sound excessively angry, or at least not as angry as I've sometimes heard him, he didn't sound pleased, either. It wasn't an inquiry, as if he truly didn't know where I was or what I was doing there. His voice was sort of tight, promising a hint of trouble if he didn't like my answer, although it lacked that icy edge of fury I'd come to recognize.

I didn't answer. Why compound my offense by spelling anything out, after all?

After a moment's silence, one that echoed loudly down the line between us, he added, "Go home, Savannah."

"Don't tell me what to do!"

There was another pause. Maybe I'd surprised him. I had surprised myself, frankly. Then again, maybe he was just thinking about what to say next.

If he was, he couldn't have made a better, or more cutting, choice.

"I can't deal with you right now. I have more important things to worry about."

Well, that was telling me, wasn't it? And for a second the pain took my breath away and made it impossible to answer.

Into the silence came movement, as the door to the daycare opened. Miss Knockers came back out on the stoop, and she wasn't alone. Next to her was a little person, a child a couple of years old, maybe. I couldn't tell whether it was a boy or a girl. The bright blue jacket, little boots and jeans could have belonged to either gender, and the hair was covered by a red hat. I could see the face, though: tiny and sweet, with caramel colored skin and big, brown eyes.

I didn't make a sound. I believed the worst, of course—Rafe's girlfriend and Rafe's child—but I didn't say anything. Instead I just disconnected the call with a finger that felt numb. And when he tried to call back, I ignored him. It was all I could do to put the Volvo in gear and pull out of the parking lot and down the street.

I DIDN'T GET FAR. TWO BLOCKS in the direction of the interstate, and my eyes were so full of tears I couldn't see where I was going. I was a danger to myself and others, so I pulled off the road into an antique mall parking lot, cut the engine, and closed my eyes.

I was still sitting there when I heard the sound of the bike approaching, and part of me wished he'd see me and pull off the road so we could talk. The other part didn't want him to see me with bloodshot eyes and tears running down my face. As if there was any doubt at all that he already knew just how much I cared about him.

But he didn't pull off and in. He probably didn't even notice me sitting there. He just zoomed past, trailing the small, white Toyota. I imagined they were headed for the interstate a half block away. This time I didn't bother following them. I didn't want to watch him follow her home and go inside with her. With *them*. I just waited until I'd stopped crying—mostly—and then I hit the road again myself.

I was a mile or two up the interstate when the phone rang again. I would have ignored it, but I hadn't bothered to put it back into my purse after hanging up with—or on—Rafe, so I could see the display. And it wasn't him.

Of course it isn't him, I chastised myself as I reached out to grab it. He had more important things to do than deal with me. He'd said so.

Like last time, I really wanted to ignore the call. I didn't need Tamara Grimaldi yelling at me on top of everything else. But I defy most people to ignore the police when they call. I found I couldn't.

"Hello," I croaked into the phone.

There was a pause. "Are you ill?" Grimaldi asked suspiciously.

I cleared my throat. "No."

I felt sort of ill, admittedly, nauseous and sort of woozy, not to mention that my head was pounding. But it was mental anguish, not physical. And my nose was stuffy from the crying, which was what had led her to ask, I imagine.

Her voice softened. "What happened?"

"He has a girlfriend."

"Who?"

"Rafe." I hiccupped.

"No, he doesn't," Grimaldi said. And added, "Not apart from you."

"A girlfriend *and* a child."

There was another pause. "Have you been drinking?"

I couldn't help it, I laughed. Darkly. Or maybe hysterically. "I wish."

Grimaldi hesitated. "Have you eaten?"

Had I? "No," I said.

"Why don't we grab a late lunch and you can tell me what's going on."

It wasn't a question. "You don't have to be nice to me just because you're dating my brother," I said.

"I'm not dating your brother," Grimaldi informed me. "Your brother lost his wife four months ago. It's too soon for him to date again. And anyway, we're just friends."

Sure. "Where do you want to meet?"

"Where are you?"

I told her I was on my way north on I-65 close to downtown, and we settled on a small hole-in-the-wall not too far from MNPD headquarters. I wended my way through the downtown streets to a public parking lot, paid to leave the car there for an hour, and walked the block and a half to the restaurant. She was there before me, seated at a table in the corner with her back to the wall. It was such a Rafe-like thing to do that I wanted to kick her.

"Why do you do that?" I grumped when I tossed my bag and coat over the chair on the other side of the table and plopped my butt down.

"Do what?"

"Sit with your back to the wall. Rafe does it too. Always."

"Because there's less chance anyone will shoot us in the back," Grimaldi said calmly.

"So you'll let *me* get shot instead?"

"And also so we can keep an eye on the door and see who comes in. So we can shoot first." She looked me up and down, what she could see of me over the table. "You look like hell."

I felt like it, too. "I followed him. To this strip club south of town. It's called the Booby Bungalow."

"I'm familiar with it," Grimaldi nodded.

"It wasn't even like I was trying to spy on him, you know? I was on my way to Mrs. J's house when he came tearing out of the driveway like a bat out of hell. So I followed. Across town and down to the Booby Bungalow."

"What happened?"

I grimaced. "He went inside and came out with a girl. She couldn't have been more than twenty two or twenty three. They drove to a daycare facility near the fairgrounds and picked up a small child. One that looked like Rafe."

Grimaldi arched her brows. "You got close enough to see who it looked like?"

Well, no. Not exactly. "She was a fair-skinned blonde. The baby was light brown."

"Your boyfriend isn't the only person of color in Nashville," Grimaldi told me. "This city is full of black men and Hispanic men and even a few Asian and Arabic and Native American men. A brown baby doesn't mean anything."

"It's not like I suspect him of having fathered every light-skinned brown baby I see. Just the ones he has some sort of connection to." Like David Flannery. And the toddler I'd seen today.

172 | Jenna Bennett

"You're jumping to conclusions," Grimaldi said. "Have you spoken to him?"

I made another face. "He called."

"Let me guess," Grimaldi said. "He saw you."

Of course he did. "I'm not as good at sneaking around as he is."

Grimaldi gave me a look. When I stared back, stonily, she asked, "What did he say?"

"He told me to go home, because he couldn't deal with me just then. He had more important things to do."

Grimaldi's eyes widened. "You're joking."

I shook my head.

"He said that?"

I nodded, as tears flooded my own eyes again.

"Christ," Grimaldi muttered, and pushed a couple of napkins across the table toward me. "Don't cry."

"He doesn't love me."

"Of course he loves you. How old was this baby?"

I buried my nose in the napkins and sniffed. "Two years, maybe."

"Nothing to do with you, then. Two years ago, you didn't know each other."

Not precisely true. We'd met when I was a freshman in high school and Rafe was a senior. But it was certainly true that two years ago we hadn't been involved. Two years ago I was in the middle of divorcée blues six months after my marriage crashed and burned. Rafe Collier was, pretty literally, the furthest thing from my mind.

"I'm not worried about what he did two or three years ago," I said. "I'm not worried about what he did in high school either, that resulted in David. I know he hasn't been celibate his whole life. I *am* worried about the fact that he's lying to me and going to see her every day. He's been MIA during the same time every single day this week."

"Maybe there's something going on you don't know about."

Sure. Like, he was getting some on the side. And I had my mouth open to say so when the waitress materialized next to our table. I ordered a Diet Coke. They didn't have one, so the waitress offered Diet Pepsi instead. Grimaldi told her I'd have sweet tea.

"I don't need the sugar," I objected.

"For the shock." She nodded to the waitress, who arched her brows but withdrew.

No arguing with that, I guess, although I was angry more than I was in shock. It wasn't worth making a fuss over, however. "Decide what you want to eat," Grimaldi told me, "then we can talk more when we've ordered. She'll be back in a minute."

Sure. I opened the menu and perused the various salad options. I had to make up for the sweet tea somehow.

The tea was good, though. And it actually did make me feel a little better. Once the waitress had taken the salad-order—and Grimaldi's order of a roast beef sandwich with melted cheddar cheese—we got back to talking again.

Apparently the subject of Rafe and his extracurricular activities was closed. "I got your message," Grimaldi said.

Uh-oh. I'd almost forgotten about that, with everything else that had happened.

I must have paled, because she added, "Don't worry, I'm not going to yell at you."

"You're not?"

She shook her head. "I have bad news."

My heart started thumping, a dull, heavy feeling against my ribs. "What?"

"We finally tracked down your buddy Riggins."

Beau wasn't exactly my buddy, but OK. "Yes?"

"He's dead."

Sixteen

I don't think I fainted, but things went a bit dark for a few seconds, and when I came back to myself, Tamara Grimaldi was staring at me with a whole lot of worry on her face. "Miss Martin? Savannah?"

"Sorry," I managed. My lips felt stiff, like I couldn't quite form the words. But I was still upright on the chair, which was something.

"Have some tea." She pushed the glass closer to me, close enough that I didn't have to pick it up, I could just lean down and suck through the straw.

The sugar must have had some kind of restorative quality, I guess—and now I knew why she'd insisted on ordering it. Not because of Rafe, but because of this news.

"Beau…" I swallowed; my voice sounded very far away, "is dead?"

"I'm afraid so." Grimaldi's voice came from farther away than the other side of the table, too.

I had more tea. And while I did, images flashed through my mind.

Standing on the steps outside the house where I'd first met him, and watching him get out of his little Mini, in faded jeans and a leather jacket with no shirt underneath. All smoothly tanned skin and white teeth and glossy brown hair. Young. Beautiful. And alive.

"I'm sorry," Grimaldi said, watching me. "I didn't know you knew him well."

I blinked away the tears. "I don't. I didn't. I just met him a few times. But I liked him." Sort of. With reservations about his choice of career and his choice to sleep with Mrs. Fortunato. He'd been charming. Sort of impossible not to like, in spite of his morals, or lack thereof. "What happened?"

"It looks like suicide," Grimaldi said.

I bit back the instinctive rejection. I hadn't really known Beau well enough to say whether he might have been suicidal or not. He hadn't struck me as the type, like he enjoyed life too much, but what did I know?

"I find that hard to believe," I said instead, neutrally.

Grimaldi's gaze was steady. "If he had killed Brian Armstrong and knew I was looking for him?"

"Do you have any reason to think he killed Armstrong?"

"They frequented the same club," Grimaldi said, "and according to Sally, they were both there Friday night. So, of course, was your friend Briggs."

My friend Briggs. Right. "I thought the assumption was that Tim had killed Armstrong and asked Beau to clean up after him."

"That's another possibility. Or maybe they were together in it. They could have hooked up at the club and gone back to Briggs's place for a threesome. And then something happened, and Armstrong ended up dead. Briggs dumped the body while Riggins cleaned up."

It made a certain sort of sense, even as my mind balked at the idea of a threesome. "Why?"

She just stared at me, and I clarified, "Why would Armstrong end up dead? What could have happened to make either of them stab him multiple times? I don't... I didn't know Beau well, but he didn't strike me as the violent type. And I've known Tim for a while. He doesn't seem like someone who'd stab someone to death, either." Too squeamish by far, I would have thought.

Then again, our one-time boss and broker, Walker Lamont, had been as gay, well-dressed, and elegant as Tim, and it hadn't prevented him from dispatching several people with the help of a straight razor. He would have dispatched me too and not batted an eye had it not been for Mrs. Jenkins.

"Word at Chaps," Grimaldi said, "is that Armstrong was a dominant, and not shy about it. His wife claims to know nothing about any homosexual or sadistic tendencies. The picture I'm putting together is of a man who had spent a lot of years suppressing his natural inclinations."

"He was a dentist. I'm not surprised he was a sadist too."

Grimaldi's lips twitched, but she didn't comment. "There were no marks on him, other than the stab wounds."

Someone who liked to dish it out but didn't like to take it.

"I can't imagine Tim allowing anyone to hurt him. Not like that." Rafe had mentioned that some people like to be hurt, but Tim hadn't struck me as that type. He might not be what Grimaldi called a dominant, but he wasn't a masochist either.

"No," Grimaldi agreed, and waited until the waitress had deposited her sandwich and my salad in front of us before she continued, "that isn't my impression of him. Sally said he wasn't a regular at Chaps. She'd never seen him before."

"She had seen Beau. Did she tell you?" I lifted my fork and picked at the salad.

Grimaldi nodded, reaching for the ketchup to squirt her fries. "Good thinking on your part, showing her the pictures."

"Thank you." The salad looked great, but I found I had no appetite. I forked up a slice of strawberry anyway, and put it in my mouth. It tasted like cardboard, and was hard to swallow. I don't think the fault was in the berry, however. "I can't imagine Beau letting anyone hurt him, either."

"There were no marks on him either," Grimaldi confirmed, attacking her sandwich. "My impression is that he liked to be seen, but he wasn't into anything kinky."

I hadn't thought he was. He made his living by being beautiful, and he was too proud of that admittedly gorgeous body to want to risk bruises or any other kinds of marks.

"So maybe the two of them—Tim and Beau—hooked up for some fun." I could see that happening. They were both young, healthy, beautiful. They'd probably get along swimmingly, assuming Beau swung both ways. "And Brian Armstrong invited himself along. To Tim's place. Or maybe Beau's place. Have you checked it for blood?"

"The CSI team is going over it as we speak," Grimaldi said, around a bite of sandwich. "I didn't notice anything, though."

I poked at my salad some more. Moved some shreds of lettuce around and balanced a candied almond on my fork for conveyance to my mouth. It rattled, so I imagine my hand wasn't too steady. "Maybe things got out of hand once they got there. Maybe Brian got rough."

"Maybe one of them had had a fling with Armstrong at some point," Grimaldi said, swallowing, "and he didn't like that they were together. Possessive."

Maybe so. "One of them stabbed Brian, maybe in self-defense, and they helped each other cover it up."

Grimaldi nodded. "That's as good a hypothesis as any other, and one I'm going forward with."

"So you're thinking that Beau couldn't handle the guilt and ended it all?"

"It could happen."

It could. I couldn't quite consolidate it with the Beau I had known—been acquainted with—but it did make sense, at least in theory. "How did he die?"

"Poison gas," Grimaldi said.

Excuse me? "Where did he get his hands on poison gas?" That isn't something someone can go to the store and buy, is it?

"You'd be surprised how many dangerous substances most homes boast," Grimaldi said.

I thought for a moment. "Did he close himself in the garage and let the Mini run?"

Grimaldi shook her head. "He closed himself in the bathroom with ammonia and bleach and a bottle of drain cleaner."

"That's enough to kill you?"

"Not under most circumstances. Most people have the sense, when the chlorine gas and hydrochloric acid and chloramine starts wafting, to get the hell outta there. It stings and burns and makes it hard to breathe. But he didn't leave. He stayed in the bathroom until he passed out. There were some sleeping pills involved too, we think. Not enough to kill him, but in combination."

"So... maybe he didn't suffer, at least?"

"Perhaps not," Grimaldi conceded. "There was an empty container of sleeping pills in the trash can, along with the empty bottles of household cleaners. We think he took the sleeping pills so he wouldn't be tempted to change his mind, and then he mixed up the chemicals and went to sleep. Hopefully he didn't feel much pain."

God. I put down my fork. I'd only managed a few bites of food, and they were threatening to come back up. "Did he live alone?"

Grimaldi nodded. "Parents in Michigan. One sister. Calling them with the news that he was dead put the cherry on my morning."

"I'm sorry." My own discovery had been traumatic, certainly, but nothing compared to having to tell a family that their son and brother was dead.

"I hate that part of the job." She didn't meet my eyes, but kept her own on the fry she was dragging through the ketchup. It was perhaps the very first time she'd opened up about anything even halfway emotional or private, and I held my breath so I wouldn't jinx it. I'd been crying on her shoulder about Rafe for months, but she'd never returned the favor.

There wasn't anything more to come, though. She popped the fry in her mouth and chewed.

"Any sign of Tim?" I asked.

She shook her head. "There's some evidence that Riggins had company in the past few days, though. We'll be testing hair samples and taking prints."

"Yesterday morning, Tim told me he was staying with a friend."

"Yesterday morning, Riggins was still alive," Grimaldi said. "He died sometime later in the day."

So before I'd gone to Chaps. Not that me going to Chaps had anything to do with anything.

"Are you sure he did it to himself?"

"At this point," Grimaldi said, "I'm not sure of anything. The investigation is ongoing."

For a second neither of us spoke, and then she added, "You do realize that if he didn't do it to himself, your buddy Briggs is a prime suspect?"

I hadn't thought about it. I daresay I should have. But now that I did, yes, I could see why my buddy Briggs would be a prime suspect. If the friend he'd been staying with was Beau, and if he and Beau had killed Brian Armstrong and tried to cover up the murder, then eliminating the only other person who knew what he'd done, would seem like a good move on Tim's part.

"Are you any closer to figuring out where he is?"

Grimaldi shook her head. "There's an APB out on the car. And the uniforms drive by his house once an hour or so just in case he decides to show up at home. But I don't have the manpower to put someone there fulltime."

"Family?"

"Estranged. Parents are religious and seem to think this is the just reward for sin. They wouldn't take him in."

Sheesh. People are entitled to their religious beliefs, but it was hard to sympathize with parents so hardnosed that they'd cut off their own son for the crime of being gay.

Not that I had much room to talk. I was cutting my own family off because my mother was bigoted and unaccepting of my boyfriend. And at the same time, I was depriving her of the chance to get to know him, and to change. Was that any better, really?

I made the decision that I was definitely going to Abigail's birthday party on Friday, with or without Rafe. And then I turned my attention back to the conversation again. "Friends?"

"None we've been able to find," Grimaldi said. "I've gone through his Rolodex and little black book, and I didn't get a buzz from anybody. I have someone calling motels and hotels."

I pushed the salad bowl away. It had barely been touched, but I couldn't force any more of it down. Grimaldi eyed it, but didn't comment. "You want a box to take that home?"

"It'll be soggy by tonight. I should have ordered the dressing on the side."

"You didn't know you wouldn't be able to eat it," Grimaldi said and signaled for the check. While we were waiting for the waitress to bring it, she added, "What will you be doing for the rest of the day?"

I honestly didn't know. Going home had zero appeal, just in case Rafe showed up there. Sitting there waiting and have him not show up... I wasn't sure whether that would be worse or better.

"I'll probably just go back to the office," I said. "Nobody else is there, and someone ought to be. And I can sit there and do nothing as easily as I can do nothing at home."

Grimaldi nodded.

"I'll let you know if I hear anything from Tim. Or about him. As of this morning, he hadn't contacted the office again."

"I don't imagine he will," Grimaldi answered, "now that he knows you're looking for him."

We parted ways outside the restaurant. Grimaldi headed back toward MNPD headquarters on James Robertson Parkway—she'd walked the four blocks to the restaurant—while I made my own way back to the parking lot and the Volvo.

I passed her on the corner of Third and James Robertson, where she stood waiting for the light to change, and tooted my horn at her. She lifted a hand in greeting and then I zipped past, between the brown brick of the police building and the white marble of the courthouse, and headed across the bridge to East Nashville.

I passed the corner of Fifth and East Main on the way, and glanced up at the double balcony doors of my apartment on the way past. There was nothing to see, and also no sign of Rafe's Harley parked at the curb. Not that that meant anything: he could equally well have pulled it into the parking garage under the building and left it there. I doubted he was home, though. He had more important things to do. He was probably holed up somewhere with the busty blonde and the toddler.

The thought hurt, so I squashed it down and focused on something else instead. And because thinking of Beau Riggins hurt too, I concentrated on something I could actually do something about. Maybe.

Brian Armstrong had died Friday night or early Saturday morning.

If Grimaldi was right, and Tim and Beau had been to blame for Brian's death, then Tim had ditched the body in Shelby Park Saturday morning, while Beau had spent the time scrubbing Tim's guest room to within an inch of its life. But Tim's house was a crime scene, so Tim wouldn't have wanted to stay there. He might have gone home with Beau, and the two of them had spent the past three or four days together at Beau's place. I could see that making sense. Until yesterday afternoon, anyway, when Beau died.

Whether Tim had had something to do with that or not, he would have had to move on at that point. He couldn't go home, since I'd told him the police had been at his place and he had to expect they were looking for him. He couldn't bunk at the office, for the same reason. Per Grimaldi, he couldn't appeal to his family. She'd talked to his friends and hadn't gotten a "buzz" from them, whatever that meant. And she was currently in the process of calling hotels.

What was left?

I pulled the car into the parking lot behind the office and let myself in the back door. It was quiet as the grave, with only the low buzzing of office equipment and florescent lights to be heard, and I felt a frisson run down my back as I walked down the hallway to Brittany's desk in the reception area and dumped my stuff.

There was no new message from Tim in email, and no voicemail from anyone of any consequence. I leaned back in Brittany's office chair and chewed the newly applied lipstick off my bottom lip.

If Tim couldn't go home, and he couldn't go to his parents' house, and he couldn't stay at the office, and if he'd been staying with Beau but now Beau was dead... where would he go?

He was running out of options, and that meant Heidi Hoppenfeldt was a possibility. I had no idea where to find any of Tim's friends, so there was nothing I could do to track him down there, but I had Heidi's address. Or I'd have it, once I checked the employee roster.

Brittany kept it in her desk drawer, so it wasn't hard to find. I made a note of Heidi's telephone number, but I figured I'd accomplish more by actually driving out to where she lived to knock on the door. If Tim was there, at least I wouldn't warn him of my approach.

Unfortunately, the list was months out of date. It had Brenda Puckett's address on Winding Way listed, and she'd been dead for more than six months. Clarice Webb had been too, and her address in Sylvan Park was there as well. Not to mention Walker Lamont's former spread in Oak Hill. I'd been there once, for a company barbeque over the summer, but Walker had been languishing in Riverbend Penitentiary since mid-August. He'd been considered a flight risk, and a danger to himself and others—to me, specifically, since I was the one who had put him there—so the authorities had locked him up and thrown away the key.

Anyway, I hoped the listed information was still accurate for those of us who were among the living and the free, and who were still working for the company. Mine was. It listed my apartment in the complex on Fifth and Main that I still lived in.

Thinking of the complex on Fifth and Main brought to mind Rafe, and since I was sitting in front of someone else's computer, I threw caution to the wind and Googled Benny's Booby Bungalow.

It had a website, of course. Everyone has a website these days. I have one myself. Although mine isn't full of pictures of semi-naked women.

Then again, I run a respectable real estate business, not a nudie show.

The nudity took some getting used to, but after a minute or two I was mostly able to ignore the breasts staring me in the face and focus on the faces instead. And lo and behold, there was Rafe's girlfriend, strutting her stuff.

Lantana DuBois, the caption said, which couldn't possibly be anyone's real name.

Nonetheless, I put it into Google and got a few more hits. Lantana had a Facebook fan page, as it turned out. All her fans were men, naturally, and some of the comments they'd left on her page were quite explicit. One of them was named Desmond Othello, which didn't seem like it could be anyone's real name either, and he listed his employer as the Montgomery County Jail. License plate production, no doubt. The way he went on and on about what he wanted to do to Lantana when he got out of prison was almost enough to make me feel sorry for the girl.

The Nashville real estate database has rental listings, so those of us trying to drum up business can mass market to those people who rent, to try to get them to consider home ownership instead of spending their money to pay someone else's mortgage. I put Lantana's name into the database, but of course I didn't get any hits there. It couldn't be her real name, so why would she rent an apartment in it? Desmond Othello was a guest of the Montgomery County Jail, so there was no sense in looking him up. I did it anyway, and found zilch.

Typing in Rafe's name was an impulse. I certainly didn't expect anything to come up for him. I hadn't put him on my lease, and he shouldn't have had another, since he lived with me.

Imagine my surprise when his name showed up on a rental in Antioch, south of town.

For a few seconds I just sat there, staring at it.

He had an apartment apart from the one he shared with me?

How far did this double life extend?

But maybe it was left over from his previous life. When I first hooked up with him, back in August, he'd told me he was renting a room south of town. Maybe this was an old listing, and it just hadn't been updated after he moved out. Or maybe it was part of his TBI cover, and the TBI just hadn't gotten around to reeling in all the loose ends.

Under other circumstances, I would have called and asked him about it. At the moment, I was damned if I'd call him ever again. If he called me, I might answer—might—but no way was I contacting him.

Instead, I wrote the address on the same piece of paper as Heidi's address, and shut down Brittany's computer. And then I grabbed my coat and my purse and headed out.

Seventeen

I drove by Rafe's apartment first, for several reasons.

First, it was farthest away, so it seemed a good place to start. That way I could work my way back to town.

Second, I didn't think I'd be able to concentrate on anything else until I had.

And third— Well, thirdly, I just wanted to know.

The address turned out to be a brick duplex in a not-so-fantastic neighborhood off Murfreesboro Road, south of the airport. It wasn't anywhere I would have chosen to live, but I could see why it might suit Rafe. It was the kind of neighborhood where nobody owned property and everyone rented. There was probably a fair amount of turnover all the time, and no real sense of community. I imagined nobody cared overmuch what their neighbors were up to. It was perfect for someone who wanted to keep a low profile and go unnoticed.

The house itself looked just like the ones surrounding it. Low-slung brick, with a chain-link fence around the back and a narrow driveway leading up behind the house. The grass was dead and the landscaping gray and spindly instead of green. Not that that was anyone's fault in February, but it added to the general unwelcoming feel of the place.

The Harley was parked in the driveway. That came as a bit of a surprise, I admit. I hadn't expected him to be here.

Once I realized he was, the white Toyota was less of a surprise.

Upsetting, sure, but not surprising.

I drove past, feeling numb. And at the end of the street, I turned around and drove back. The bike was still there, in the driveway. So was the Toyota.

I was half a block farther by the time my phone rang.

I thought about not answering. I really did. But in the end, I couldn't resist. Honestly, I just wanted to hear his voice. And part of me hoped he would apologize. And explain.

I should have known better.

"What are you doing?" he demanded, without any kind of greeting.

"Driving away," I told him, and I'm pleased to say my voice was steady.

"How d'you find us?"

That "us" hurt, I admit.

"Your name is on the lease," I said.

He was silent for a bit. I continued driving. "It isn't what you think," he told me eventually.

"Sure." And my name wasn't Savannah Martin, never to be Collier. "You know, that's exactly what Bradley said, when I asked him about Shelby."

I hung up without waiting for him to answer, and then I turned the phone off and continued to drive away.

I reached Heidi's apartment just under fifteen minutes later. I had resisted the urge to turn the phone back on to see if he'd tried to call back. I didn't want to know, or so I told myself. I almost believed it, too.

Heidi lived in a little complex of townhouses just off I-65 South in the Brentioch area: between Brentwood and Antioch. It was the same area where St. Jerome's Hospital was located, where my late sister-in-law, Sheila, had run into trouble back in November. It was also the area where Aislynn, half of my buyer-couple of Aislynn and Kylie, worked at a small café called Sara Beth's, where Sheila had had lunch before going to St. Jerome's.

Instead of heading straight to Heidi's townhouse, I drove into the parking lot of the strip mall and parked the car. Although the idea of eating still didn't hold much appeal, my stomach was complaining loudly about being empty. It had been a couple hours since lunch with Grimaldi, and I figured I might as well try to force down a few bites of something.

As luck would have it, Aislynn was working, and she set me up with a bowl of soup and a drink. The soup was a bit easier to choke down than the salad had been. It required less effort, for one thing, and for another, the warmth in the pit of my stomach felt good.

It wasn't just the chill in the air outside. The day was gray and gloomy, with a bone-chilling sort of cold that got into my clothes and bones and didn't let go... but I think it was more that I felt cold and numb and alone with the knowledge that Rafe was spending his time with someone else.

It was like Bradley all over again. I hadn't been woman enough for my husband, and now it turned out I wasn't woman enough for my boyfriend, either.

And it hurt worse than anything Bradley had ever done. I loved Rafe in ways I hadn't realized was possible back when I was Bradley Ferguson's wife.

So the soup warmed the physical parts of me, but the emotional parts, those stayed cold and empty. Aislynn must have seen it too, because when she came to take my empty bowl away, she lingered by the side of the table, goth-girl eyes worried. "Everything all right?"

I shook my head. "My boyfriend's with someone else."

"Bastard," Aislynn said. "This is why I'm gay."

"Because my boyfriend's with someone else?"

"Because all men are swine." She took the bowl and stomped off, dreadlocks swinging halfway down her back.

When she came back a minute later, I thought she was bringing me the check. Instead, she made me an offer I couldn't refuse. "Why don't you come over to the house tonight? We're all settled in. You can see what we've done to the place. And Kyle makes killer lasagna."

That sounded too wonderful for words, actually. Not the lasagna, so much, but the company. The last thing I wanted, was to go home tonight and sit there in my empty apartment, halfway hoping and halfway dreading that Rafe would come home. To talk, or to pack his things and leave once and for all.

"I'd love to," I said.

"Six o'clock," Aislynn answered and walked away.

"Wait a second! Where's my check?"

"It's on the house." She kept walking.

All right, then. I left a five dollar bill on the table and took my leave, feeling marginally better. My stomach was full, I wasn't feeling as nauseous anymore, and I had something to do tonight, something to take my mind off Rafe.

I STOPPED BY THE PANERA BAKERY on my way to the car, and picked up a couple of pastries, just in case I needed a bribe.

Heidi's place was just a few minutes away, in a complex full of two-story townhouses surrounding a pool. The pool was covered now, of course, and the lounge chairs looked cold and a little sad in the chilly air.

I parked the Volvo next to Heidi's Honda and got out. The wind bit my cheeks as I ventured up to the front door and rang the bell.

At first I wasn't sure she was going to answer. She was here, or so it seemed, since the car was parked outside and she isn't the type to walk anywhere. Heidi is voluptuous and then some, if you catch my drift. She likes to eat and she doesn't like to exercise. I had a hard time believing she'd taken to her feet.

I rang again. And I saw the peephole in the door darken, so I knew she was inside. Or that someone was, anyway. I considered making a face, but resisted the temptation. Instead I smiled and lifted the Panera bag invitingly.

The door inched open and I stuck my foot in the opening and leaned in. "Hi." For good measure, I waved the bag back and forth so the smell of the pastries would leak out. "I brought you a cinnamon roll."

That did the trick. The door opened all the way, abruptly enough that I almost fell into the foyer and landed at Heidi's feet.

She's about my age and height, and approximately twice my weight. Her hair is brown and frizzy, and she has a round face and a round body. As is often the case, she had crumbs on her bosom, from the last thing she'd eaten. Judging from the residue, I suspected some sort of corn-based chip. Fritos, maybe.

She reached for the bag, and I handed it over, before closing the door behind me. "How are you?"

"Fine," Heidi said, opening the bag to peer in.

"You haven't been at work for a few days. I was getting worried."

"Oh." She blinked. "With Tim out, I didn't think I needed to be there."

"Did you know that Tim was going to be out?" Because, if memory served, she hadn't been there for the sales meeting on Monday morning herself, either. At that point, I'd still been hopeful that Tim would show up.

"He called me on Sunday," Heidi said, "and told me he wouldn't be in on Monday."

Ah. So instead of taking that as indication she should go to the office and take over Tim's responsibility for the meeting, she'd decided to sleep in instead.

"Have you spoken to him since?"

Her eyes shifted, sideways. That was a sign of someone lying, Rafe had told me once.

I banished the thought of Rafe and focused on Heidi.

"No," she said.

"Are you sure? Because Tim hasn't been in the office the rest of this week, either. Brittany is out as well."

"Brittany is in bed with Devon," Heidi said dismissively.

I had assumed as much. There was no reason why Heidi wouldn't simply have assumed the same thing, of course, but there was something in her tone that caught my attention. Something of the implication that Brittany was shirking her duty while she—Heidi—wasn't.

Between that and the lying, it bore further investigation.

"So Sunday was the last time you spoke to him?"

She nodded, and her eyes slid sideways again.

"Did he say what was wrong?"

"No," Heidi said.

"Because I stopped by his house, and he wasn't there. If he's sick, I'd expect him to be at home in bed."

She didn't answer.

"He isn't in the hospital, is he?"

Heidi shook her head before she made an abrupt turnaround and headed for the kitchen, bakery bag in hand.

I followed, of course, looking right and left as I went.

The place was nicer than I had expected. Nicer than my apartment. Bigger, too. There was a staircase immediately beside the door in the foyer, leading upstairs to what I assumed were a couple of bedrooms and a bath. Beyond the foot of the stairs was what looked like a formal living room with a gas-log fireplace and leather furniture. I don't have a fireplace, and I also don't have hardwood floors. My rental is all carpet, except for the bathrooms and kitchen, which are vinyl, not tile.

Down the hall from the front door was a small half bath tucked under the stairs, then a laundry closet, and a kitchen and dining room combination across the back of the townhouse. A small courtyard waited beyond the double glass doors. It looked dreary and cold now, with only spindly brown sticks in the colorful glazed pots, but I could imagine how nice it might be in the summer, with sunshine and ivy growing up the brick walls. Much nicer than my little balcony overlooking the traffic on Main Street.

"This is great." I looked around at the kitchen. Nice Shaker-style cabinets, stainless steel appliances, and a granite counter. I don't have any of those things, either.

"Thanks." Heidi put the bakery bag down on the island and ripped it open.

I continued my perusal. There was a pot on the stove, bubbling with something that smelled great. A Ziploc travel container sat on the counter, empty and waiting, and beside it sat an aluminum-foil wrapped something. From the shape of it, maybe half a loaf of French bread?

I turned back to Heidi. "Beef stew?"

She hesitated, with a cinnamon bun halfway to her mouth. Maybe she was afraid I'd ask to stay for dinner. "Yes."

She bit into the bun, and flakes of sugar scattered across her chest. "That's a big pot, for just one person. Do you freeze the leftovers?"

"Yes," Heidi said, and her eyes slid sideways.

I was tempted to ask if I could stay, just to see what she'd say, but I refrained. "I should go," I said instead, turning back toward the front of the townhouse. "I have plans for dinner. I'll leave you to get on with it."

Heidi followed me to the front door, practically stepping on my heels. I stopped on the top step and turned back to her. "If you talk to Tim, tell him I need to talk to him about Beau."

"Beau?" Heidi said.

"Beau Riggins. Don't you know him?"

She shook her head.

"He's a friend of Tim's. Or was. He died yesterday."

I waited and watched, for some kind of reaction, but she just kept chewing. So I gave up and headed down the couple of steps to the parking lot. She was still chewing when she closed and locked the door behind me.

I got in the car and cranked over the engine. Then I backed out of the parking space and maneuvered out of the lot. And once I was out on the road and halfway down the hill toward Old Hickory Boulevard, I pulled into the parking lot of a fast food restaurant and stopped again.

If I'd had the necessary equipment, I'd totally be listening in on Heidi's cell phone communications right now, because I would have wagered my left testicle, had I had one of those, that she'd be on the phone with Tim the second the door closed behind me. Or at least the second she was sure I had driven away. She'd been skulking behind the drapes in the living room window when I drove off. They were sheer drapes, and with the lights on inside, she was hard to miss.

By now, she was probably deep in conversation with Tim.

I thought about calling Tamara Grimaldi. But she had her hands full with Beau, and besides, all I knew—or thought I knew—was that Heidi had lied. She'd been in contact with Tim, maybe as recently as today.

Grimaldi might be able to haul her into the Nashville PD for questioning, and that might scare the truth out of her, but I had a better idea. That bubbling pot on the stove, along with the wrapped bread and waiting to-go container, had given me an idea. If I waited a while, what were the chances that Heidi would be coming down the hill, to bring Tim his dinner?

He was holed up somewhere. With the police looking for him, he probably wouldn't risk going outside any more than he had to. Eating in public, in a restaurant, would be dangerous, and even ordering a pizza for delivery might be too big a chance to take. The delivery guy might recognize him. But if he were in contact with Heidi, he could get her to bring him food. She relied on him for her living, so she wouldn't want to refuse.

It was only 3:30. I had two free hours before I had to leave this part of town to get to Kylie and Aislynn's by six. And I certainly didn't want to go home in the interim. I settled in to wait.

With nothing to do but peer out the window for Heidi's Honda, the temptation to turn the phone back on was too much to resist. I pushed the power button with great trepidation, but I pushed it nonetheless. And I wasn't sure whether to be disappointed or relieved when Rafe hadn't called and hadn't texted.

No one else had called or texted either. I dropped the phone back into the car console with a sound somewhere between a sigh and a huff.

Time passed. Cars passed. None of them were Heidi's Honda.

I got tired and sick of waiting. I eyed the phone balefully, thinking critical thoughts about Rafe and Lantana.

Good Lord, didn't he have better taste than that? A stripper, for God's sake?

How could he do this to me? He knew Bradley had cheated. He knew how that fact had messed with my mind and my self-esteem and my confidence in the aftermath of the divorce. He'd spent months telling me what a jackass Bradley was and how there was nothing wrong with me. How could he turn around and do the same thing Bradley did?

And how was I going to explain this to my mother? Dix and Catherine had been supportive of my relationship with Rafe because they loved me. They'd accepted him because I'd made it clear I wanted them to. I knew they'd had reservations, but they hadn't voiced them, out of respect for me and because they acknowledged my right to make my own decisions—or mistakes. But mother had been vocal, and staunchly opposed to my getting involved with Rafe. This development probably wouldn't surprise her at all.

It surprised me. I hadn't thought he'd do this. Not in a naive way, because I'd been pretty sure I wouldn't be able to hold on to him forever. He'd get tired of me eventually, and probably sooner rather than later. I wasn't—couldn't be—as exciting as the other women he'd known. But I hadn't thought he'd cheat. I'd trusted him to tell me if he wanted out, not to continue to live with me while he got some from someone else on the side.

I glared at the silent phone and almost missed the small, blue Honda coming down the hill. By the time the sight registered, Heidi was halfway through the intersection and on her way up Old Hickory Boulevard toward the interstate and Franklin Road.

I breathed a word of the sort that would have caused mother to click her tongue, and cranked the key in the ignition.

I didn't have to be as careful with Heidi as I'd been when following Rafe earlier. She wasn't trained to pick up a tail, and she probably wouldn't even consider the possibility of one. I'd have to be pretty blatant to catch her attention, I figured, and if I'd managed to follow Rafe all the way from Potsdam Street to the Booby Bungalow without him seeing me—and if he had, surely he would have stopped before getting there?—I shouldn't have any problems tailing Heidi to wherever she was going.

She headed straight up Old Hickory Boulevard toward the shops in Brentwood. Past the entrances to Interstate 65 north and south, past Franklin Road, and past the stores and business buildings of Maryland Farms. I made sure to keep two cars between us whenever I could, and when I couldn't, I slowed down until I wasn't directly behind her. It helped that she'd gotten a head start, and the cars coming off the interstate ramp that lodged between us helped too.

At Granny White Pike she took a right. Luckily a few other cars were in line behind her, so it wasn't just the two of us heading north.

Granny—Lucinda—White was a poor widderwoman who came to the Nashville area from the Carolinas in the early 1800s sometime, after her husband died. At one point, she ran a still and a tavern in the hills just north of Radnor Lake, in what is now the Inns of Granny White subdivision. Her grave is still there, behind a little fence, in the median halfway up the hill.

Closer to town, Granny White Pike becomes 12th Avenue South, and leads to Tim's house in the 12 South area. For a minute or two, I thought Heidi might be headed there. But then she took a right on Tyne Boulevard and headed east.

I slowed down. None of the other cars turned, and once I did, it would be just the two of us on the road. At that point, she couldn't really miss seeing me behind her.

By now, I was starting to develop a sneaky suspicion where we were headed. After a couple of minutes, when she turned onto Chatsworth Drive, that clinched it.

It was just this afternoon that I'd thought about a house on Chatsworth Drive. It used to belong to Walker Lamont, my old broker, now a guest of the state of Tennessee. I had assumed he'd had to sell it to pay legal fees, but perhaps not. He'd pleaded guilty, so maybe there hadn't been a trial and so no need for a financial sacrifice. Maybe Walker still owned the place.

Maybe Tim had a key.

I idled in front of the neighbors' while I watched the Honda pull into the driveway and disappear behind the house, and while I tried to decide what to do.

I could drive up behind the house myself, and perhaps catch Heidi in the process of aiding and abetting a fugitive.

Or I could wait until she left, and tackle Tim on my own.

If I went up there now, there'd be two of them against one of me. Tim was probably pretty desperate to avoid trouble by now, and Heidi was something of a loose cannon. She was also sizeable enough to make it impossible to breathe if she sat on me. Much as I was tired of sitting in my car, it might be better to wait for her to leave again.

As luck would have it, she didn't stay long. It was only five minutes later when she came back down the drive. I ducked down below the dashboard and crossed my fingers that she wouldn't stop to investigate the Volvo parked on the side of the road.

But she must have been eager to get out of there, because she just drove by. I waited until her taillights had disappeared around the corner onto Tyne, and then I started the car and made my way up the winding driveway toward Walker's elegant home.

Eighteen

Tim must have thought Heidi had forgotten something, because he flung the door open as soon as I knocked, without bothering to check who it was. His consternation when he saw me made it abundantly clear that if he'd realized who was outside, he wouldn't have answered.

"We need to talk," I informed him.

He glanced around the parking pad. "Are you alone?"

"Of course I'm alone. Who'd be with me?"

As the words left my mouth, I realized that maybe I shouldn't have admitted that. If Tamara Grimaldi was right and Tim had killed both Brian Armstrong and Beau Riggins, he probably wouldn't quibble about killing me.

He stepped back. "Come in, then."

Now it was my turn to hesitate. Going inside an empty house with a suspected murderer probably wasn't the smartest move I'd ever make. I'd done it before, but then I hadn't actually realized what I was doing. This time I did. And this time, there was no chance that

Rafe would show up in the nick of time to save me, either. If anything happened, my body would lie on the floor of Walker's house until there was nothing left but bones. All Tim had to do was kill me and leave. Nobody would think to look for me here.

"Hurry!"

He peered out, nervously shifting from one foot to the other.

He looked horrible. Although not as horrible as he had the other morning, in his ratty jeans and sweatshirt. Or at least now he looked horrible in a different way.

He was dressed with a semblance of care, in dark slacks and a crisp, striped dress shirt. His hair was clean and so were his hands; it was the face that looked ravaged.

I was used to Tim being gorgeous, or as gorgeous as a gay man can look to a straight woman.

He didn't look gorgeous today. He looked every day of his thirty-some years, plus another decade thrown in for good measure. He looked like he hadn't slept since the last time I'd seen him, with circles under his eyes that weren't just dark, but that looked like the pits of hell. The eyes themselves were bloodshot, and there were lines carved into his face.

"You look horrible," I said.

He immediately turned peevish. "You should talk. Have you been crying?"

Yes. And since I didn't want to talk about why—not to Tim—I said, "Are you going to kill me if I come inside?"

"What do you think?"

I made a decision. "I'm coming in." I wanted to hear what he had to say, and he wasn't going to talk to me standing on the doorstep. Besides, it was cold.

Tim stepped aside and I crossed the threshold into the mud room.

I'd been to Walker's place once before, but it had been for a cookout in the summer, and I hadn't spent much time inside. Enough to get a good look around, of course—I'm a realtor because I enjoy looking at other people's houses—but I hadn't been able to snoop too much, both because Walker was my boss, so it was unseemly, and because I was afraid someone might catch me.

It looked much the way I remembered it. A big, sprawling mid-century ranch, with large open rooms, tall ceilings, and gleaming oak floors. Walker had excellent taste, so everything—furniture, paint colors, artwork—was exquisite.

"Nice place," I said, falling further and further behind as I looked around.

"I'd rather be home," Tim answered.

Well, of course. I glanced at his back. "Why aren't you?"

He sent me a glare over his shoulder as he passed through the kitchen door. "You know why. You're the one who told me the police had been there."

I followed, and looked around, at the marble counters and big butcher-block island, before I answered. "Did you kill Brian Armstrong?"

He slammed the glass he'd just taken out of the cabinet down on the counter hard enough that I worried it would shatter, and put both hands on his hips to scowl at me.

"Sorry," I said, "but you did dump the body in Shelby Park, didn't you? You can't blame me for asking."

He must have seen my point of view, because he shrugged and started dishing beef stew out of the Tupperware container and into a bowl. He glanced up at me. "You want some of this?"

"No, thank you. I have dinner plans." I took my coat off, draped it over the nearest chair, and took a seat. If nothing else, he didn't look like he planned to kill me anytime soon. Not unless he assumed Heidi's stew was poisonous and would do me in. But just in case I was wrong, I did keep an eye on the big butcher knife on the counter.

Tim smacked his lips, and I don't think it was over the stew. "How is Rafael doing?"

"Rafe's fine," I said. In fact, he was probably more than fine, over there on the other side of town with his stripper.

"Yes," Tim agreed with another approving murmur, "he certainly is."

I resisted the temptation to roll my eyes. "So you're telling me you didn't kill Brian Armstrong?"

"No," Tim said.

"No, you didn't kill him?"

"No, that's not what I'm telling you."

I tensed as he picked up the big knife, but when he just used it to slice the hunk of bread into a couple of pieces, I relaxed again. "So you did kill Brian Armstrong?"

"No," Tim said. He put his bowl and the slices of bread on the table and took a seat across from at me.

"But..." I stopped and shook my head. Never mind. "You either did or you didn't. Which is it?"

Tim hesitated. "I don't know," he said eventually.

"How can you not know?" I mean, killing someone isn't something that should slip someone's mind. Is it?

"I'm not sure," Tim said.

I watched as he dipped his spoon into the stew and tasted it. It was either too hot or too spicy, because he grimaced and blew on the spoon. "How can you not be sure?"

"I don't know."

Argh. "Let's go back to the beginning. You had an appointment at Chaps on Friday night, right?"

He glanced up at me. "How do you know about that?"

"I put together your calendar page," I said.

"The one I shredded?"

I nodded. He smirked, probably at the effort I'd gone to, and I added, a little defensively, "I wanted to know where you were."

There was a pause. "Do you know what kind of place Chaps is?" Tim asked eventually.

"Gay bar," I answered. "Leather."

He looked surprised, and I added, "I went there a couple of nights ago. With Rafe."

Tim put down the spoon to give me his full attention. "You took Rafael to Chaps?"

In a manner of speaking. I nodded.

"Oh," Tim breathed, an unholy light in his baby-blue eyes, "I wish I could have been there to see that!"

"It was... interesting." In the moment, I'd been too relieved at Rafe's sudden appearance to notice many of the other details, but the instant awareness in the faces and postures of the other men had been amusing in retrospect.

Tim grinned. "I can imagine."

I let him bask in the fantasy for another moment, and then I gently yanked the conversation back on track. "You did go there on Friday, right? Someone told me you sat at the bar and that you looked like you were waiting for someone."

"Brian," Tim said with a sigh. "He asked me to meet him."

"For a date?"

"I assumed it was professional," Tim said. "I wouldn't have gone otherwise. I'm not into kink. Not on that level. A pair of handcuffs and a blindfold is one thing, but I don't bottom for anyone who's into inflicting pain."

Too much information. "Was Brian into inflicting pain?"

"He was a dentist," Tim said. And then he seemed to remember the food in front of him again, because he dipped his spoon back into the stew. I let him take a few bites before I asked my next question.

"So was it professional? The date?"

"I'm not sure," Tim said.

"Didn't he show up?"

"I think he did."

"You don't remember?"

"Yes," Tim said. "I think I do."

"You spoke to him?"

He nodded. "I'm pretty sure I did. And... no, it wasn't professional."

"He was hitting on you?"

"I think he was."

"So what happened?"

"I don't know," Tim said.

I took a deep breath and held it, to keep from screaming at him. "Let's talk about Saturday morning instead. When I saw you at the office, you were rinsing blood off your hands. And there was a big bloody handprint on your trunk. You'd just come from dumping Brian in Shelby Park, right?"

Tim shuddered and pushed the bowl of soup away. "Yes."

"How did you end up with the body?"

"He was there," Tim said.

"Where?"

"Next to me."

"At Chaps?"

He shook his head. "In bed."

Now we were getting somewhere. "Your bed?"

He nodded.

"So you took him home with you? From Chaps?"

"I don't know," Tim said, and rubbed his forehead. "I must have, I guess. I just... don't remember."

"Well, how else could he have gotten there?"

Tim shrugged and kept rubbing. I waited for him to say something else, but when he didn't, I tried again. "So... he was next to you in bed? When?"

"When I woke up. Early."

Yikes.

"It was in the guest bedroom. I don't remember going to bed there. I don't remember bringing Brian home, either. I don't know why I would have brought Brian home. I didn't like him."

"Did he..." I hesitated. It was a delicate question, and I didn't quite know how to phrase it. Furthermore, I didn't know if I should ask. Frankly, I wasn't sure I wanted to hear the answer.

"No," Tim said, glancing at me.

"He didn't—?"

"If you're asking if we had sex, no."

"Oh. No. I actually wanted to know whether he hurt you."

"Oh," Tim said. "No. Not that, either."

"No bruises or anything?"

He shook his head.

I sat back on the chair, chewing on my lip and trying to make some sense of this.

So Brian was into rough sex, but Tim wasn't, and Brian had gone home with Tim, but Tim couldn't remember it, and they hadn't gotten around to either the sex or the rough stuff, but somehow Brian had ended up dead.

"Did you kill him before he could... you know... hurt you?"

Tim paled. "I don't know."

"Do you remember stabbing him?"

Tim shook his head, not just pale now, but a lovely shade of almost green.

"All you remember is waking up, and he was there. Already dead."

He nodded.

"Was there a knife?"

"I tossed it in the river," Tim said faintly.

"Was it yours?"

"From the butcher block in the kitchen."

Tamara Grimaldi's CSI team had undoubtedly noticed that. I wondered why she hadn't mentioned it to me.

"Now you know why I can't go home," Tim said.

Oh, yes. Because the police would arrest him for murder. And he wouldn't be able to prove he didn't do it. Because he probably did, even if he couldn't remember it.

"What about Beau?"

Tim looked surprised. "Beau Riggins? What about him?"

"Was he there?"

"I should be so lucky," Tim said. "Listen, if I could have taken Beau Riggins home, I'd have done it in a heartbeat, and to hell with Brian Armstrong. But he doesn't swing my way."

"So he wasn't there on Friday night."

Tim shook his head. "I don't remember seeing him. But if you want to know, why don't you just call and ask?"

"He's dead, too."

There was a beat. "Beau's dead?"

I nodded.

"How?"

"Suicide," I said. And qualified it, "Maybe."

When he didn't say anything, I elaborated a little. "A mixture of sleeping pills, ammonia, bleach, and drain cleaner."

Tim winced. "Jesus."

I nodded. "I don't suppose you have an alibi for yesterday?"

He looked at me as if I'd grown an extra head. "No."

"You've been here since Saturday?"

He nodded. "I've spoken to Heidi on the phone a couple of times a day, but I haven't seen anyone else."

So if Beau had been killed, Tim could have killed him. Or at least he couldn't prove that he hadn't. Just like with Brian.

"Is there any chance that Beau could have killed Brian?" I asked.

Tim looked at me.

"I was just thinking... if the three of you went to your house, and Beau killed Brian, and then left him there..."

He didn't say anything. No denial, but no confirmation, either. If he'd been guilty of murder, wouldn't he have grabbed the chance to pin the blame on Beau?

"I should go," I said. And I admit it, when I got to my feet, my knees were a little wobbly. If he'd been stringing me along this whole time, and he knew exactly what had happened to both Brian and Beau, because he had killed them both, now was the time when he'd have to kill me too, before I could leave and tell anyone where he was. "Just... stay here, OK? I won't tell anyone where you are."

He looked at me.

"I won't. I swear." I'd just call Grimaldi and tell her what he'd told me. And deal with her trying to browbeat his location out of me.

Or maybe it would be better not to tell her. Maybe I should just give it some more thought first, and try to come up with a good scenario that explained what had happened. I could wait until tomorrow to call her. I had things to do tonight anyway.

I grabbed my coat off the back of the chair. "Just stay here a few more days. I'll try to figure out what's going on."

He peered up at me. "Why?"

"I don't want you going to jail for something you didn't do," I said. "Rafe's been to prison, and he said you wouldn't like it."

"If they have men like Rafael there, I wouldn't mind," Tim informed me. "I'll be your boyfriend's bitch anytime, darling."

Gack.

"I'll make sure he knows," I said, and on that note, I made my way to the door and out. Tim didn't make any move to stop me, just shut and locked the door as soon as I was outside. I got in the car and drove away.

Nineteen

A islynn and Kylie's new house used to be one of Tim's listings. It was located in Edgefield, just a few blocks from the office, and half mile or so from my apartment, as the crow flies. It wasn't very far from Erin Armstrong's house on Forrest, either.

I got there at six o'clock sharp, after driving past my own apartment on the way. The lights weren't on upstairs, and there was no sign of Rafe's Harley on the street. I didn't stop, of course.

The Victorian was redolent of tomato sauce and spices, and it looked great. They'd managed to unpack all their boxes in the couple of weeks since they'd moved in, and the place looked like they'd always lived there.

"We love it here!" Aislynn confided as she showed me around. "So much better than that Stepford place you showed us."

The Stepford place was a planned community on the south side of town. Very pristine and orderly, and closer to Sara Beth's than we were now. The left-brained Kylie would probably have been quite happy there, but Aislynn was more of a free spirit.

"It looks fantastic." I turned away from the big king-sized bed in the master bedroom. "How's Kylie doing? Any problems after the accident?"

Back before Christmas, someone had fiddled with the brakes on Kylie's blue Volvo, thinking it was mine, and she and Aislynn had crashed on their way home from making the offer on the house. Aislynn had walked away mostly unscathed, with a few cuts and bruises from the seatbelt and airbag, but Kylie had had broken ribs and a concussion and had spent a few days in the hospital.

Aislynn shook her head. Her multiple earrings danced. "She's fine. Great. You saw her."

I had, when I first walked in. And she'd looked just like she used to, before the accident. A lot like me, with shoulder-length blonde hair—an inch or two shorter and a bit lighter than mine—and about my height and size.

"I'm glad you guys are happy with the house."

"We're thrilled," Aislynn assured me. "Couldn't be better."

Good. At least something had gone right lately.

The food was good too, and I found I had recovered enough of my appetite to do it justice. And after dinner we curled up in the sofa with a glass of wine each to watch a movie.

They'd chosen the most recent James Bond action thriller, which was fine with me. When you're a lesbian, I guess a straight romantic comedy doesn't really blow your skirt up, and in the frame of mind I was, I had no desire to watch one. Someone else's happy ending was likely to set me off bawling.

Not that watching 007 work his way through the usual array of gorgeous Bond girls made me feel much better, either.

I must have ground my teeth loud enough for Kylie to hear, because halfway through the movie she turned to me. "Everything OK?"

"Fine," I said.

"Don't you like James Bond?"

Handsome, larger than life, and a womanizer? "What's not to like?"

"It's just that you're grinding your teeth," Kylie said.

"Boyfriend trouble."

"Ah." She exchanged a glance with Aislynn, who said, "I told her."

"Told me what?"

"That's why we're gay."

Because all men are swine. I remembered.

"I don't think I have it in me to be gay," I said.

"That's OK." Kylie patted my hand. "It isn't for everyone."

We went back to watching the movie.

They offered me the use of the couch, and I guess maybe I should have taken them up on it. But I hadn't brought a change of clothes, and I hadn't had that much to drink. The apartment was only a few blocks away. I figured I could make it there in one piece. And it was late enough that I wouldn't have to worry about sitting around waiting for Rafe to show up—or not—when I got home. I could just fall into bed, and into oblivion.

So I said thank you and good night, and made my way out to the Volvo. And drove carefully through the dark streets in the direction of home.

I noticed the car behind me the first time I made a turn. With the second turn, I noticed it again. With the third, I was pretty sure it was following me.

By the time I made the fourth turn, my heart was beating faster.

Not all of it was terror. It could just be Rafe behind me, tracking me down because I hadn't come home. And if so, the terror was more of an anger-fueled excitement.

Although it was definitely a car behind me, not a motorcycle. Two headlights instead of one. He had borrowed a Town Car from Wendell a couple of times before, though. He could have done so again. Or he could be driving Lantana's white Toyota.

I glanced in the rearview mirror as the car behind me passed under a streetlight. It was dark in color. Black or maybe dark blue. Not white.

So not the Toyota. It could still be the Town Car, though. Then again, it could be someone else. It could be Tim. It wasn't his baby blue Jag behind me either, but maybe he had borrowed Heidi's Honda. Maybe he really had killed Brian, in spite of pretty much convincing me that he hadn't, at least not while he was conscious, and now he wanted to silence me before I could tell anyone about it.

But if he'd wanted to kill me, why not just kill me before I left Walker's house? No one knew I was there. No one would ever find my body. It didn't make sense for him to let me leave, and then follow me here.

So maybe it was someone else entirely. Maybe it was Brian's real killer, assuming Tim had told me the truth.

The headlights followed me around another corner. I was in the middle of a quiet, residential neighborhood full of parked cars and cats, with a stop sign on every corner. I couldn't punch the gas and get out of there no matter how much I wanted to.

I was also a little leery of driving home. If whoever was behind me didn't know where I lived, I didn't want to take him—or her—there.

At the same time, I couldn't keep driving around forever. I'd run out of gas sooner or later, for one thing, and for another, I was tired and I wanted to go home and sleep.

I headed for the office. It was nearby, and there'd be people there. Five Points is alive into the wee hours, with bars and restaurants, a gas station, and lots of funny little stores.

The parking lot behind the office was half full. I didn't kid myself that anybody was inside, though. No, it was just people using our lot during off-hours, while they shot the breeze at Beckett's or at the FinBar down the street.

I pulled into a slot and cut the engine and the lights. Behind me, the car that had been following slid up to the curb and idled.

I didn't recognize it. It was dark, a sedan of some sort, bigger than Heidi's Honda, and with a vaguely ghetto-look to it. Lots of shiny chrome on the wheels and tinted windows.

Nobody came out. I wondered if he—or she—was waiting for me to make the first move. I wondered what would happen if I did.

If I ran, could I make it into the office before he—she—could catch up?

Not likely, I figured. Not with having to unlock the regular lock and the deadbolt on the back door. And while I was doing that, he—or she—would corner me in the out-of-the-way niche where the door was.

Conversely, what would happen if I just stayed where I was. Would he—she—get tired of waiting and drive away eventually?

There were a few people out and about, but the area wasn't as populated as I had hoped it would be. I could hear music from the FinBar down the street, and loud voices from the gas station on the next corner, but there was nobody right here. When the door to the sedan opened and a man got out, there was nothing I could do to avoid the confrontation.

HE WAS BIG AND BLACK AND muscular, dressed in saggy jeans and an oversized sweatshirt with the hood up so I couldn't get a good look at his face. When he rapped on my window, it was with a metallic sound, from the gun in his hand.

I rolled the window down two inches, with my heart thudding against my ribs. "Can I help you?"

He bent down and peered in. "I'm looking for Tanya."

Tanya? "I'm sorry," I managed. "I don't know anyone by that name."

"Open the door."

I turned on the interior light instead. No way was I giving this guy the opportunity to grab me. If he wanted me, he'd have to try to haul me out through the window, and I doubted my posterior would fit. "There's no one else in the car. Check the trunk if you want."

I popped it, before I remembered that I'd have to close it again before I could drive away.

He peered inside. With the light on, I could see his face. Broad, dark, with a square jaw and flat, hard eyes.

Vaguely familiar, but not someone I'd ever met before, to my knowledge.

"Why were you following me?" I inquired, while I ran mental mugshots past my eyes. There was no match, just that vague feeling of familiarity.

He turned back to me. I wished he hadn't, because the flat snakelike hardness of those eyes was disturbing. "Looking for Tanya."

"I don't know Tanya. Or where she is."

"The house you were at…"

"Belongs to Aislynn and Kylie," I said firmly, or as firmly as I could, with my heart in the back of my throat. "Not Tanya."

He hesitated. "You don't know Tanya."

I shook my head. "I really don't."

There was a moment of silence before he stepped back. I kept my eyes on the gun, in case he thought to do something with it. Like shoot me.

But he walked away. Away from the Volvo, across the parking lot, across the sidewalk, and into the street. Just got into his car and drove off.

I sat there for quite a few minutes before I dared to open the door and drag myself around to the back of the car to slam the trunk shut. And I scurried back inside and closed and locked the door in record time. And then I sat for another minute to get my breathing under control again before I managed to turn the key in the ignition and pull the car out of the lot and onto the street.

Nothing happened on the way home. Nobody followed me, at least not that I could see. I debated on whether or not to risk the underground parking garage—someone hit me over the head there once—and decided to check the front of the building for any available spaces instead. When I found one right in front, I slid the car into that, with hands that shook.

There were no lights on in my apartment. I hadn't expected there to be, but I wasn't sure whether to be disappointed or not. On the one hand, I didn't really want to see Rafe. On the other, knowing that he was spending the night with her and not me had to be worse than anything else.

I opened the door to the apartment carefully. There was no sound of movement from inside.

I slipped across the threshold and closed and locked the door behind me before unbuttoning my coat and hanging it on the hook in the hallway by feel. I unzipped my boots the same way, and padded down the hallway toward the living room/dining room combo on stocking feet.

I was halfway to the bedroom when the light flicked on, almost blinding me.

I threw a hand up to cover my eyes, and it took a few seconds before I could see anything but spots.

"Where the hell have you been?" Rafe asked, his voice tightly controlled.

I turned to him, where he was sitting in the sofa, and put my hands on my hips. "That's rather rich, coming from you."

His voice stayed even. "It's past midnight."

"So? I'm a grown woman. If I want to stay out late, I can."

There was a pause, during which he looked me up and down. I wasn't wearing anything special. Just the same type of skirt and blouse combo I usually wear to work. Gray skirt, pink blouse, in this case.

"Dinner with Satterfield?" he inquired.

I hesitated. Part of me wanted to throw it in his face that I had other options, as well. That I hadn't been sitting at home pining for him. But he already knew that, so there was no point in lying.

"No."

I thought I saw an infinitesimal softening in his lips, but I couldn't be sure. "New boyfriend?"

"I thought I'd try the gay lifestyle," I told him. "I spent the evening with Kylie and Aislynn."

This time he almost smiled. "How was it?"

"Not the same," I said.

There was a few seconds of silence.

"About what happened earlier..."

"I don't want to talk about it," I said.

"That's too bad," Rafe answered, but not in a way like he was agreeing to let it go. This was more the, 'I'm gonna talk about it whether you want me to or not,' kind of 'too bad.'

"You said it yourself. You have more important things to do than explain anything to me."

"Savannah..."

"Just get your things and go." I turned away, toward the bedroom, so he wouldn't see the tears in my eyes.

"Not until you agree to listen." He didn't move. And since I knew very well how stubborn he could be—he really wasn't going to go until he'd had his say—I did the only thing I could.

"Fine." I folded my arms across my chest. "Talk. Get it off your chest. But I don't care. It's none of my business."

"No, it isn't. But since it's my fault she's in the position she's in..."

Of course it was. Every other woman in creation seemed able to have his children, just not me.

I tried to blink away the tears, but it didn't work.

"I love you, Savannah."

"Don't tell me that!" I dashed at my eyes with the back of my hand. "Just go. Be with her."

"I don't wanna be with her," Rafe said. "I wanna be with you."

"Maybe you should have thought of that before..."

But what could I say, after all? The kid was a couple years old. Back then, I hadn't given him a thought for at least a decade.

He didn't say anything, just looked at me. I couldn't bear to look at him, so I looked around.

"How d'you find me?" he asked eventually. "This afternoon?"

"I followed you."

"From?"

"Mrs. J's house. I was on my way to tell you something." At this point I couldn't even remember what, it seemed so long ago. "You came tearing out of the driveway like a bat out of hell. So I followed."

"I didn't see you." There was something almost like approval in his voice, and in the look in his eyes.

"Sure you did," I said.

"Not until we got to the daycare."

I shrugged. "How did you hook up with a stripper, anyway?"

"She didn't used to be a stripper. When I met her, she was a waitress in Clarksville."

Clarksville.

It's a town roughly forty five minutes from Nashville. Northwest, on the border to Kentucky. And other than the song, it's mainly known for being the home of the 101st Airborne, the Screaming Eagles. There's a big military base up there, called Fort Campbell.

Something about Rafe and the military base in Clarksville rang a faint bell. Something about Todd Satterfield, sitting across the table from me at some restaurant or another, telling me...

"She was involved with this guy I was after." His voice was faint and far away.

Ah, yes. Now I remembered. Once upon a time—five months ago, maybe—Todd had hired a private detective to look into Rafe's past, in an effort to prove to me that he wasn't someone I should be interested in. (As if I didn't already know that.) One of the things the PI dug up, was Rafe's involvement in a gang which was ripping off weapons from the military base. At the time Todd—and I too—thought Rafe was a criminal. Now, of course, I knew better.

"She got me what I needed to turn him in. Him and everyone else."

Yes, Todd's PI had made mention of that. Everyone but Rafe had been arrested and sent to prison. Rafe had skated through and surfaced a few months later in... Knoxville, was it? Somewhere else in Tennessee, anyway, where someone else was doing something nefarious. Todd had found that fact extremely sinister. I had found it sort of funny. If the police hadn't even bothered to arrest him, how bad could he be?

By now I knew that he always slipped through the police's fingers not because he was a particularly good criminal, or a particularly bad one, but because the TBI needed him on the loose to reel in the next thread in the South American Theft Gang they were after.

"When did she come to Nashville?" I asked, trying to keep up with the conversation.

"After the baby was born," Rafe said.

"Why is she working as a stripper?"

"Easy money?" He shrugged.

"Doesn't it bother you?"

"Why would it? It's legal."

Yes, but... he wouldn't let me go to a gay bar by myself, yet he let her take her clothes off in front of a bunch of drooling deviants? And she was a mother, too!

"How old is the baby?"

"Two," Rafe said.

"What's its name?"

"It's a boy. His name is Justin."

I nodded. Part of me wanted to be snide and congratulate him, but the other part couldn't quite manage. And because I wanted to shake him up a little, I said, "A man with a gun followed me earlier."

The reaction was all I could have hoped for. Something moved in his eyes, something flat and deadly, and his whole body tightened. "When?"

"Just now. When I left Aislynn and Kylie's house."

"Are you all right?"

He was on his feet, and moving toward me. I took a step back. "I'm fine. It was just a misunderstanding."

"What kind of misunderstanding?" He stopped two feet away, and I could see his hands clench at his sides, but I wasn't sure whether it was because he wanted to reach for me and knew I didn't want him to, or because he wanted to punch someone.

"He was looking for someone I don't know. Someone named Tanya."

For a second he just stared at me. "Tanya?"

"That's what he said."

"Shit," Rafe said. He swung on his heel and grabbed his phone from the coffee table. While he dialed, he asked me, "What did he look like?"

"Big guy. Black. Saggy pants. Hoodie. It was dark."

"Car?"

"Some kind of sedan. Not a compact. Dark. Do you know him?"

He held up a finger and spoke to the phone. "Everything OK?"

The phone quacked.

"You sure?"

The phone quacked again.

"I'm on my way. Don't open the door till I get there."

The quacking took on a shrill note.

"Dunno," Rafe said. "But someone's seen him. And if he's this close..."

The phone quacked, alarmingly. Rafe rolled his eyes, but kept his voice even. "I'm on my way. Just hang tight until I get there."

He disconnected the call and turned to me. "I have to go."

"Back to her?"

Much as I tried, I couldn't keep that little hiccup out of my voice.

He looked at me for a second. Just looked. Then he seemed to make a decision. "Get your shoes back on."

"Excuse me?"

"You're coming with me."

"I am?" I trotted after him into the hallway, where he grabbed his leather jacket from the hook and shrugged it on.

"Unless you don't want to."

"No." I wanted to. I wasn't sure why, when he'd spent the day—and yesterday, and the day before—with another woman, but I'd rather be with him than without him.

"C'mon, then." He opened the door while I stuffed my feet back into the boots and snagged my coat and bag from the hooks. By the time I moved through the door, he was halfway down the hallway. "Where's your car?" he asked me over his shoulder.

"On the street." I hurried to catch up as the door to the apartment slammed shut behind me. "I was too nervous to park in the garage."

"Good thing. Makes it easier to leave." He held the door on the first floor for me and then, when we were on our way across the courtyard, held out his hand. "Keys."

I dug them out of my purse and handed them over. He peeled away from the curb before I had my seatbelt fastened. And then he dropped something in my lap. "Hold onto that."

I stared at it and up at him. "Your gun?"

"You never know when you might need to shoot someone."

It was the same thing he'd said yesterday. It hadn't struck me as funny then either. I don't think it was supposed to be.

"Who are you planning to shoot tonight?"

"Nobody," Rafe said, "I hope. The guy you saw—" He stuck a hand inside his jacket and pulled out a piece of paper, "this him?"

I unfolded it and looked at the picture. "Yes."

And now that I saw it again, I knew why the guy had seemed familiar, too. I'd never met him before, but I had seen his picture—this very picture—just this afternoon. Rafe must have snagged it off Lantana DuBois's Facebook page and blown it up a few times before printing it.

"Who is he?" I asked.

Rafe shot me a sidelong look as he took the left onto Interstate Drive on two wheels. "Name's Desmond Johnson. One of the guys I put away three years ago."

"Lantana's boyfriend?"

"Tanya." He nodded. "Yeah."

"And... he's the baby's father?"

Rafe nodded. I didn't say anything, but he must have been able to read my mind—not for the first time—because after a moment he turned to me. "What, you thought it was mine?"

"I... yes."

He shook his head. "Christ, Savannah. I've told you, I don't have any kids. Not that I know of. Other than David."

"I'm sorry. I just... I saw you together, and I thought..."

He didn't answer. I'm not sure whether it was because he was busy merging with the cars on the interstate—at a higher speed than he should have been—or whether he didn't want to talk, or just didn't know what to say.

I looked down at the picture in my hand. "This guy wrote some pretty creepy stuff on her Facebook page."

Rafe nodded, and then realized what I'd said. "How d'you know about that?"

"I looked her up," I said. "If my boyfriend's seeing someone on the side, I want to know who she is."

"Your boyfriend ain't seeing anyone on the side." When I didn't answer immediately, he shot me a look. "I don't spend the day with another woman and then come home and make love to you, Savannah."

I was beginning to realize that. "How about you just tell me what's been going on?" The way he should have done from the beginning.

He sighed. "I got a text from Wendell Friday night, that Desmond was out of prison. Some sort of work-release program he'd walked away from. He shouldn't have been allowed outside at all, not with the way he's been cyber-stalking Tanya, but she didn't want to cause a fuss and make him even more angry, so she never reported it."

"That doesn't sound smart."

"No kidding," Rafe said. "She's barely twenty one and takes her clothes off for a living. Ain't nothing smart about that girl."

I tried my best not to smile a bit happily at the description, but I don't think I managed completely. "So...?"

"Wendell stayed with her overnight to make sure nothing happened, and I went to her place on Saturday to help move her out and into the apartment she's in now."

Moving a witness. In the very basic sense of the word: actually moving her from one residence to another. Along with her assorted belongings.

"Wendell and I have been trading off watching her for the past couple days. Getting her to work and home. Picking up the kid. Just until we... until *they* track down Desmond."

"That's all?"

He nodded.

"You could have told me."

He glanced at me. "I didn't want you to worry."

How could he imagine I wouldn't?

I had my mouth open to ask when he turned to look at me again, and the expression on his face took my breath away. "I don't know about this, Savannah."

This? As in, him and me?

"Rafe..."

He shook his head, hands flexing on the steering wheel as we flew down the interstate. "I know I promised you I was done. But I ain't cut out to paint walls and finish floors for the rest of my life. I'm sorry, darlin'. I know you worry when I'm out there, but I'm dying doing nothing."

I wasn't sure whether to laugh or cry. "What do you want to do?"

He glanced at me, so maybe it showed in my voice. "It won't be undercover work. I wouldn't do that to you. I won't be gone for weeks or months at a time. But it prob'ly won't be nine to five, either."

I nodded.

"And I can't see myself taking that desk job they offered. Maybe I can do training, or be a handler. Ten years of undercover work oughta be good for something."

"I'm sure they can learn a lot from you," I managed.

He peered at me. "Are you crying?"

"No," I said, dashing tears from my eyes.

"Darlin'..."

"I'm happy. I thought you were going to tell me you were leaving me. That I wasn't interesting enough."

"Darlin'..." But he ended up just shaking his head.

"You can do anything you want. Just as long as you come back to me at the end of the day." And if I worried about him while it was going on, well... that was par for the course, when you fell in love with someone whose idea of being alive was carrying a gun and chasing down bad guys.

Twenty

Rafe slowed down when we turned onto the street where the duplex was. Everything looked quiet. There were lights on in some of the houses we passed, and the blue flicker of televisions behind drawn curtains. Someone was playing music—Spanish mariachi—and somewhere, not too close, a dog barked.

The duplex also looked quiet. One side was completely dark, while the other had a flickering blue light in what I assumed was the living room. That must be where Lantana—Tanya—lived.

"Who lives on the other side?" I asked Rafe, my voice low.

He glanced at me. "Nobody."

"How come?"

"I moved in with you."

Oh.

I didn't say anything, and he added, "We didn't wanna risk somebody moving in next to me. So I rented both sides."

Good thinking. Not that I would have expected any less. "It's empty, then."

He nodded. "Should be."

"Is there furniture?" Like maybe a bed? Or at least a sofa?

His teeth flashed white in the darkness, as if he knew what I was thinking. "It don't do no good to be on the other side of the wall from someone you're trying to protect, darlin'. But hold that thought for later."

"How long do you think this will take?"

He shrugged and pulled the car into the driveway. "No way to know. Get ready to take the wheel."

"What?"

"I'm getting out," Rafe said. "I need you to drive away."

What? "Why?"

He glanced at me. "He's been tailing us from East Nashville. But he ain't gonna make a move unless he thinks we've checked that everything's OK and left again. So one of us'll have to drive away. And it can't be me."

Obviously not. "He's been following us?"

"Black Buick," Rafe said, "five or six years old."

"I didn't notice."

"You're not used to looking for a tail."

"I spotted him last time!"

"It's easier to stay back on the interstate. Harder on the smaller roads." He opened his door and the overhead light turned on.

"If you knew he was there, why did you bring him here? Why didn't we just go back home?"

"Cause this way I have a chance to catch him," Rafe said and swung his legs out. I watched as he stood up and then bent. "C'mon. Scoot over."

I scooted. "What do you want me to do?"

"Gimme my gun. Thanks." He stuffed it into the back of his pants. "Wait for me to get inside and give you the all clear. And then you leave. Drive far enough that he thinks you're gone and wait for me to call you."

"Don't you want me to take Lan... Tanya and her baby out of here?"

"Do I look stupid to you?" Rafe demanded. "If you've got 'em in the car, he'll stop you. I ain't risking your life like that."

"They could hide in the back. And won't he notice that you're not with me?"

"Not if you drive fast." He shut my door and took a step back. I rolled the window down, of course. "Go," he told me. "Get the hell outta here. Wait for me to call you."

I hesitated, of course. I didn't want to leave him here to face Desmond-AKA-Othello on his own. Not that I imagined I'd be able to do anything helpful, but I just didn't want to leave.

He must have known it, because he took a step forward and dropped a quick, hard kiss on my lips. "Don't make me worry about you too, Savannah. Let me do my job."

Of course. "Just be careful."

"Always." He winked and headed for the door. Tanya opened up, in sweats and a T-shirt, looking both ways before stepping back to let him in. He slipped across the threshold, gun in hand, while down on the road, the sleek shadow of a car rolled by, slowly.

The door closed, and I put the car in reverse. If that was Desmond going by, I might be able to get onto the road and turned in the other direction while he was down at the end of the street, and where he wouldn't be able to tell that I was alone in the car.

I rolled down the hill toward the road and took a left. Behind me, I could see the dark shape of the sedan coming back up the road, lights off.

I stepped on the gas and took off up the street.

Up until that point, it hadn't occurred to me to question Rafe's plan. It made sense. Driving away would make it seem like we'd checked to make sure everything was all right, and now we were going back home.

You can imagine my surprise when the sedan followed me instead of going up to the house.

My first reaction was disbelief. Then worry, when I realized that just because Rafe said Desmond wouldn't bother stopping me when I didn't have Tanya and Justin in the car, didn't mean anything. He had no idea whether I did or not. He wouldn't know until he stopped me.

The fear didn't really kick in until he put on a burst of speed, two blocks away from the house, and hit the back of my car with the front of his.

It doesn't look like much in the movies. In reality, it knocked me forward against the seatbelt, which made my foot slam down automatically on the brake, which threw my head back again against the seat—hello, whiplash—at least until he hit the back of the Volvo one more time, since I'd now come to a complete stop and he didn't have a choice...

I bounced forward again, squealing across the blacktop, and ended up with the nose of the car against a telephone pole. There were only two saving graces: one, that I was driving a Volvo, the safest car on the road, and two, that I'd been standing still when he hit me. The impact wasn't enough to do much damage at all. Both headlights kept shining into the night, one on each side of the pole, and the engine even kept grinding until I shook off the shock and confusion and turned it off.

That took a few moments, and by the time I got the door open, Desmond had exited his own car and was stalking toward me, gun in hand.

He reached in for me.

I batted his hand away. "Knock it off. What's wrong with you?"

"Where's Tanya?"

"I told you," I said, "I don't know Tanya. See for yourself. There's no one else here."

There wasn't, and he could see it clearly with the door open, since the interior light was on, illuminating the clearly empty car.

It had worked once, but I guess it was too much to expect it to work again. He wrapped a ham-sized hand around my upper arm and yanked.

"Ow!" I protested, but I popped out of the car like a cork out of a bottle. "What are you doing?"

"I want Tanya."

Yes, I'd caught that. "I'm not Tanya. I don't know her."

"You gonna get her." He pulled me, stumbling, over to his own car, idling by the side of the road. The driver's side door was open, and—

"In." He gave me a push, and I scrambled into the sedan ahead of him.

We talked a lot about safety during real estate training. A lot of realtors are women, and a lot of us move around on our own, without the benefit of male protection. Among other things, I've been told that getting into a car with an abductor is the worst thing you can do for your own safety. Letting him take you out of your familiar territory and into his, is practically tantamount to signing your death warrant. It sounds good on paper. But when you're in the middle of the situation, and it's a decision between getting into the car or getting shot... well, let's just say that the choice becomes a little more complicated than that.

I thought about fighting. I did. Turning around and kicking at him. Or trying to open the door on the other side of the car and getting out that way, while he was getting in.

But in the end, it came down to not wanting to risk him using the gun on me. He didn't really want me, he wanted Tanya. If I didn't do anything to upset him, maybe I'd survive.

So I did as he said, and crawled across the gear shift into the passenger seat. He got in next to me and we were off, back in the direction we'd come, before I'd even managed to straighten up.

It was a weird sensation, sitting there next to a man with a gun in his hand. A man with a gun who wasn't Rafe, I mean. Desmond didn't talk to me. Didn't seem to notice I was there, to be honest. I knew he had to know I was in the car—he had put me there, after all—but it was like I didn't quite exist.

Like I wasn't really human, just a means to an end.

226 | Jenna Bennett

It was a pretty uncomfortable feeling, to be honest.

I was fairly certain I knew what he planned to do. It came as no surprise at all when we pulled up outside the duplex and he pointed the gun at me. "Stay."

I stayed. Until he walked around the car and opened my door. This time the command was, "Get out."

I got out, on legs that were shaky. He yanked me around and held me in front of him like a shield, with the muzzle of the gun cold against my temple, and raised his voice. "Tanya!"

Shades of Marlon Brando...

The bellow was loud enough that for a moment, I found myself worrying about my eardrum. Loud enough that surely one of the neighbors would hear him. Maybe they'd call the police.

And then I remembered that the TBI was already here. And besides, a busted eardrum was really the least of my concerns. A bullet through the brain would do a lot more damage.

"Tanya!"

There was the sound of a baby crying from inside the house. Justin must have woken up from the ruckus. And there was a sense of movement behind one of the darkened windows. I could almost feel the force of Rafe's chagrin at the miscalculation we'd both made, and I was certain he was cursing me.

"What d'you want?" a male voice came from the house.

It startled me for a second, before I realized what was going on. Desmond's grip tightened on my arm, as if he suspected me of trying to get away. "I want Tanya!"

"You can't have her."

"I wanna talk to her!"

There was no answer from inside. I could imagine the conversation. Or rather, I could imagine Tanya refusing and the arguments as to why she should allow it. Including the one that came next.

"I'll kill her if I don't get to talk to Tanya!"

It must have been compelling—it certainly had an effect on me—because a moment later, Tanya's voice floated out of the house. "Don't hurt her, Des."

Desmond stiffened. "Hello, bitch."

There wasn't much anyone could say to that, and Tanya didn't try.

"You can't talk to her like that," I managed. "Not if you want her to talk to you."

Desmond growled, and the pistol dug into my temple. "Shut up." He raised his voice. "Get out here!"

It wasn't Tanya who answered. "Can't let her do that, Desmond. You'll have to talk to her through the door."

"Fuck that!" Desmond said, and yanked me up straight. I squeaked. "You can have this one if I get Tanya. If not, I'll kill her."

The voice was still even, though I could hear the tightness in it. "You'll go back to prison for the rest of your life if you do."

"I ain't going back at all!" Desmond hollered, so spittle flew out of his mouth and hit my shoulder and hair. "You have five seconds to send Tanya out before I put a bullet through her brain!"

As he began to count, time stretched to infinity and my mind blanked.

I'd been here once before, although it hadn't been my life on the line then. Back in Rafe's childhood home, a trailer in the Bog in Sweetwater, Jorge Pena had given Elspeth Caulfield five seconds to get out of his way and leave a clear shot so he could kill Rafe.

"Four."

Elspeth had refused, and he'd ended up shooting her instead. Rafe had killed him, with a gun I hadn't even realized he'd had, and somehow Jorge had managed to clip Rafe in the shoulder too, before going down. I knew from personal experience, gleaned since, that getting shot in the shoulder hurts like hell, but isn't fatal. However, when I stepped out of the closet where he'd hid me, the room had looked like a mini-massacre had taken place.

"Three."

In just a few seconds, it could be me on the ground, with my brains spattered across the blacktop. And unlike Elspeth, I didn't have a weapon I could use. She'd had a gun. She could have shot Jorge any time between five and one. Under those circumstances, I think I would have. It wasn't as if there'd been any doubt he'd been serious. But now there was nothing I could do. Desmond had made me leave my purse in the Volvo, so I didn't even have my handy little lipstick cylinders from Sally's store to help me.

"Two."

There was a sound from the house. Voices. Arguing. And what might have been a scuffle over the door. Either Tanya was trying to get outside, or resisting being shoved.

Desmond hesitated. But when nothing happened, he said, "One."

Everything happened at once.

"Wait!" sounded from the house. The door opened. I took advantage of Desmond's momentary distraction to grind my heel, hard, into his foot, and at that exact moment, there was a sound from behind us. I didn't even have time to turn my head before something heavy hit Desmond from behind and knocked him forward, and me along with him.

He let go of both his grip on the gun and on me. I fell to my knees and scrambled out of the way on all fours, as quickly as I could and barely even noticing the cold blacktop against my knees and palms.

Safely out of the way, I turned around.

Rafe was busy trying to subdue Desmond and put a pair of handcuffs on him. It took effort, because Desmond was big—heavier than Rafe—and had nothing to lose. He obviously didn't want to go back to prison, and who could blame him? So he bucked and cursed and did everything he could to toss Rafe off.

Rafe, meanwhile, did his best to keep a knee planted in the middle of Desmond's back while he struggled to get the cuffs on, and muttering a litany of threats and curses of his own. "A little help?" he asked breathlessly after a particularly vicious move on Desmond's part threatened to dislodge him completely.

He wasn't asking me. Wendell was on his way out of the house and toward him even as he spoke. Beyond Wendell, I could see Tanya in the now lighted window, holding Justin and cooing to him. The little boy was dressed in footed pajamas with dinosaurs, and he had his head on his mother's shoulder and his thumb in his mouth. His head was full of tight, dark brown curls.

I turned back to Rafe, who with Wendell's help managed to get the cuffs fastened around Desmond's beefy wrists. Between the two of them, they hauled the big man up. "I'll get him in the car," Wendell grunted.

Rafe nodded and turned to me.

For a second neither of us said anything. I was glad to be alive, and that he was alive, not that I'd really expected him to be otherwise. He was probably happy that I'd come through mostly unscathed, too. My hands and knees smarted a little from contact with the blacktop, and my nerves were shot, but other than that I was fine. I managed a tentative smile, and saw some of the tension ease.

He came toward me, slowly. I don't know why, but it was almost as if he was reluctant, or fearful of his reception. For a second I worried that he didn't want to embrace me in front of Tanya, but then I pushed it aside as silly. When I reached out, he pulled me into his arms, carefully. I could feel his breath against my hair, and hear his heart beating double-time, but he didn't speak. Just held me.

"Are you OK?" I asked against his shoulder.

He nodded.

"Are you sure?"

Another nod.

"I love you," I said.

He took a breath. It shuddered through his chest. His arms tightened and he seemed to find his voice, finally. "I'm sorry."

"For what?"

"I didn't think he'd stop you."

"I didn't either," I said.

"I wanted to get you outta here before anything happened."

"I know." I stroked his back through the T-shirt. His muscles were bunched hard as rocks.

"I should have realized—"

"How could you? It made sense that he wouldn't bother if Tanya wasn't with me." He didn't answer, and I added, "Did he hurt you?"

He chuckled. It sounded half-choked. "Less than I deserve."

Oh, God. I pulled back to look at him. "Are you in pain?"

"Just my pride, darlin'."

"Why?" I said, stepping in to put my head on his shoulder again. For comfort, both because I wanted it and I figured he could use some. "You didn't do anything wrong."

He spoke into my hair. "I shoulda protected you. Not sent you away so he could get at you. It was my fault. If something happened to you.."

"It didn't. You saved me. You saved Tanya, too."

She was still standing in the window, looking out. Justin seemed to be asleep by now. Wendell had stuffed Desmond into the back of the Buick and was standing by with his gun at the ready.

"Oh, no," I said.

Rafe lifted his head. "What?"

"My car."

"What happened to it?"

"I ran into a telephone pole two blocks away. Desmond hit me."

I felt him turn to stone, and added, "I was practically standing still when it happened. I didn't get hurt. The car was still running when I left it, but it didn't sound happy. Grinding, you know?"

He hesitated a moment. "I'll go look at it."

"I'll come with you," I said.

He glanced down. "In those?"

"They're only a couple inches tall. And I've had training." Hours of deportment in finishing school. With a book on my head. Going up and down a spiral staircase. Yes, in three-inch heels. I'd also practiced how to dance in them for a couple hours and keep a smile on my face. They don't call Southern Belles steel magnolias for nothing. "A few minutes' walk is not going to hurt me."

He hesitated.

"Please," I said. "I don't want to stay here." And besides, Tanya would probably be happy to put Justin back to bed and go to sleep herself, with no worries about Desmond coming to get her.

"I've got this," Wendell told him. "Take her home."

Rafe hesitated again, but eventually he nodded. We walked down the driveway with his hand on my lower back, leaving Wendell to deal with Tanya and with Desmond. Once we hit the street, however, he turned to me. "Darlin'..."

"I know," I said. "If something goes wrong—if Desmond makes it out of those handcuffs and hurts Wendell—you'll never forgive yourself."

Rafe nodded.

"Call him. Then we'll keep going to the car. It's only a couple of minutes. He can stop on his way past and make sure I can get home on my own. And then the two of you can go off with Desmond. And do your job."

He smiled. "Thank you."

I shook my head. There was no need to thank me. I was feeling guilty enough. My voice had a catch when I told him, "I never wanted to stop you from being who you are. I just wanted you to be safe." And I was trying to keep my heart safe at the same time. Because if something happened to him, I wouldn't know what to do.

But I didn't want to hamstring him. Didn't want him to feel like he couldn't be himself because I'd worry. That was the last thing I wanted.

I didn't want him domesticated. It occurred to me, much too late, that that's what I'd been trying to accomplish, with my home-cooked meals and regular sex.

And in an ironic and quite uncomfortable twist, it was also one of the things that drove me the craziest about Todd Satterfield. I'd told Rafe once that if I married him—Todd, that is—he'd wrap me in metaphoric cotton wool and put me on a metaphoric shelf, and never, ever let me do anything. Because he cared.

Now I was guilty of the same thing.

Rafe was busy talking to the phone, and wasn't looking at me. When he finished the conversation, he reached out and took my hand. "Thank you, darlin'."

"Don't mention it," I managed.

He peered more intently at me. "Are you crying?"

I sniffed. "No."

"Liar." But his voice was warm, and so was his hand around mine. "He's gonna pick me up at the car. He's settling things with Tanya right now."

"What's going to happen to her?"

Rafe shrugged. "I guess she'll just stay here. She's settled. I'll transfer the lease. Not like I need the place anymore."

"Why did you keep it?" Was it a safeguard in case things didn't work out between us?

But no, he had Mrs. J's place for that. And LaDonna's trailer in Sweetwater, since the people who had bought the Bog with the intention of building a subdivision there, seemed to have dropped off the face of the earth.

"Not sure," Rafe said. "I used it off and on up to Christmas. Whenever I didn't wanna stay at my grandma's place. Whenever I was dealing with someone I didn't wanna bring there. Someone I wanted to keep away from you and my grandma and David."

Understandable. "Is it OK to give it up now?"

"I ain't undercover anymore," Rafe said. "Tanya's welcome to it. And it's paid for through July, so maybe she can get ahead a little."

Fine with me.

We turned the corner and saw the Volvo up ahead. The lights were still on and shining into the night, the door still open. "The battery's probably dead," I muttered.

"If the battery was dead," Rafe answered, "the lights would be off." Of course.

I checked my watch, and was astonished to see that it hadn't even been twenty minutes since I'd run the car into the telephone pole in the first place. It seemed like a lot longer.

Behind us, a car came around the corner from the road we'd just exited. "Here's Wendell," Rafe said and picked up speed. "Just let me make sure she'll drive and won't break down on you between here and home."

I nodded, and watched as he got in, maneuvered the car away from the pole, and popped the hood. After a look at the engine, he pronounced the car ready to go. "I'll take another look tomorrow. But she'll get you there."

I nodded. I was already behind the wheel, strapped in and ready to take off.

"Park on the street. If she doesn't start in the morning and we have to have her towed, it'll be a lot easier if she isn't in the garage."

Indeed. "Just go," I said. "I'll see you at home."

"This could take a while."

No problem. "I'll be in bed," I said.

"I'll see you there." He walked off. I moved the gearshift into drive and rolled away with the Buick keeping pace behind me.

Twenty-One

It was the next morning before I had the chance to tell Rafe about my adventures the day before. The adventures I'd had between following him to the Booby Bungalow and being followed home by Desmond Johnson, that is.

Or more specifically, about Tim. How Sally had said she'd seen him at Chaps on Friday night, how I had deduced that Heidi was bringing Tim food, and how I had shadowed her to Walker's old house in Oak Hill and had my tête-à-tête with him.

Rafe wasn't amused, of course. "Have you lost your mind?" he demanded. "He could have carved you up and left you for dead and nobody would have found your body until Lamont gets out of prison in twenty years. I wouldn't have known to look for you there."

Since the very same thought had crossed my own mind yesterday, there wasn't a whole lot I could say except, "I'm sorry." And then I added, "But nothing happened. I'm fine."

"No thanks to you."

No arguing with that.

"You didn't really think he was a murderer, did you?"

"I don't know that he ain't," Rafe said tightly. "And I don't want you taking stupid chances. Especially because you're pissed off at me."

He had me there. I'd done it partly because I was angry with him. Or if I hadn't been angry with him, I would at least have told him where I was going and why, before I went. So that if something had happened, he'd know where to start looking for my butchered body.

"I'm sorry about that too. I should have let someone know where I was."

"Yeah," Rafe said. "You shoulda."

"Do you want to know what he said?"

"Soon as I calm down."

He looked calm to me. It was early, or at least semi-early, considering how late we got to bed. We were still under the blankets, and the time was just after eight. And he looked perfectly relaxed, all dusky skin and hard muscles against the white sheets. Except maybe the eyes. His eyes were roiling with an emotion that wasn't the heat I usually see there when we're naked in bed together.

"I'm sorry," I said again, and snuggled close.

He let out a breath and then wrapped his arm around me. "Me too. I ain't used to worrying."

I shifted my head on his shoulder to peer up at him. "You're not going to turn into Todd, are you? Telling me that I can't go out and do things?"

His mouth curved. "No, darlin'. Don't think I have it in me to turn into Satterfield."

"Thank God." I rubbed my nose against the side of his neck, and followed up with a brush of lips. He tilted his head to catch them, and a little time passed.

"He said he didn't remember killing Brian Armstrong," I told him after I'd gotten up for air.

"Course he did."

"He said he didn't kill Beau either."

"Beau?"

"Didn't I mention that?" I guess I hadn't. "Tamara Grimaldi and I had lunch together yesterday."

He quirked a brow. "Ragging on me, darlin'?"

I flushed. "I was upset."

"Guess I'm lucky she didn't hunt me down and slap me in a cell."

"She doesn't like me that much," I said, although I must admit the thought appealed.

"She likes you more than you think." He added, "Beau?"

"He's dead. An overdose of sleeping pills mixed with a poisonous mixture of bleach, drain cleaner, and ammonia."

"Chlorine gas?"

I blinked, surprised, and he smiled. "I like chemistry."

"I didn't think you liked any part of school."

"Chemistry's OK," Rafe said, and proceeded to show me just what he meant by chemistry. Which we had, in spades.

It was a while before we returned to the conversation, and by then we were out of bed and dressing. It would be only too easy to spend the day under the covers, but I had places to go and people to see. "Do you think I should tell Grimaldi about Tim?" I asked while I watched Rafe put his clothes on. "Where he is, and what he told me?"

"Yes," Rafe answered, pulling a T-shirt over his head, "I think you should."

"He won't be happy with me."

"If he didn't kill nobody, he ain't got no cause not to be happy."

It took me a second to decipher what he'd said. Most of the time I have no problem understanding him, but once in a while the multiple double negatives trip me up.

"He said he didn't," I answered eventually. "Or at least that he doesn't remember."

He shrugged. "Then he's safer talking to Tammy."

"Safer?"

"If somebody dumped the body on him, it was to set him up. If it was Beau, then Beau killed himself when it didn't work. If it was somebody else, Tim could make for a pretty good next-in-line. Specially if they could pin Beau's murder on him, too."

"You think Beau was murdered?"

"Seems like he might be. Though you'd be a better judge of that than me. I never met the guy."

"I find that easier to believe than that he committed suicide," I admitted. "He seemed like he enjoyed life too much to kill himself. I could see him killing Brian Armstrong, maybe. In self-defense. If Brian tried to force him to do something he didn't want to do."

Rafe nodded.

"And if he did, and then felt guilty, I guess he might have killed himself. Maybe. But I'd rather believe someone else did it. And then killed Beau. I liked him. I don't want him to be guilty of murder."

"What about Tim? You think he killed Beau?"

I hesitated. "No. He seemed genuinely shocked when I told him Beau was dead. I could believe that he killed Brian, maybe. Same scenario as Beau. Brian tried to hurt him, and Tim defended himself. And then blocked the memory of it."

Rafe nodded.

"But I can't see him killing Beau. He liked Beau. And he kept telling me he didn't remember anything that happened on Friday night, until he woke up and found Brian next to him in bed. But he knew exactly what he did on Tuesday night, when Beau died. So he didn't block anything then."

Rafe nodded.

"Do you really think he's in danger?"

"If he didn't kill either of them, and somebody else did," Rafe said, "then yeah."

I pulled a blouse out of the closet and shrugged it on. "I should go back there and tell him that. See if I can't convince him to turn himself in."

"Not without me, you won't."

I stopped buttoning to look at him. "Don't you have other things to do?"

"More painting."

"What about Wendell and the TBI?"

"Got an appointment tomorrow," Rafe said. "Wendell said he'd set it up and call me with the time." He peered at me. "You OK with that?"

"Fine. I just want you to be happy. And here. With me."

"You ain't getting rid of me that easy, darlin'."

Good to know.

"And I don't want you going there on your own."

"It's Tim," I said. "How dangerous can he be?"

"Not sure. But I don't aim to find out when the hospital calls to say he's stabbed you twelve times. So just put up with me breathing down your neck today."

No problem at all. "You're welcome to breathe on me anytime you want."

"Glad to hear it," Rafe said. "I'd like to ask Tim a couple questions myself too. Let's go."

We went. Down the stairs and across the courtyard, out the gate to the Volvo.

"Oh." I stopped. "I forgot. Do you need to look it over?"

"Any problems getting home last night?"

I shook my head.

"Grinding noises? Flames shooting out from under the hood?"

"Lord, no."

"Then I think we're good," Rafe said and held out his hand for the keys. "She ain't sexy, but she's solid."

And in a car, maybe that isn't a bad thing.

I directed him down the interstate to Battery Lane, and down Granny White Pike into Oak Hill. We drove up to Walker's not-so-humble abode about thirty minutes later.

"Nice place," Rafe said, looking around at the acre-plus lot and the many upscale houses dotting the landscape in every direction. Pseudo-chateaus, English manor houses, and a fair few overgrown mid-century ranches like Walker's.

"Way out of my price range."

He shot me a look. "Would you wanna live here if you could?"

"In this neighborhood? It's very nice. Peaceful. Lovely. Probably quite safe. As safe as anywhere is these days." And with a great big yard for a passel of kids.

He nodded.

"I'm not that girl anymore." And I'd rather be with him, wherever that was. Clearly not here, though. I couldn't imagine Rafe fitting in in a neighborhood like this, nor could I imagine him wanting to.

I left him looking at his surroundings and wandered over to the kitchen door. While I waited for Tim to respond to my knock, he joined me. "No answer?"

"Maybe he's still in bed." I knocked again.

"Maybe he's gone," Rafe said. He fished in his pocket. "Keep an eye out."

"For...? Oh." He went to work on the lock while I looked left and right to make sure no one was watching. There wasn't much chance of that. With the size of the properties in this part of town, the nearest neighbor was a quarter mile away.

It took him less than a minute to open the door. "Shit," he added when an alarm cut through the air. "You know the code?"

I shook my head.

"Lucky guess?"

"Um..." I rattled off the street number. I rattled off the alarm code we used at the office. I rattled off the street number for the office, and the phone number for the office. I rattled off Walker's birthday, best as I could recall it. Nothing worked.

Rafe started keying in numbers at random while he told me over his shoulder, "You have three minutes before the cops get here. See what you can find."

"If he's not responding to this, he's—" I stopped before I uttered the dread word 'dead.' "Uh-oh."

"I'm sure he's just gone," Rafe said calmly. "Or I'd be right behind you."

Right. I ran off.

The kitchen was empty, and pristine. No sign that anyone had been there at all. Tim must have washed the dishes and put them away after I left last night.

The bedrooms were equally spiffy. If he'd spent the night in one of Walker's beds, either last night or the night before, he'd done a stellar job of remaking the bed afterwards.

The bathrooms were spic and span, the living room pillows fluffed and fabulous. It was as if no one had ever been there at all.

Throughout it all, the alarm kept blaring.

I ran back to Rafe, who was still keying numbers into the keypad. By now, the expression on his face was morose, and his other hand was fisted, as if he'd much rather just punch the keypad until it stopped wailing, than try to hit on the right combination. "Anything?"

I shook my head. "It's like he's never even been here."

"Probably decamped as soon as you were outta sight last night," Rafe said, scowling at the keypad.

I tilted my head. "Why don't you just rip it out of the wall? That would shut it up, wouldn't it?"

"Might be a little hard to explain when the cops show up, though."

"Don't we want to be out of here by then?"

"It's prob'ly too late for that. Scuse me."

He walked off, just as a police cruiser rolled around the corner of the house and onto the parking pad.

"Where are you going?" I called after him.

He glanced at me over his shoulder. "You're better off without me. They see me, they'll think we're breaking in. Just spin'em a story, get the hell outta here, and come back for me."

He ducked through the door and out of sight. I squared my shoulders and went to talk to the cops.

Only to sag with relief when I saw the car doors open and officers Spicer and Truman get out.

I met Lyle Spicer and George Truman the first Saturday in August last year, upon the occasion of having discovered Brenda Puckett's butchered body. When Rafe called it in, they were the first officers on scene. I've run into them several times since then. Not only were they on hand to arrest Walker after he came close to killing me back in August, but they have a habit of catching me doing things I shouldn't be doing, like kissing Rafe and committing B&E. It wasn't the first time they'd caught me somewhere I technically wasn't supposed to be.

"You again," Spicer said when he spotted me. He's the senior partner, in his late forties or early fifties, with frizzy ginger hair turning gray and a little paunch. Truman is younger, straight out of the police academy, and he blushes if I look at him too long.

I looked from one to the other of them. "What are you two doing here? This isn't your usual area, is it?" Normally I'd see them in and around East Nashville, while now we were ten miles or so south of that.

"The detective sent us to check out the place," Spicer said. To hear him talk about it, it's as if Tamara Grimaldi is the only detective on the Nashville force.

I kept my voice light. "Great minds."

He chomped on his gum. "Whatcha here for, Miz Martin?"

"Looking for Timothy Briggs," I said.

He didn't answer, just chewed. I felt compelled to continue. "This is Walker's house. Walker Lamont, my old broker. Then one who killed Brenda Puckett, remember? Tim has been taking care of the place since Walker went to prison."

"And you thought he might be here."

It wasn't a question, but I nodded. And focused on looking as innocent as I could manage.

"How d'you get in?" Spicer asked.

"Oh. Um..."

As Rafe frequently informs me, I'm a lousy liar. Can't tell a fib without blushing and fiddling with my hair. I felt my hand sneaking up to twirl, and managed to force it back down, but there was nothing I could do about the blood rushing to my cheeks.

Truman grinned. Spicer sighed. "Where's your boyfriend?"

"What boyfriend?"

Of course Rafe chose that moment to return to my side. I guess he'd recognized Spicer and Truman, and realized that his arrest wasn't imminent. I don't think he would have dared to show himself to anyone else, since your average Oak Hill cop would have assumed that a black man setting off the alarm on a three quarters of a million dollar house would be reason enough to arrest him. But Spicer and Truman know better. Or so I sincerely hoped.

Indeed, Spicer grinned. "Mr. Collier."

"Officers." Rafe nodded back. "Tammy having you run errands again?"

"The detective sent us down to check out the place. Just in case Briggs was holed up here."

"You can tell her she's too late," Rafe said. "He was here, but he ain't here now."

Both cops stiffened like pointers. "How d'you know he was here?" Truman asked.

Rafe glanced at him. "Shower curtain's wet. Hard to imagine who else it'd be."

So Tim had washed and put away the dishes, made the beds, taken his trash with him and probably wiped down the walls and chrome in the shower... but he hadn't been able to do anything about the shower curtain, so he'd left it, thinking it would dry and nobody would notice the difference.

"At least he left under his own steam," I said. All three of them turned to me, and I added, flushing, "Rather than someone dragging him off, kicking and screaming."

Spicer's eyes sharpened. "D'you have reason to think someone would wanna drag him off, Miz Martin?"

"He—" I caught Rafe's eye and stopped short of telling them that Tim had told me he couldn't remember committing murder. "If he didn't kill Brian Armstrong or Beau Riggins, whoever did do it might be after him."

"You got a reason to think he didn't kill Armstrong and Riggins?"

I hesitated.

"What about other suspects?" Rafe asked.

Spicer shook his head. "Can't tell you that, Mr. Collier."

Rafe nodded, so he probably hadn't expected anything else, nor for that matter cared whether he got an answer or not. "We'll leave you to it. Unless you're bringing us in?"

Spicer and Truman exchanged a look. "The detective would love that," Truman muttered. Spicer grimaced and raised his voice.

"Not this time."

"You'll tell her we were here, though?"

Spicer nodded. "No way around that."

Good. I wouldn't have to call Grimaldi myself, then. I could just wait for a phone call this afternoon. Spicer and Truman would let her know Rafe and I had been together, so she'd know things were back on track, and I could reliably expect a call in a couple hours, ostensibly to yell at me for being at Walker's house before her cops got here. In the process of talking, she'd get around to making sure I was OK with whatever Rafe was doing, too. I was getting to know the way she operated, little by little.

"We'll have to go through the place ourselves before we leave," Spicer said. "Can't take your word for it, Mr. Collier."

"Course not."

"Scram before I change my mind about hauling you in." He looked around the living room. "Nice place."

Truman nodded. Rafe nodded toward the back door and we tiptoed out.

Twenty-Two

"That could have gone worse," I said when we were in the car and on our way down the road.

He nodded. "Anybody else, and I'd have been on my way to lockup."

"You? What about me?"

"Ain't nobody wanna arrest you," Rafe said.

"You're not a criminal anymore, you know. You don't have to worry about anybody arresting you."

"There are people would arrest me for being in the wrong place at the wrong time, darlin'. For breathing the wrong air. Driving the wrong car. Looking at 'em wrong."

Maybe so.

"And besides, I just broke into a house. Burglary is a felony."

"We weren't going to steal anything."

"Don't matter," Rafe said. "Still a crime."

Huh. It certainly wasn't our first time making our way—or the first time I'd made my own way—into someone else's space. I'd never really considered that I was committing a crime before, though, since I'd never broken and entered with malice aforethought. It was always for other, nobler reasons. But if he was right...

"I'm a criminal?" I said.

"Fraid so, darlin'."

"Wow."

He grinned. "You prob'ly shouldn't sound so happy about it."

"Wait until my mother hears!"

The look he shot me was concerned, as if he wasn't quite sure I was joking. "You know who'll get blamed for this, don't you?"

He would. "I won't tell her," I said. "I'll just enjoy the knowledge in peace and quiet."

He looked relieved.

"And if Todd ever gives me a hard time about choosing you over him—" At the moment Todd and I weren't on speaking terms. Easier for both of us that way, "—I might mention it then."

"He prob'ly won't believe you," Rafe said, hitting the entrance ramp for I-65 north.

"Probably not. But you and I know better." I looked around. "Where are we going?"

"Back to East Nashville."

"Back to bed?"

He slanted another look my way, and a grin. "For such a nice girl, you're shameless."

"I told you before, I'm not that nice. And I have a lot of years to make up for."

"I'll make it up to you later. In the meantime, text Tim. Tell him I wanna see him."

"Oooh." I dug my phone out of my purse. "He won't be able to refuse that."

"That's the hope," Rafe said and concentrated on merging the car into traffic as we approached 100 Oaks Mall.

I sent my text, and it wasn't even a minute later that my phone signaled an incoming message. It was no surprise at all to see it was from Tim. *Where/when?*

"You've made his day," I told Rafe. "Where do you want to meet him?"

He shrugged. "Somewhere he'll feel comfortable."

I told Tim to choose, and a minute later, had a time and location. "Twenty minutes, Fort Negley."

Rafe made a face but changed lanes so the car was pointed in the right direction.

"He probably just wanted somewhere without a lot of people," I said.

"Pain in the ass," Rafe answered.

"It's not that bad. And you can't blame him for being cautious."

Rafe looked like he could, but he didn't say anything else, just maneuvered the car off the interstate at Wedgewood Avenue and proceeded in the direction of Fort Negley.

Nashville was occupied by Union forces during the War Against Northern Aggression—that's the Civil War to those of you on the other side of the Mason-Dixon line—and Fort Negley was part of that. The Union built it in 1862, of limestone and earth, using free blacks and conscripted slaves, and named it after Union Army Commander General James S. Negley. They were preparing for an attack by the Confederates, certain the South would want Nashville back under their control again. But when the Battle of Nashville finally began in December 1864, the fighting took place mostly farther south, so Fort Negley didn't end up playing a big part in any of it. The fort was abandoned after the war, although in an ironic twist, it served as a meeting place for the Ku Klux Klan during the reconstruction period.

People tried for a long time to do something with it, but for one reason or another, nothing ever happened. The Nashville Sounds baseball stadium was built on one side of St. Cloud Hill, and the Adventure Science Center, a children's museum, on the other, but most of Nashville forgot that Fort Negley existed, up there on top. But a few years ago a visitors' center appeared beside the big stone gates. Effort was made to clear off the trees and brush that had grown on the hilltop over the past century, and after many years of being inaccessible, it's now possible to climb the hill to the fort again.

The visitors' center is open longer hours during the summer, but now, on a sour February morning, it was closed. The parking lot was deserted when Rafe pulled the Volvo to a stop in the far corner.

"Looks like he isn't here yet," I said, pointing out the obvious.

Rafe nodded. "You wanna stay in the car, or go up the hill?"

I hesitated. It was cold and dreary, and I was wearing suede boots with heels, and aside from that, I'm not really the type to climb hills. Tim isn't either, so he might just want to talk in the car. But on the other hand... "Have you been here before?"

Rafe shook his head.

"Then let's go up. You should see it."

He opened the car door and came around to open mine. "Is it worth seeing?"

I shrugged. "The view is nice. Though it's a bit chilly."

"I'll keep you warm." He put an arm around my shoulders. I snuggled into his side as we headed up the paved path circling the top of the hill.

It took a few minutes to get there, and once on top, there honestly wasn't much to see. I imagine the fort might have been impressive back when it was built, but all that's left is a lot of low limestone walls, mostly overgrown, and two or three remaining doorways and staircases. Newly built wooden walkways snaked over and through the site so most of the time, we didn't actually set foot on the hallowed ground, we just sort of floated above it. There were signs posted everywhere, telling visitors to stay off the limestone walls and keep to the walkways.

The view was nice, though. On the side of the hill facing downtown, we could see the pyramid shaped roofs of the Adventure Science Center through the bare branches of the trees. And the downtown skyline stretched in front of us from side to side, the buildings spiky against the iron gray of the sky.

Back in the old days, the soldiers at the fort would have been able to look down on downtown Nashville. Not so these days: aside from the trees obscuring the view, the buildings were taller than the hill, so we looked straight at the middle to upper floors.

On the interstate circling the north side of the hill, tiny Matchbox cars chased one another from I-65 onto I-40 to the east and west. Beyond, I could see the church towers of Edgefield rising out of the gray tangle of branches on the other side of the river.

On the other side, the parking lot side, we could see further. There were no trees, and all of South Nashville was spread out below and beyond, with Peach Orchard Hill in the distance. To our right was Reservoir Park with the remains of Fort Casino, and to the left, the giant floodlights of the baseball stadium, taller than we were.

Directly below us, at the bottom of the hill, was the roof of the visitors' center and the big stone gates. As we watched, a pale blue car pulled into the lot and parked.

"There he is," I said.

Rafe nodded. "Think he'll come up here? Or wait in the car?"

"I guess that depends on how much privacy he wants. How afraid he is of being arrested."

"Not like I couldn't arrest him," Rafe said dryly.

"I don't think he's thought of that." I hadn't thought of it myself, if it came to that. "Could you?"

"Sure. You could arrest him too. Citizens arrest."

"That's different."

"Comes to the same thing in the end," Rafe said. "Tammy wants him, so she ain't gonna quibble about who brings him in."

Down in the lot, a small figure got out of the car and slammed the door. We watched as Tim crossed the lot and began trundling up the hill. He was dressed in an oversized plaid jacket that looked like something a lumberjack might wear, nothing he'd have in his own closet, and he had his hands stuffed in his pockets and his head drawn in like a turtle. The mist glistened like diamonds in his hair.

"Are you planning to arrest him?" I asked.

He shook his head. "I just wanna talk to him."

"About?"

"Turning himself in."

"He's not going to agree to that," I said.

"I have an idea."

"What kind of idea?"

"One that might help."

"Unless you're planning to bribe him with yourself—" and he'd better not be, "—I don't think that's going to work."

"We'll see." He turned me around, away from the view. "Let's go meet him."

I glanced over my shoulder down the hill. Tim was no longer visible. "OK."

We headed across the grass toward the Sally Gate, and the paved path beyond.

We'd walked for about a minute, surrounded by the soft whisper of rain and the low hum of cars from the interstate, when a shot rang out, shattering the silence of the Civil War shrine.

Tim had just come into view, just in time to shriek and fall to the ground.

"Shit!" Rafe took a few quick steps to the right, pulling me along with him, and tumbled us both into the wet bushes at the edge of the path. Spiky sticks poked at my face and hands.

Rafe fumbled behind himself and looked chagrined when he realized he didn't have his weapon. Nonetheless, he turned to me. "Stay here."

I clutched at his sleeve as he made to move away. "Where are you going?"

He glanced over his shoulder, down the path to where Tim was lying in a crumpled heap. It was impossible, from here, to see whether he was alive or dead. "Someone's gotta check on Tim."

"Someone has a gun!"

"And if I don't stop whoever it is, Tim's gonna be history. Stay."

He moved away, sticking close to the edge of path, but moving at a good clip. I hissed, but stayed. I've learned that he's more effective—and more prone to take care of himself—if I don't put myself in danger. It took everything I had to stay where I was, on my butt on the wet ground, with rain seeping through my coat into my buttocks, but I didn't follow him.

Another shot rang out. It came nowhere near me, but I lost my breath at the thought that the unknown gunman might be aiming for Rafe. Tim was down, already hit, and I was still and not very exciting, but Rafe was moving, determinedly making his way closer to Tim. If any one of us made for a good target, it was him.

Tim yelled, so at least he wasn't dead—and hopefully he didn't get hit again, either—and Rafe flattened himself against the ground. My heart stopped beating, until he lifted his head again. When nothing happened, he continued moving south.

I fumbled for my phone. I couldn't do anything else, sitting here, but I could call for help, without attracting the attention of whoever was shooting at us. At them.

But my pockets were empty, and I realized, with chagrin to match Rafe's upon realizing he'd left his gun behind, that I'd left my phone in my bag in the parked car down by the gates.

Rafe was almost on top of Tim now, and there had been no more shots, so I decided it would be safe to follow. But just in case, I moved on my hands and knees along the side of the path, shredding my nylons and snagging the edges of my coat on branches along the way. That way, at least Rafe couldn't yell at me to get down. Unless he wanted me to slither, commando-style, on my stomach, I couldn't get any closer to the ground.

Nothing happened. Nobody shot at me. Nobody shot at them again, either, not even when Rafe moved across the path to crouch next to Tim. I held my breath—now would definitely be the time to try for him, if he unknown gunman wanted to—but everything stayed quiet.

I moved into a crouch myself, so I could move a little faster, and reached them just in time to see Rafe shrug out of his leather jacket before peeling the snug T-shirt up over his head.

However badly Tim was hurt, it wasn't bad enough that he didn't manage a choked laugh. "That's almost worth dying for."

"You ain't dying." Rafe pulled the leather jacket back around his naked upper body before wadding the T-shirt into a ball and pressing it against Tim's stomach. Tim sucked in a breath and turned a shade paler. Not an easy task, when he was already the color of rice pudding.

Rafe glanced at me. "Hold this in place."

I swallowed back nausea and placed trembling hands on the wadded-up T-shirt and pressed down. The fabric was slowly soaking through with blood. It was pouring out rather fast, for a man Rafe had said wasn't dying. "I was going to call 911, but I don't have my phone. I left it in the car."

His voice was as even as mine was jittery. "I'll take care of it. Just stay with him."

"You're going?"

"Someone's gotta," Rafe said, "and I ain't letting you."

"Are you sure he's gone?" Or she, since shooting is an equal opportunity method of committing murder.

"Nobody's shooting at us anymore. Just keep him alive until I get back." He moved away, sticking to the treeline on the south side of the path, but going faster now.

I concentrated on keeping the T-shirt in place against Tim's stomach. He was so pale he was practically colorless, his eyes closed and his lashes spiky against sunken cheeks. I wasn't sure whether the wetness on his face was sweat, rain, or tears.

"Hang in there," I told him. "We'll get you to a doctor as soon as it's safe."

He nodded, but without opening his eyes.

"How do you feel?"

He licked dry lips before answering. "Like I'm dying."

"I don't think you are. Rafe said you weren't."

I lifted the T-shirt and peered underneath. Blood was still seeping sluggishly out of a wound low on Tim's flank, just above his hip. The sight turned my stomach, but it seemed as if the flow had already slowed. I lowered the T-shirt and applied pressure again. Tim turned white around the mouth,

"What happened?" I asked, both because I wanted to know and to take his mind off the pain.

He tried to shrug, but must have thought better of it. "No idea."

"Who wants you dead?"

"Nobody," Tim whispered.

"Someone must. They were aiming for you, not Rafe or me. Unless whoever it was has *really* bad aim."

Tim didn't answer, and I added, "Did you notice anyone following you?"

He shook his head, not surprisingly. If he had noticed someone following him, presumably he wouldn't have gone up here. It was a perfect place for an ambush. I wondered whether the unknown assailant had thought the place was empty or just hadn't cared that Rafe and I were here.

In the distance, I heard the sound of a car starting up.

I glanced over my shoulder, down the path, and saw that Rafe stiffened. He must have heard it too. After a moment he took off, out from the shelter of the trees and down the path at a dead run.

I just hoped whoever was in the car would be too concerned with trying to get away to see him coming.

And I also hoped that whoever was in the car—whether Rafe had gotten a good look at it or not—had actually been the gunman, and that he or she hadn't just been waiting for Rafe to leave to come out of hiding and finish Tim off, and me along with him.

But that didn't happen either. There were no shots, not up here where we were, and not down at the bottom of the the hill where Rafe was going. Everything was still, the silence broken only by the soft pitter-patter of rain, the chirping of birds, and Tim's belabored breathing.

"We'll get you to the hospital soon," I told him. "Rafe must be down in the parking lot by now. I'm sure the ambulance will be here in a few minutes."

Tim nodded. "Hurts," he told me, and now I was pretty certain at least some of the moisture on his face was tears.

I nodded. "I know. I was shot a couple of months ago. You'll feel better in a few days, I promise."

I lifted the T-shirt again. It was disturbingly soppy, and my palms were stained red, but the wound didn't look too bad. The flow of blood had definitely slowed. Hopefully that meant Tim wasn't in any danger of bleeding to death. Whether the bullet had nicked any internal organs was a different story, but I didn't figure there were too many of those down on his left side. Heart and lungs and kidneys were all farther north. And if his appendix had been hit—well, we all know they're useless anyway.

"Cold," Tim muttered, his teeth chattering. I wasn't sure whether it was the chilly air hitting the wound that bothered him, or whether it was just the shock of being shot in the first place, combined with the blood loss, the misty rain, and lying on the cold ground, but I lowered the wad of fabric again, before struggling out of my coat.

Rafe came loping back as I did my best to drape it over Tim without taking my hand off the sodden T-shirt. And I might as well admit it: without trying to touch the coat too much. Blood is almost impossible to get out of fabric, and my hands were almost dripping with it. And although my cashmere coat is several seasons out of fashion, I don't have the money to replace it with anything even remotely comparable right now. I didn't want to smear blood all over it if I could help it.

When I heard the sound of approaching footsteps, I jerked, and my heart starting up a limping run. Then came Rafe's voice. "Everything OK?"

I started breathing again. "Fine."

Tim's eyes fluttered open, and I figured Rafe probably tried to give him—and maybe me—something else to focus on when he shrugged out of the leather jacket to drape it over Tim in lieu of mine. "Put your coat back on, darlin'. You're getting wet."

"So are you," I said. "And at least I'm wearing something else. You're not. You'll catch your death out here in the rain with no clothes on."

"You can warm me up later." He winked.

Tim mumbled something, but I didn't ask him to repeat it, since I figured I already knew what it was.

"Did you call 911?" I asked instead, draping the coat over top of Tim, on top of Rafe's leather jacket.

Rafe nodded. "Ambulance is on its way. Let me take a look."

He nudged me aside, pushed away the coats and lifted the sodden T-shirt. Tim sucked in a breath and gritted his teeth.

"Looks good."

"I'll live?"

Rafe grinned. "Yeah. You'll have a scar, though."

"Like yours?"

Tim tried to lift his arm, but managed just a weak flutter and a grimace. Rafe glanced down at his own shoulder. "Yeah."

"Hot." Tim's lips curved.

So did Rafe's. "You're doing great. Just hang in there. The ambulance is coming."

Tim nodded and closed his eyes again. I tilted my head and listened. Far away, in the distance, I could hear the sound of sirens approaching.

"I'll go down and meet them," I said. "Show them where to go." And give Tim the thrill of having Rafe—a topless Rafe—all to himself for a few minutes.

"Be careful," Rafe told me.

"Always."

The ability of throwing his own standard response back at him gave me no little satisfaction as I headed down the walkway and the hill toward the parking area and gates.

Twenty-Three

"What was that all about?" Rafe asked some twenty minutes later.

We were standing in the lobby of Vanderbilt University Hospital's emergency room, after watching Tim being taken inside for bullet removal. The attending physician had been kind enough to stop for a moment to reassure me that he'd be just fine, and now Rafe was arching his brow at me.

"What do you mean?" I turned in the direction of the double doors. "He was just telling me not to worry."

He followed me toward the outside. "You never mentioned this guy before."

I glanced at him over my shoulder. Surely he wasn't jealous? Was he?

"I've only met him once. He was the attending physician when Kylie Mitchell had her car accident back in December. Simon Ramsey. I had to tell him I was Kylie's sister so he'd let me—and Aislynn—in to see her."

We passed through the sliding doors and out.

"He remembered you," Rafe said.

"So? I remembered him, too."

"That's different. He was your friend's doctor. You were just one of, I'm sure, a lot of friends and relatives coming through the ER."

I shrugged. "So maybe he likes blondes."

"Yeah," Rafe said. "Maybe he does."

I glanced at him. Opened my mouth to inquire how he could possibly be jealous of a man I'd met only once, and closed it again.

"Do you think he'll be OK?" I asked instead. "Tim?"

He glanced at me. "He'll be fine. The doc said so."

Right. "What happened?"

"Somebody shot him," Rafe said.

"Beyond that."

He shrugged. The open leather jacket slithered over wet, naked skin. "You were there. You know as much as I do."

"You're sure they were shooting at him, right? And not you?"

"If they were shooting at me," Rafe said, "they missed by a football field. Anybody coming after me has better aim than that."

Good to know. Or not.

"Anyway, ain't like nobody's gonna look at Tim and think he's me."

No. Nobody in his right mind would make that kind of mistake.

I turned my head to look at him, at those faded jeans hanging low on his hips, wet on the bottoms, and the smooth skin and ridged abdomen visible under the open leather jacket. And felt my body get warmer in spite of the chilly air and misty rain. "Aren't you cold?"

"I could zip up," Rafe said, without making any move to actually do so. He held my gaze for a moment. "You want me to?"

"Are you cold?"

"Not when you look at me like that."

"We should go home and get out of these wet clothes. Maybe get under the blankets for a while. To warm up."

He grinned. "You want me."

"Always. And I want to wash my hands. They're bloody."

His face sobered when I held them up. "You did a good job, Savannah. I'm proud of you."

"Thank you." That actually meant a lot, coming from him. Gave me a nice, warm glow inside, different from the glow I got from watching him naked under the black leather.

He put an arm around my shoulders and steered me toward the Volvo. "Let's get you home and cleaned up. Out of those wet clothes. And under the blankets."

"You want me," I said, even as I felt just a little bit stupid, and maybe a bit risqué, doing so.

He grinned down at me. "Always. And I gotta remind you why you picked me, don't I, and not one of the doctors or lawyers?"

I hadn't picked him because he was good in bed—although it hadn't hurt—but I didn't bother telling him so, just let him put me inside the car and close my door. If he felt the need to prove something to me, who was I to tell him not to exert himself?

I HAD GOTTEN RID OF AS much of the blood on my hands as I'd been able to in the emergency room sink, but there were still traces of it stuck underneath my nails and my cuticles, and I didn't want to touch anything until I'd washed with bleach and about a gallon of antibacterial soap. So I stood just inside my front door and watched Rafe shrug out of the leather jacket and hang it on the hook in the hallway. My knees went weak at the sight, and I wanted to touch him, to throw myself in his arms and have him take me to bed, but I couldn't.

He turned to look at me, and he must have read the feelings on my face because he chuckled. "Let me help you with that, darlin'."

I wasn't entirely sure what 'that' was, whether he was referring to my frustration or the fact that I couldn't get undressed, but he started by helping me out of my coat. He pulled it carefully down over my arms and hands and hung it, equally carefully, on a hanger so it wouldn't lose its shape while it dried.

Then he got down on his knees in front of me, and pulled my boots off, one after the other. He shook his head over my shredded nylons and dirty knees, before he skimmed his hands up the outsides of my thighs under the skirt.

I lost my breath, of course, although all he did was peel the ruined pantyhose down and off. "Lift your foot, darlin'. Good girl. And the other one."

I lifted each foot in turn, bracing my wrists on his shoulders since I couldn't brace my hands there, and since I doubted I could have managed to stay upright without the support.

When he got to his feet again, I wasn't sure whether I was disappointed or not. When his fingers went to the front of my blouse, I decided I'd reserve judgment.

He made short work of the buttons, and pushed the still damp blouse off my shoulders and down to the floor. The skirt was next: a quick tug on the zipper on his part and a hip-wiggle on mine, and I stood in front of him in a virginal white lace bra and matching panties.

He smiled, of course, even as I blushed and resisted the urge to try to cover myself. Two months of regular nudity hadn't been enough to turn the good girl I'd been brought up to be into a wanton seductress. I was still a little uncomfortable with the way I wanted him. I had certainly never wanted anyone else the same way.

He tilted his head. "Did you and Bradley ever have shower sex?"

I shook my head. "I told you. Bradley was traditional in bed. That meant doing it in bed."

"Good," Rafe said and gathered me up. I wrapped my legs around his waist and my arms around his neck and hung on, monkey-style. "I won't have to worry about measuring up."

"You've never had to worry about measuring up." The personal equipment that was currently nestled against the apex of my thighs, nudging me with every step he took toward the bathroom and the shower, blew Bradley's out of the water. And he more than measured up in every other way too. I couldn't imagine Bradley ever undressing me so sweetly and carefully, and with so much banked heat in his eyes. And I certainly couldn't imagine Bradley ever turning on the shower to the perfect temperature before stripping off my lingerie and carrying me into the spray without bothering to take his own jeans off.

Not that Bradley had ever worn denim. He was a slacks-and-khakis sort of guy. No black leather, and no faded jeans hanging low on his hips, dipping ever lower as they took on water.

"What about...?" I gestured.

"Later." He filled his hands with soap and began washing me, big, hard hands slipping slickly over my skin. The only blood was on my hands, but I wasn't about to complain. "Over," he mumbled, "under, below, between..."

Since action was suited to words, it was hard for me to get my voice to cooperate, but I managed a single word. "Poetry?"

The corner of his mouth quirked up. I wondered whether it was something he told all the girls—I wondered whether it was *his* first time for shower sex too, and decided it probably wasn't; he was too good at it—and then I decided it didn't matter. He was mine now, and he was obviously enjoying himself. Did it really matter what he'd done, and with whom, before?

When I reached for the waistband of his now soaked-through jeans, the muscles in his stomach quivered and he growled a warning. "Careful."

"Why?" Doubt reared its head immediately, of course. Doubt and insecurity.

He pinned me with a glance. "The second those come off, it's all over. They're the only thing that stands between you and being nailed to that wall behind you."

"But..." Didn't he want me to return the favor? I'd rather been looking forward to soaping my hands and washing him, too. Over, under, below and between. All that soft skin and hard muscles under my now-clean hands.

"All I want is inside you," Rafe said. "And the second you take those off, that's where I'm gonna be. So you'd better make damn sure when you pull that zipper down, you're ready."

I grinned and pulled down the zipper.

"Did you get a look at the car?" I asked an hour later. We were naked, under the covers, warm and mostly recovered.

"Car?"

"The one the gunman at Fort Negley drove."

"Damn." He turned toward the night stand and swore.

"What?" I said.

He glanced around. "My phone."

"It wasn't in your pants pocket, I hope?" Because if so, it was dead by now, drowned in the bottom of the tub.

Chagrin flashed across his face before he shook his head. "Jacket."

"Hallway."

He slipped out of bed and padded toward the door. I watched, while I lamented the fact that playtime seemed to be over for now.

He came back a few seconds later, to toss the phone on top of the covers. "Tammy must be talking to Tim. Her phone went to voicemail."

"You didn't answer my question," I said, as he sat down on the edge of the bed.

He nodded. "Yeah, I saw it. That's why I wanted to call her. To let her know. I forgot all about it till you asked."

"What kind of car was it?"

"Mini Cooper," Rafe said.

I stared at him. "What kind?"

"A blue Mini Cooper. With a white stripe down the middle."

"You're kidding."

He shook his head. "Why?"

"That's the kind of car Beau Riggins drives. Or drove."

"He wasn't driving it this morning," Rafe said.

Obviously not, since he was dead. "The police would have confiscated his car, surely?"

"You'd think. Unless it wasn't at his house when they got there."

"I saw a car like that a couple days ago. Monday night. When I was leaving Mrs. Armstrong's house. I thought maybe it was Beau coming to visit the widow."

He arched a brow. "What gave you that idea?"

"She'd mentioned having a cleaning service. I saw the car turning down the street when I drove away. And I knew he slept with Connie Fortunato last year. I guess my mind added two and two together."

Rafe was silent for a moment. "Did you go back around the block?"

"Of course. And knocked on the door and told her I'd lost my cell phone. She wouldn't let me in. Left me standing on the porch. Didn't I tell you this?"

"You didn't mention what kind of car it was," Rafe said and stood up. "C'mon."

"Where?" I watched as he opened a bureau drawer and pulled out a pair of black boxers.

"Mrs. Armstrong's place. I want a look around for that car." He reached into the drawer again and grabbed a bra—blue satin—and tossed it my way. It hit the bed with a plop. A pair of panties—pink lace—followed a second later.

"Those don't match," I pointed out.

He shot me a glance, in the process of tugging the snug cotton up over his legs. "I won't tell nobody. Unless you wanna stay here and have me go alone?"

"No." I scrambled out of bed and began putting the mismatched lingerie on. It wasn't like my mother would ever know, after all. And the chances that I'd have an accident and would end up in the hospital, where Simon Ramsey would see my underwear, was surely a long shot.

Five minutes later we were in the car on our way to Erin Armstrong's house. I was driving, so Rafe could keep dialing Tamara Grimaldi. She must have turned off her phone, however, and wasn't simply screening calls, because if she'd noticed the back-to-back calls from his number, I don't think she would have ignored him.

Eventually, when he couldn't get through, he ended up calling the Metro PD and leaving a message for Spicer and Truman, telling dispatch to let them know where we were going and why. And since that was all we could do, he settled back to wait.

He didn't have to wait long. Another minute or two, and we pulled up to the curb across the street from the Armstrong residence.

"No Mini Cooper," I said. "There wasn't the other night either. I probably just made a mistake and it belonged somewhere else." Erin Armstrong might just have been rude to me because she'd thought she was settled for the night, in her robe with her wine, and then I came back to disturb her again.

"Maybe," Rafe said, "maybe not. Drive around the block and see if there's an alley."

I took my foot off the brake and the Volvo slid away from the curb. "I'm sure there is. This is an old neighborhood. Pre-1900. They built in grids back then, with alleys."

"Let's see if there's a garage back there."

Sure. I turned the corner and took a left into the alley behind the Armstrong house.

As it turned out, there were a lot of garages fronting the alley, including one that belonged to the Armstrongs. A nice, big two-story one, with two bays and what was either guest quarters or storage up above. Or maybe just a vaulted ceiling in the garage itself, although that didn't make a whole lot of sense, I guess.

Rafe slipped out of the car and over to the garage. I idled while he disappeared around the side and back.

A minute later he came back, and bent to talk to me through the window. "Car's there."

"Beau's car? A Mini Cooper? Blue with white stripes?"

He nodded. "I don't think it's Beau's car, though. This one has California tags."

"Beau's from Michigan. Grimaldi told me." And I think I would have noticed if Beau's car had had anything but the normal Tennessee plates. I'd only seen it a few times, but that's the kind of thing you notice. And remember. "That's quite a coincidence, isn't it?"

"Not that big," Rafe said. "The factory did produce more than one blue Mini Cooper."

Well, sure.

"Come take a look." He held out a hand.

I turned the Volvo off and made my way over to the back of the wooden building, where there was a high window. Rafe gave me a boost so I could see in, and sure enough, there was a blue Mini Cooper inside the garage. With a California license plate clearly visible. H0TSH0T, it said, with zeros in place of the O's.

"Someone thinks highly of himself," I remarked when Rafe lowered me back to the ground.

He nodded. "Could be Armstrong's car. Or Mrs. Armstrong's."

"Erin drives a Lexus SUV. She parked it at the curb the other night. And it wasn't Brian Armstrong who drove this on Monday night. He was already dead."

"Helluva lot of dead people driving around in this car."

I nodded. "Is this the Mini Cooper you saw leaving Fort Negley this morning?"

Rafe shrugged. "Looks the same. But I didn't get a look at the tags. Wrong angle."

I glanced around. And called up the mental picture of the front of the house. "The Lexus isn't here." Not in the garage and not parked at the curb out front.

He glanced at me. "So?"

"She must be at work. The place is empty. We could go inside the garage and see if the Mini's been outside in the last couple of hours. If it has, there might be water and sand in the tires, right?"

He nodded.

"If the car stays inside the garage much longer, that might dry up."

He grinned. "You asking me to commit another felony, darlin'?"

"Well..." It wasn't like I was asking him to break into the house, right? That seemed a lot worse. This was just the garage. And we weren't planning to steal anything. I just wanted to look at the car.

Maybe it was a felony, as he'd pointed out several times now. But it didn't feel like one.

"While you stand there and dither," Rafe said mildly, "how about I just go open the door?"

I dithered some more. He shook his head and walked away.

I trotted after. "Shouldn't we at least make sure the place really is empty?"

"Sure," Rafe said. "Give her a call. Make up an excuse. Find out where she is."

Easy for him to say. I'm not used to fibbing. But I squared my shoulders, scanned through my call logs until I found Erin's number, and dialed.

She picked up a second later, her voice brisk and businesslike when she introduced herself.

"Hi," I said apologetically. "This is Savannah Martin, from LB&A. We met a few days ago?"

There was a pause, while she either tried to place me or wondered why I called.

"I... um... just wanted to check in with you. See how you were."

"I'm fine," Erin said. And added, "Everything considered."

"I took the house off the market two days ago. By now it should have trickled down to all the websites. I hope you've stopped getting requests for showings?"

"Yes, thank you," Erin said.

Not much I could say to that, beside, "Good." While I racked my brain for something else to move the conversation forward, she interrupted. "This isn't a good time to talk. I'm at work."

"Oh." *Thank you.* "Of course. I'm so sorry. I'll let you go. Please let me know if there's anything else I can do for you."

Erin promised she would and hung up, but not before giving me a little parting shot. "I'm glad you found your cell phone, Savannah."

The smirk was evident in her voice. I grimaced and dropped the phone in my pocket before turning my attention to the garage.

Rafe hadn't waited for me. The garage door stood open and he was already inside the dusky room, peering at the Mini's tires. As usual, I took a moment to enjoy the way his jeans fit across his posterior before pulling the door shut behind me, just in case someone should happen to walk by and notice the garage sitting open. "How does it look?"

"Good," Rafe said. "Water and dirt in the tires. Mud spatters on the chassis. We have a winner."

"I wonder whose car it is. Erin drove an SUV the other day, and when Brian moved out, I'm sure he took his car with him. He'd need it to get around." Nashville isn't the kind of town where anyone who doesn't have to chooses to use public transportation.

"Might be a toy," Rafe said. "Maybe she or Brian brought it from California to drive on the weekends. While they kept the fancy cars for work."

Maybe. But— "If so, the plates would be expired or changed to Tennessee plates by now. Grimaldi told me the Armstrongs had been here a couple years."

"Tags are current," Rafe said.

"Maybe there's registration information in the glove box."

He reached for the passenger door handle. The door opened, and he leaned in and came back with a handful of papers. Registration, proof of insurance, even a photo ID card, all in the same of— "Neil Donnelly," Rafe read.

"Irish name. Like Erin. Maybe it's her brother." I reached for the paperwork. While he handed it over, I added, "Unless she has another brother, he's also her alibi for her husband's murder. She was on the phone with him at 1 o'clock on Friday night. 11 PM on the west coast."

"If he got the news Saturday morning," Rafe said, obviously reading my mind, "he coulda made it here by Monday night, when you saw the car."

"If he drove straight through and didn't sleep for three days straight."

Rafe shrugged.

I peered down at the paperwork in my hand and added, "Anyway, he didn't."

"How d'you know?"

"Because if this is him," I brandished the ID card; it showed him as a card-carrying member of Bottoms Up, an exclusive gay hangout in L.A., "he was here long enough to get friendly with Beau Riggins."

"No kidding?"

"None at all. This is the twink from Beau's Facebook page. Sally said she'd seen him at Chaps."

Rafe had his mouth open to answer, but he never got to say a word—not about that—because there was a sound from above— where I had surmised that there might be an apartment—and there stood Neil Donnelly himself, in the flesh.

Twenty-Four

It was rather nice flesh, too, if you happened to go for that kind of thing.

He looked just like his picture: young, cute, and gay, in slightly too tight pants and slightly too well-coiffed hair, with a shirt that was open several inches too far down his chest. He was almost angelic-looking, with that golden crown and those bright blue eyes.

The only thing that detracted from the picture was the gun in his hand. It looked too big and heavy for his rather slender wrist, although in justice to him, he had no problem keeping it pointed. As he came down the stairs and stopped in front of me, the gun didn't waver at all.

I've looked down the barrels of a few guns over the past six or seven months—more than I'm comfortable with, strictly speaking—but it never gets easier. At least not until you've looked down the barrels of as many as Rafe has, and between you and me, I hope I never get to a point where being threatened with another gun becomes commonplace.

But I digress. And anyway, Rafe turned rigid at the sight of this one too, although I think it was more because it was pointed at me than for any other reason. And probably because there was nothing he could do, not with the gun pointed squarely between my breasts. From the other side of the car, he couldn't even step in front of me, and by the time he'd made it over here, Neil would have had time to pump a half dozen bullets into me. I could see Rafe's body tense, as if he was thinking about it, but he didn't actually move.

Neil glared at him. "You again. I should have put a bullet in you when I had the chance."

"You tried," Rafe answered. His voice was light and his lips curved in a smirk, although I recognized that stone cold fury in his eyes that I've never seen on his own behalf, only ever on mine. "I can't help it that your aim's for shit."

Neil flushed angrily. "It isn't too late."

Rafe actually grinned and spread his arms. "Take your best shot. If you think you can manage to hit me this time."

Neil's eyes narrowed and the gun wavered, from me and in the direction of Rafe.

"Have you lost your mind?" I exclaimed, and Neil's attention turned back in my direction again. Rafe scowled, but I'm used to that.

Under other circumstances, I might have tried to talk my way out of there. Pretending I had no idea what Neil was guilty of, and just trying to get out of the garage with our skins intact. But he'd already given himself away when he recognized Rafe, so that was not an option.

The second best thing would be to keep him preoccupied and distracted, I figured. Maybe Rafe could figure out a way to take him down without getting either of us shot in the process.

I prepared to build rapport. I've been brought up to put a man at his ease, although I don't think my mother ever imagined the training would come in handy in situations like this. "You're Erin's brother, right?"

He nodded.

"How long have you been in Nashville?"

"A couple of weeks," Neil said.

Since before Brian died, then. Not that that came as a surprise, since I was beginning to realize some things I hadn't realized before, when I hadn't known he was here.

"What I don't understand," I told him, not only to draw his attention away from Rafe but also because I really did want to know, "is how Tim got involved in this."

Neil contemplated me in silence for a few seconds before he deigned to answer. "He was in the wrong place at the wrong time."

"You mean, he was at Chaps on Friday night? You didn't plan that?"

He shook his head. "I was going to pin the murder on Beau, but then Tim got into it with Brian and it seemed like fate." He shrugged, the motion spare and elegant.

"They got into it?"

"Brian wanted Tim to go home with him," Neil said. "He wasn't inclined to take no for an answer."

"So they argued?"

"And everybody saw and heard them. It was too good an opportunity to pass up."

"So until then you were going to pin the murder on Beau? Why?"

"It was his fault," Neil said, boyish face darkening.

"What was his fault?"

"He slept with Erin," Neil said. "If it hadn't been for that, none of this would have happened."

"What do you mean?"

He squinted at me. And then I guess he decided that if he was going to shoot me anyway, he might as well satisfy my curiosity. "If Beau hadn't slept with my sister, Brian wouldn't have moved out and started divorce proceedings, and if he hadn't done that, we wouldn't have had to kill him."

"So it was for the money?"

"No," Neil said, "it wasn't for the money. I wanted to kill him all along. It was Erin who told me to wait, to make him suffer. But if he was leaving, we couldn't make him suffer anymore. So he had to die."

I understood all the words he used, but I had no idea what he was talking about. "What do you mean, you wanted to kill him all along? Since when? Since your sister married him?"

That was rather extreme, if you asked me. My family wasn't thrilled about my involvement with Rafe, but I sincerely hoped that none of them would ever consider murder to rid themselves of him.

"Before that," Neil said.

Before Erin married him? "Why?"

"Because he ruined my life."

I looked at him. He didn't look ruined. He was young and handsome and seemed to be healthy. Granted, best as I could figure it, he was also headed to jail for the rest of his life for a couple of murders, but really, apart from that, he didn't seem like he should be complaining.

As Rafe often tells me, I'm not a good liar. My face gives away my feelings in a most unladylike manner, according to my mother.

Neil flushed. "Six years ago," he said, his voice almost choked with anger, "I was sixteen. I knew I was gay, and I was just starting to figure things out, to experiment. And I met Brian."

Ouch. I could imagine what happened only too well, from what he said, and what he didn't. Young, impressionable Neil going out looking for understanding and reassurance and guidance, maybe even hoping for love, to figure out who he was and how he fit into the world, and instead falling into the greedy mitts of an experienced, older, seasoned sexual sadist. "I'm sorry."

"He hurt me," Neil said, his voice brittle. "He hurt me, and he liked it. He told me I had to learn to like it too. He didn't let me leave until I told him I did. Until I thanked him for hurting me. And until I signed a paper saying I'd submitted voluntarily."

My stomach twisted, and I had to focus on keeping my voice level. "Did you report him to the police? Afterwards?"

"No," Neil said.

"Why not?"

"Because they wouldn't believe me. They would say I was looking for it. That I agreed to it by being there, and being drunk, and not fighting hard enough..."

"You were sixteen. Underage. They would have listened."

He shook his head. "Erin was raped once. That's what happened to her. They made it sound like it was her fault."

"I'm sorry." It does happen that way sometimes. I've heard of it myself. The whole idea of putting the victim on trial because she's wearing a tight dress and high heels and because she was there and drinking and that must mean she wanted it. It isn't good, and it isn't right, but it happens.

"We decided to take care of things ourselves instead," Neil said. "We got pictures of the way I looked, and we told him we had DNA he'd missed, that proved he was guilty. He offered to pay, but not enough. And I didn't want his money. I wanted him to suffer."

"So Erin married him?"

Neil smirked. "She got access to everything he owned. No prenuptial agreement. Full reign of everything. And she could make his life as miserable as she wanted. As *we* wanted. He's had to keep his pecker in his pants for six years now. No going around hurting anyone who couldn't fight back."

"But then they moved to Nashville?"

Neil nodded. "And my stupid sister started fucking the help. And when Brian found out, he moved out and filed for divorce. Adultery is still reason for divorce in this God-forsaken backwater. There was nothing Erin could do. I wanted to kill her."

"You would have lost everything. The money. The hold over Brian. The chance to make him suffer."

He nodded. "Couldn't have that. The bastard had to go, before he could leave us with nothing."

"So you and Erin decided it was time to kill him."

He shrugged, as if it was no big deal. "I always assumed we'd have to. I was looking forward to it. This just meant picking up the pace a little."

Of course. He had to assume Brian was looking for a way out, and would find one sooner or later. I was honestly surprised Brian hadn't just killed Erin first, and gotten out from under. Then again, he couldn't have imagined he'd get away with that, I guess. He probably figured Neil would get him if he did. "So you came to Nashville too. And made friends with Beau?"

Neil's mouth twisted. "We had so much in common. Even drove the same kind of car."

Sure. "So what happened Friday night?"

"We went to Chaps," Neil said. "I figured Brian would be there, and I was going to give him Beau. Beau deserved it, after ruining everything."

"I didn't think Beau was gay."

Neil giggled. "You slip enough roofies in a guy's drink, he doesn't care what he does. Or who."

Yowch. I tried not to let my reaction show, but I'm afraid I didn't quite manage.

Neil didn't seem to notice. "But then we saw Brian hitting on this guy who wanted nothing to do with him, and Beau told me it was the real estate agent. The fucker who was selling my sister's house."

"It wasn't his fault about the house," I said. "The realtor has nothing to do with it."

"Bullshit," Neil answered succinctly. "When he left, I told Brian I'd make a deal with him. I'd get him the guy if he'd stay married to my sister."

"And he believed that?"

"Of course not," Neil said. "But he believed that I believed it."

Ah.

"He said he would, and I took Beau and followed the realtor to the Cock-Pit."

"Didn't Beau think that was strange?"

"I told him I wanted to meet the guy," Neil said with another elegant shrug. "So Beau introduced us."

"Why doesn't Tim remember that?"

"Probably because of the roofies I put in his drink." He smiled.

Roofies. Rohypnol. And here I thought only women had to worry about that.

It certainly explained why Tim couldn't remember anything that happened Friday night, though. I've never been on the receiving end of date rape drugs, but I've heard they make you do things you'd never do under normal circumstances, and that they have the additional benefit—to whoever slips them to you—of making you forget everything you did, and with whom.

"Beau showed me where the realtor lived," Neil continued, "and then he left. I got the guy inside and into the bedroom. He was so out of it by then, he had no idea what was happening. When I let Brian in he didn't say a word."

God. My face twisted. And I wanted to ask whether he'd let Brian have his way with Tim before he—Neil—killed him, but on the other hand I didn't want to know, so I didn't ask. Tim had said no, so I figured I'd just go with that.

"And then I stabbed him and left him there," Neil said, in the same tone of voice as he'd told me about Beau showing him where Tim lived before driving away. As if it were no more significant than that.

I pulled it together enough to ask another question. "What about the phone call to your sister? You were her alibi, right? I guess nobody realized, when she spoke to her brother in California, her brother was actually just a few miles away."

He smiled, as if I'd complimented him. In a sense, I guess I had. "That was my idea. She couldn't leave the house. The police would see that the alarm system had been turned on and off and on again in the middle of the night. But I wanted her to hear him scream."

I opened my mouth, but nothing came out. After a second I closed it again.

During this conversation, Rafe had been so quiet I had almost forgotten he was there. Now he spoke into the silence. "And then you had to kill Beau cause he knew you'd been at Tim's house that night?"

Neil nodded. "I used the sleeping pills from six years ago. Turns out they were still strong enough to knock him out. And then I mixed up a little gas to finish the job. Cleaned up after myself and left."

He sounded so cool and calm about it all. So reasonable, like it all made perfect sense and only someone with no sense of reason or justice could possibly object to what he'd done.

"I suppose you didn't have a choice when it came to shooting Tim, either." I could hear the edge in my voice; I just hoped Neil wouldn't take objection to it.

"He might remember something," Neil said earnestly. "He saw me, you know. Spoke to me. Might remember that I took him home."

"But why shoot him? How did you think you'd get away with that?" Surely random violence would be stretching credulity a yard or two too far at this point.

"It was supposed to look like he shot himself," Neil said, irritated. "I had it all planned out. He'd be found, whenever he was found, with the gun beside him. Everyone would think he'd committed suicide out of guilt for killing Brian and Beau."

"With your gun? Or is it your sister's gun?"

Neil smirked. "It's Beau's gun. I took it with me from his place."

Of course. And since it was supposed to look like Tim had killed Beau as well as Brian, it would make perfect sense that he'd kill himself with Beau's gun. When in actuality, Tim had been nowhere near Beau's house at all. The 'friend' he'd been staying with all along had been the absent Walker.

"So what happened? This morning?"

Neil's face darkened. "You were there. I didn't see you until it was too late. I couldn't finish the job when you were there."

So we'd actually saved Tim's life. That made me feel a little better about not telling Grimaldi that he was camping out at Walker's place last night. I hadn't risked his life by not speaking up; I had actually saved it by being at Fort Negley.

"I guess that's it," Rafe said with a glance at me across the Mini's roof rack.

I nodded. I'd gotten all my questions answered, and there was no sign of the cavalry. "What now?"

"Now," Neil said, "we get in the car and drive somewhere where I can kill you without alerting the neighbors."

Rafe smirked. "Hard to get away with much in these upscale neighborhoods."

Indeed. "That isn't going to work," I told Neil when he made shooing motions toward the Mini.

He squinted at me. "Why is that?"

"My car is parked in the alley. It's blocking your garage doors. You won't be able to get out."

Chagrin crossed his face, or maybe it was annoyed petulance, like the look Dix's youngest, three-year-old Hannah, gets, when she's refused another cookie.

"I can go move it," I suggested, while I reflected that if we didn't get out of this situation alive, I could forget about getting to Sweetwater for Abigail's birthday party tomorrow.

If I were found in a ditch tomorrow morning, my mother would probably blame Rafe. And Rafe would probably agree with her, except he'd be dead too. He'd got to his death believing he'd failed in protecting me, though.

However, the fact that Rafe was with me, actually made me feel better about my chances—our chances—of survival. We'd taken down Perry Fortunato together. And Hector Gonzales. And most recently, Desmond Johnson. Bigger baddies than Neil Donnelly could ever hope to be.

The only reason he was still in the driver's seat, metaphorically speaking, was because of the gun. If I could get the gun away from him, he didn't stand a chance against Rafe. Rafe had him by five inches or more, and probably thirty or forty pounds, all of it muscle. If it hadn't been for the gun, and especially for the fact that it was pointed at me, Neil would have been a smear on the concrete by now.

He was, understandably, more concerned about Rafe than he was about me. Which meant that when he told us we'd take my car, and gestured with the gun toward the doorway, most of his attention was on Rafe. "You go first."

The gun was on me, as insurance that Rafe wouldn't do anything stupid on his way through the door, but Neil wasn't actually looking at me. He was watching Rafe, preparing for an attack. Which made it pretty easy, everything considered, to swing my purse and knock the gun out of his hand.

It went off, of course, and the bullet whizzed past me with a few inches to spare before punching through the blue metal of the Mini Cooper, leaving a jagged hole. And the car wasn't the only thing that took a hit. A second later, Rafe's fist hit Neil's jaw with enough force to knock the young man off his feet and onto the concrete garage floor. I had to jump out of the way to avoid being felled like a bowling pin. Rafe landed on top of him, and if Neil hadn't already been unconscious, from the double whammy of a fist to the jaw and the back of his head meeting the concrete, that would have done it.

Rafe glanced up at me. "You OK, darlin'?"

He wasn't even breathing hard.

"Fine," I said. "Should I get the gun?" It had landed a few feet away, halfway under the car.

He shook his head. "He ain't going nowhere for a while. And when he does, that gun's gonna be the least of his concerns. Toss me that fishing line over there."

I fetched the line from the hook on the wall and handed it to him, and watched as he secured Neil's hands, none too gently. Unconscious, with his face smooth and those angry eyes closed, Neil looked younger than twenty two, almost innocent.

"Don't start feeling sorry for him," Rafe said, clearly reading my face, or else my thoughts. "He did this to himself."

"Of course. Although it was horrible, what happened to him. What Brian did to him."

Rafe shrugged. "Stuff happens. That ain't no excuse for killing innocent people."

It wasn't. "I'll go try see what's taking Spicer and Truman so long," I said. "And if I can't get hold of them, I'll call 911 and request a pickup for Neil."

Rafe nodded. "I'll stay with him. If he wakes up, I'll put him back under for a while. Don't wanna risk him trying to escape."

No, indeed. "Enjoy yourself," I told him, and headed out of the garage and into the alley, where I hoped the cell phone reception would be better.

Twenty-Five

I went to Abigail's birthday by myself the next evening, since Wendell had called to say that Rafe's interview with the TBI had been scheduled for 4 o'clock that afternoon. Inconvenient, but I didn't want him to miss it, so I told him that of course he had to go, and I'd see him when I got home. Part of me hadn't expected him to come with me anyway, although of course I'd been hopeful. But it was going to take time, I was slowly coming to realize that. We'd jumped one hurdle this week, and made it safely to the other side. Getting him used to dealing with my family, and them used to seeing him, could wait. God willing, we'd have plenty of time yet to accomplish that.

So I made the drive to Sweetwater by myself.

It's a small town a little more than an hour south of Nashville, southeast of Columbia and on the way to Pulaski, famous for being the birthplace of the Ku Klux Klan. Pulaski, I mean, not Sweetwater. Sweetwater isn't the birthplace of anyone or anything particularly well known, unless it's Rafe. He was certainly infamous in and around Maury County ten or fifteen years ago.

My siblings and I grew up in the Martin Mansion, a big antebellum house on a little knoll outside town, on the Columbia Highway. Back in the day, it was a full-fledged working plantation, and after the Civil War, during which the then-owner of the mansion perished, my great-great-great-grandmother Caroline had a relationship with one of the grooms, which resulted in my great-great-grandfather William. My mother doesn't know this, but that's the reason my sister Catherine, who takes after our father, is short and curvy with sallow skin and coarse, dark hair. Dix and I, who take after the Georgia Calverts, mother's family, are taller and blond.

I'm keeping the information in reserve, for whenever mother steps inexcusably out of line as far as Rafe is concerned.

I wasn't going to the mansion. I would end up there later, after the family party, to spend the night in my old room, but Abigail's birthday celebration was at Dix's house.

He lives in a pseudo-Tudor in a subdivision of other brick McMansions: English manor homes and French Chateaus and Tuscan villas. They're all located on postage-stamp sized lots, with so little room between them that you could stand in the living room in one and hand a cup of sugar to your neighbor in the other without ever leaving your house... had it not been for the fact that there are no windows. All the windows are either in the facade or the back wall. If there were windows in the side walls, you could also stand at your own window and look directly into your neighbors bedroom, and nobody wants that.

I was the last one there when I pulled up to the curb just before six. The usual rush hour traffic had been made even worse by the rain, and I'd been delayed by two separate accidents, one of which involved multiple cars. Best as I could make out, it was just a chain reaction of fender benders and nothing serious. But it had blocked a couple of lanes, and backed up traffic for several miles.

Dix's driveway was full of cars. I recognized my sister Catherine's minivan, my mother's Chrysler, and Sheriff Satterfield's truck. My heart sank when I recognized Todd's SUV.

I had expected him to be here, of course. Not only because his father is my mother's main squeeze, but because Todd has been Dix's best friend since they were both in diapers. And with Sheila gone, Dix needed all the support and love he could gather around himself and his daughters.

Nonetheless, I wasn't happy to realize I would have to deal with Todd. We hadn't spoken since Christmas, since Rafe and I made things official between us. It was funny, but for someone who had suspected I had feelings for Rafe long before I had recognized anything but curiosity and a certain self-destructive fascination myself, Todd had been remarkably unwilling to take my word for it once I had admitted it to myself. For several months last autumn, he had clung stubbornly to the hope that my feelings for Rafe was something I'd outgrow if he gave me enough time. He'd probably be watching me like a cat at a mousehole all evening, just waiting for a sign of weakness, so he could explain to me, yet again, why I'd be happier with him. The fact that I was here alone would definitely fuel that fire. And not just for Todd, but for mother too.

There was nothing I could do about it, though. I couldn't turn around and drive back. Especially not after the curtains fluttered and someone realized I was there. I pulled the key out of the ignition, grabbed my purse and Abigail's gifts from the passenger seat, and stepped out.

IT WAS CATHERINE WHO MET ME at the door.

She peered over my shoulder into the road. "Are you alone?"

If I hadn't known better, I'd have said she sounded disappointed. Or maybe that's unfair: when we had Christmas dinner at Catherine's house on Christmas Day, and I insisted that Rafe accompany me since he was in Sweetwater anyway, the two of them had gotten along rather well. Well enough that I'd felt just a touch of jealousy because of the easy way my sister related to my new boyfriend.

My siblings may have had some reservations about my new relationship initially. Not like mother, but enough to cause concern, Dix in particular was hesitant to give us his blessing, both out of loyalty to Todd and because he's my brother and as such doesn't appreciate Rafe the way another woman would. But Catherine is a year older than Rafe, so the two of them spent three years together at Columbia High before my sister graduated. She knew him a lot better than I did back then, which is probably why that meeting at Christmas went so well.

"Rafe had an appointment with the TBI this afternoon," I explained. "We didn't know how long it was going to take, so I came down on my own." He and Wendell would probably grab a beer and some food later, hopefully to celebrate.

"Bummer," Catherine said and relieved me of my coat.

"Why is that?"

"Todd's here. It amuses me to see them together." She grinned.

I lowered my voice, with a guilty look at the door to the dining room. "I thought you liked Todd."

"I don't mind Todd. I just don't like him for you. You were so miserable with Bradley even I could see it—"

"I wasn't miserable," I protested, but not very strongly, since I knew she had a point. If I hadn't been exactly miserable, at least I'd been a bit unfulfilled.

Catherine shrugged. "I'm just glad you found someone who makes you happy. Never in my wildest dreams did I think it would be Rafe Collier, but if he's who you want, more power to you."

"He's who I want. And I wish he could have been here. Mother won't ever learn to accept him if he's never around. But this meeting was important."

"Finalizing things?" Catherine asked, and waved me to follow her down the hallway to the family room in the back.

It trotted along while I answered her question. "The opposite, actually. He's going back to work for the TBI."

She glanced at me over her shoulder. "Undercover?"

I shook my head. "Oh, no. We're not sure as what. Trainer, maybe. Or handler. But not undercover. Too many people know who he is, for that to be possible."

"So he's going straight?"

"He's always been straight," I said, and stepped around the corner to see every eye in the room focused on me. "Oh. Sorry."

Catherine grinned, of course, and went to sit by Jonathan.

"Savannah," mother said, her lips tight.

I nodded back. "Mother."

She too glanced past me. "Are you alone?"

"I wouldn't talk about him if he were here. That would be rude. If he were here, I would expect him to speak for himself."

Mother's lips compressed, but she didn't say anything else. I nodded to the man next to her. "Good evening, Sheriff."

He nodded back, a tall, gray-haired version of his son.

"Todd." I smiled, while making sure I only met his eyes for a tenth of a second; just long enough to keep up appearances.

"Savannah." Todd inclined his head in what was more than a nod, but not quite a bow. I was relieved that he remained seated. Had he still been courting me, he would have gotten up. So maybe something was finally starting to sink in.

"Dix." I grinned at my brother, who grinned back. He's only a year and a half older than me, so we've always been close. I lifted the gift bags in my hand. "Where's your daughter?"

"The kids are up in the bonus room," Catherine said, before Dix could open his mouth. "We're opening presents a little later."

Sure. "I have ours and one from Det... um... Tamara."

Dix, bless him, blushed. "Just put it with the others."

"Tamara?" mother repeated, a tiny wrinkle between her elegant brows. "Isn't that the woman who gave the girls those horrid dolls for Christmas?"

"I had Barbies when I grew up," I said, and went to sit next to Catherine and Jonathan in the sofa. "They're not horrid. I mean, I know they give little girls a skewed image of women, with those perfect breasts and that impossibly tiny waist and those permanently deformed feet..."

Mother sniffed.

"...but they're much less damaging these days. There are Attorney Barbies now. Veterinarian Barbies. Police Barbies." Those same Police Barbies mother objected to. "G.I. Barbies. You know, the kinds of professions that little girls can actually aspire to these days."

Next to me, Catherine—herself an attorney—was vibrating with suppressed mirth. I grinned at Todd, in the other sofa. "How many women in the district attorney's office in Columbia, Todd?"

"Four," Todd, assistant to the D.A., said, a little stiffly. He doesn't like being made to disagree with mother.

"See?" I smiled sweetly. Mother eyed the bag with Grimaldi's gift balefully. I put it beside me for safe-keeping rather than leaving it with the others, as Dix had told me to do. I didn't want to turn around and find it missing, after all.

I behaved after that, though. I didn't pick any fights, and I didn't bandy Rafe's name about when it wasn't absolutely necessary, just so I could watch mother's eyes narrow. I didn't even bring up controversial subjects, like Police Barbies or murder. It wasn't me who asked about Brian Armstrong and Neil Donnelly a few minutes later.

"I hear they made an arrest in the murder of the orthodontist," Sheriff Satterfield said.

Mother clucked and shook her head, probably at the idea that someone could murder a dentist. In mother's world, our kind of people—doctors, lawyers, and dentists—aren't victims of violent crime. One might have thought that Sheila's murder, at the hands of a doctor, had cured her of that tendency, but one would be wrong.

I nodded. "Tamara Grimaldi arrested the brother-in-law yesterday."

"His brother-in-law did it?"

"His brother-in-law stabbed him. His wife listened on the phone."

Mother winced, and so did all the lawyers. The sheriff didn't. "So it was the money?"

"Partly. But it was revenge more than anything. See, Brian Armstrong—the dentist—raped Neil Donnelly when Neil was sixteen. He was a sexual sadist, and to hear Neil explain it, he was lucky to get out alive."

"How do you know that, Savannah?" mother asked.

I decided to pretend I hadn't heard her. "Instead of reporting him to the police, Neil and his sister forced Brian to marry Erin. They were busy making his life a living hell—"

"Savannah, dear..." mother protested weakly.

I glanced at her, but didn't stop talking. "—until they moved here, and Erin started sleeping with her housecleaner. He was the second victim."

"Did Donnelly kill him too?" the sheriff asked.

"Neil Donnelly killed everyone. Brian threatened to divorce Erin, since adultery is reason for divorce in the state of Tennessee, so Neil and Erin decided to kill him. Beau—the housecleaner—happened to know that Neil was there the night Brian was killed, so Neil had to kill him too. And then Neil had to try to kill my broker, who was supposed to be the fall guy for everything."

Well, really, I guess it was Beau who had been supposed to be the fall guy for everything. And if Neil had stuck to his original plan, things might have worked out better for him. He could have taken Brian to Beau's place, killed him, left him for Beau to deal with—Beau, who wouldn't remember anything thanks to the dose of roofies Neil had given him—and he'd have been home free. It was improvising—deciding to frame Tim after the public argument at Chaps—that had tripped him up.

"How do you know this, Savannah?" mother asked again, and this time I had no choice but to answer.

"It was Rafe and I who figured it out."

"Savannah...!"

I wasn't entirely sure whether the undertone was shock, exasperation, or horror. In any case, I was happy when the doorbell rang and I had an excuse to jump up. "I'll get it."

"It's probably the pizza," Dix said. "It's already paid for. I gave them my credit card number when I placed the order."

"Pizza?" Mother sounded as if he'd offered her gruel.

"It's Abigail's birthday," Dix said. "She likes pizza."

I hid a smile. "I'll be right back."

I barely made it around the corner before I started giggling. Pizza! My mother would be eating pizza. With her fingers. Maybe even from a paper plate. Mother, who was used to foie gras and Chardonnay, and who could differentiate between a dozen different tableware patterns by sight. I could barely wait.

I had a big grin on my face when I yanked the door open. It didn't diminish at all when Rafe grinned back. "Evening, darlin'."

My heart gave an actual skip. "You came!"

"It's been long enough. We gotta deal with this sooner or later."

True. Even if I still had a hard time wrapping my brain around the fact that he was actually here. "Come in, then. Let me take your coat. How did it go this afternoon?"

He shrugged out of a rather upscale wool peacoat and let me hang it next to mine in the coat closet. Under it, he was still dressed in the dark suit and white shirt and tie he'd been wearing to the interview.

"You look wonderful." Not as wonderful as he would later, naked in my bed at the mansion, but pretty darned good.

He grinned at me. "I thought your mother would appreciate the suit."

She wouldn't. It made him look too respectable, and that would challenge mother's preconceptions. But if nothing else, it would show her that he cleaned up rather nicely. "You didn't answer my question. How did it go? Do you have a job again?"

"What are you gonna do if I say yes?"

"Kiss you," I said, since I hadn't yet.

"What if I say no?"

I'd probably kiss him then too. Since I hadn't yet. But— "You got the job, didn't you?"

"Would you be worried if I did?"

"I want you to be happy. As long as you're happy—and as long as you come back to me at the end of the day—I can deal with a little worry."

"In that case—" He took a breath. "I took the job."

"Trainer?"

He nodded.

"Handler?"

He shook his head. "Not yet. I haven't been off the streets long enough. They're gonna keep me behind the scenes awhile."

"Nine to five?"

He nodded.

"I'll dig out the pipe and slippers."

"Let's get a dog," Rafe said. "That way you can stay in bed. Naked."

He grinned at me. I grinned back. "Remember what I said?"

"You were gonna kiss me?"

Precisely. I was on my way up on my toes when Dix appeared at the other end of the hallway. "Sis? What happened to the... oh."

Rafe laughed against my lips, but by then it was too late to pull back. His hands were at my waist, I was swaying toward him, and his lips were close enough to mine that all I had to do was stretch another centimeter to get what I wanted.

The last thing I heard before it all faded to black was Dix's voice down at the end of the hall. "Sorry, folks. False alarm."

ABOUT THE AUTHOR

Jenna Bennett writes the *USA Today* bestselling Savannah Martin mystery series for her own gratification, as well as the *New York Times* bestselling Do-It-Yourself home renovation mysteries from Berkley Prime Crime under the pseudonym Jennie Bentley. For a change of pace, she writes a variety of romance, from contemporary to futuristic, and from paranormal to suspense.

FOR MORE INFORMATION, PLEASE VISIT HER WEBSITE:
WWW.JENNABENNETT.COM

CPSIA information can be obtained at www.ICGtesting.com
Printed in the USA
LVOW12s1613110215

426636LV00008B/853/P

9 780989 943437